MR VERTIGO

MR VERTIGO

Paul Auster

faber and faber

LONDON · BOSTON

First published in 1994
by Faber and Faber Limited
3 Queen Square London WC1N 3AU

Phototypeset in Palatino by Intype, London
Printed in England by Clays Ltd, St Ives Plc

© Paul Auster, 1994

Paul Auster is hereby identified as author of this work
in accordance with Section 77 of the Copyright,
Designs and Patents Act 1988.

A CIP record for this book is
available from the British Library

ISBN 0–571–17092–7

2 4 6 8 10 9 7 5 3 1

I

I was twelve years old the first time I walked on water. The man in the black clothes taught me how to do it, and I'm not going to pretend I learned that trick overnight. Master Yehudi found me when I was nine, an orphan boy begging nickels on the streets of Saint Louis, and he worked with me steadily for three years before he let me show my stuff in public. That was in 1927, the year of Babe Ruth and Charles Lindbergh, the precise year when night began to fall on the world forever. I kept it up until a few days before the October crash, and what I did was greater than anything those two gents could have dreamed of. I did what no American had done before me, what no one has ever done since.

Master Yehudi chose me because I was the smallest, the dirtiest, the most abject. 'You're no better than an animal,' he said, 'a piece of human nothingness.' That was the first sentence he spoke to me, and even though sixty-eight years have passed since that night, it's as if I can still hear the words coming from the master's mouth. 'You're no better than an animal. If you stay where you are, you'll be dead before winter is out. If you come with me, I'll teach you how to fly.'

'Ain't nobody can fly, mister,' I said. 'That's what birds do, and I sure as hell ain't no bird.'

'You know nothing,' Master Yehudi said. 'You know nothing because you are nothing. If I haven't taught you to fly by your thirteenth birthday, you can chop off my head with an axe. I'll put it in writing if you like. If I fail to deliver on my promise, my fate will be in your hands.'

It was a Saturday night in early November, and we were standing in front of the Paradise Cafe, a slick downtown gin mill with a colored jazz band and cigarette girls in transparent dresses. I used to hang around there on weekends, cadging handouts and running errands and hustling cabs for the swells. At first I thought Master Yehudi was just another drunk, a rich booze hound stumbling through the night in a black tuxedo and a silk top hat. His accent was strange, so I figured him to be from out of town, but that was as far as I took it. Drunks say stupid things, and the business about flying was no stupider than most.

'You get too high in the air,' I said, 'you could break your neck when you come down.'

'We'll talk about technique later,' the master said. 'It's not an easy skill to learn, but if you listen to me and obey my instructions, we'll both wind up millionaires.'

'You're already a millionaire,' I said. 'What do you need me for?'

'Because, my wretched little thug, I barely have two dimes to rub together. I might look like a robber baron to you, but that's only because you have sawdust for brains. Listen to me carefully. I'm offering you the chance of a lifetime, but you only get that chance once. I'm booked on the *Blue Bird Special* at six thirty a.m., and if you don't haul your carcass onto that train, this is the last you'll ever see of me.'

'You still haven't answered my question,' I said.

'Because you're the answer to my prayers, son. That's why I want you. Because you have the gift.'

'Gift? I ain't got no gift. And even if I did, what would you know about it, Mr Monkey Suit? You only started talking to me a minute ago.'

'Wrong again,' said Master Yehudi. 'I've been watching you for a week. And if you think your aunt and uncle would be sorry to see you gone, then you don't know who you've been living with for the past four years.'

'My aunt and uncle,' I said, suddenly realizing that this man was no Saturday-night drunk. He was something worse than that: a truant officer or a cop, and sure as I was standing there, I was up to my knees in shit.

4

'Your Uncle Slim is a piece of work,' the master continued, taking his time now that he had my attention. 'I never knew an American citizen could be that dumb. Not only does he smell bad, but he's mean and ugly to boot. No wonder you turned into such a weasel-faced guttersnipe. We had a long conversation this morning, your uncle and I, and he's willing to let you go without a penny changing hands. Imagine that, boy. I didn't even have to pay for you. And that dough-fleshed sow he calls his wife just sat there and never said a word in your defense. If that's the best you can do for a family, then you're lucky to be rid of those two. The decision is yours, but even if you turn me down, it might not be such a good idea to go back. They'd be plenty disappointed to see you again, I can tell you that. Just about dumbstruck with sorrow, if you know what I mean.'

I might have been an animal, but even the lowest animal has feelings, and when the master sprang this news on me, I felt as if I'd been punched. Uncle Slim and Aunt Peg were nothing to write home about, but their home was where I lived, and it stopped me in my tracks to learn they didn't want me. I was only nine years old, after all. Tough as I was for that age, I wasn't half as tough as I pretended to be, and if the master hadn't been looking down at me with those dark eyes of his just then, I probably would have started bawling right there on the street.

When I think back to that night now, I'm still not sure if he was telling me the truth or not. He could have talked to my aunt and uncle, but then again, he could have been making the whole thing up. I don't doubt that he'd seen them – he had their descriptions dead on – but knowing my Uncle Slim, it strikes me as next to impossible that he would have let me go without wheedling some cash out of the bargain. I'm not saying that Master Yehudi welshed on him, but given what happened later, there's no question that the bastard felt wronged, whether justice was on his side or not. I'm not

5

going to waste time puzzling over that now. The upshot was that I fell for what the master told me, and in the long run that's the only fact that bears telling. He convinced me that I couldn't go home, and once I accepted that, I didn't give a damn about myself anymore. That must have been how he wanted me to feel – all jangled up and lost inside. If you don't see any reason to go on living, it's hard to care much about what happens to you. You tell yourself you want to be dead, and after that you discover you're ready for anything – even a crazy thing like vanishing into the night with a stranger.

'Okay, mister,' I said, dropping my voice a couple of octaves and giving him my best cutthroat stare, 'you've got yourself a deal. But if you don't come through for me like you say, you can kiss your head good-bye. I might be small, but I never let a man forget a promise.'

It was still dark when we boarded the train. We rode west into the dawn, traveling across the state of Missouri as the dim November light struggled to crack through the clouds. I hadn't been out of Saint Louis since the day they buried my mother, and it was a gloomy world I discovered that morning: gray and barren, with endless fields of withered cornstalks flanking us on both sides. We chugged into Kansas City a little past noon, but in all the hours we spent together I don't think Master Yehudi spoke more than three or four words to me. Most of the time he slept, nodding off with his hat pulled down over his face, but I was too scared to do anything but look out the window, watching the land slip past me as I pondered the mess I'd gotten myself into. My pals in Saint Louis had warned me about characters like Master Yehudi: solitary drifters with evil designs, perverts on the prowl for young boys to do their bidding. It was bad enough to imagine him taking off my clothes and touching me where I didn't want to be touched, but that was nothing compared to some of the other fears knocking around in my skull. I'd heard

6

about one boy who had gone off with a stranger and was never heard from again. Later on, the man confessed he'd sliced up the lad into little pieces and boiled him for dinner. Another boy had been chained to a wall in a dark cellar and given nothing to eat but bread and water for six months. Another one had had the skin peeled off his bones. Now that I had time to consider what I'd done, I figured I might be in for the same kind of treatment myself. I'd let myself fall into the clutches of a monster, and if he turned out to be half as spooky as he looked, the odds were I'd never see the dawn rise again.

We got off the train and started walking down the platform, wending our way through the crowd. 'I'm hungry,' I said, tugging on Master Yehudi's coat. 'If you don't feed me now, I'm going to turn you in to the first flatfoot I see.'

'What's the matter with the apple I gave you?' he said.

'I chucked it out the window of the train.'

'Oh, not too keen on apples, are we? And what about the ham sandwich? Not to speak of the fried chicken leg and the bag of doughnuts.'

'I chucked it all. You don't expect me to eat the grub you give me, do you?'

'And why not, little man? If you don't eat, you'll shrivel up and die. Everybody knows that.'

'At least you die slow that way. You bite into something filled with poison, and you croak on the spot.'

For the first time since I'd met him, Master Yehudi broke into a smile. If I'm not mistaken, I believe he even went so far as to laugh. 'You're saying you don't trust me, is that it?'

'You're damn straight. I wouldn't trust you as far as I could throw a dead mule.'

'Lighten up, squirt,' the master said, patting me affectionately on the shoulder. 'You're my meal ticket, remember? I wouldn't hurt a hair on your head.'

Those were just words as far as I was concerned, and I

wasn't so dumb as to swallow that kind of sugary talk. But then Master Yehudi reached into his pocket, pulled out a stiff new dollar bill, and slapped it into my palm. 'See that restaurant over there?' he said, pointing to a hash house in the middle of the station. 'Go in and order yourself the biggest lunch you can stuff inside that belly of yours. I'll wait for you out here.'

'And what about you? You got something against eating?'

'Don't worry about me,' Master Yehudi replied. 'My stomach can take care of itself.' Then, just as I was turning to go, he added: 'One word of advice, pipsqueak. In case you're planning to run away, this is the time to do it. And don't worry about the dollar. You can keep it for your trouble.'

I walked on into the restaurant by myself, feeling somewhat mollified by those parting words. If he had some sinister purpose, then why would he offer me a chance to escape? I sat down at the counter and asked for the blue-plate special and a bottle of sarsaparilla. Before I could blink, the waiter shoved a mountain of corned beef and cabbage in front of me. It was the largest meal I had ever encountered, a meal as large as Sportsman's Park in Saint Louis, and I wolfed down every morsel of it, along with two slices of bread and a second bottle of sarsaparilla. Nothing can compare to the sense of well-being that washed through me at that filthy lunch counter. Once my belly was full, I felt invincible, as if nothing could harm me again. The crowning touch came when I extracted the dollar bill from my pocket to settle the tab. The whole thing toted up to just forty-five cents, and even after I threw in a nickel tip for the waiter, that left me with four bits in change. It doesn't sound like much today, but two quarters represented a fortune to me back then. This is my chance to run, I told myself, giving the joint the once-over as I stood up from my stool. I can slip out the side door, and the man in black will never know what hit him. But I didn't do it, and in that choice hung the entire story of my life. I went back to where the master was waiting because he'd promised to turn me into a millionaire. On the strength of those fifty cents, I figured it might be worth it to see if there was any truth to the boast.

We took another train after that, and then a third train near the end of the journey which brought us to the town of Cibola at seven o'clock that night. Silent as he had been all morning, Master Yehudi rarely stopped talking for the rest of the day. I was already learning not to make any assumptions about what he might or might not do. Just when you thought you had him pegged, he would turn around and do the precise contrary of what you were expecting.

'You can call me Master Yehudi,' he said, announcing his name to me for the first time. 'If you like, you can call me Master for short. But never, under any circumstances, are you to call me Yehudi. Is that clear?'

'Is that your God-given name,' I said, 'or did you choose that moniker yourself?'

'There's no need for you to know my real name. Master Yehudi will be sufficient.'

'Well, I'm Walter. Walter Claireborne Rawley. But you can call me Walt.'

'I'll call you anything I like. If I want to call you Worm, I'll call you Worm. If I want to call you Pig, I'll call you Pig. Is that understood?'

'Hell, mister, I don't understand a thing you're talking about.'

'Nor will I tolerate any lying or duplicity. No excuses, no complaints, no back talk. Once you catch on, you're going to be the happiest boy on earth.'

'Sure. And if a legless man had legs, he could piss standing up.'

'I know your story, son. So you don't have to invent any tall tales for me. I know how your pa got gassed over in Belgium in 'seventeen. And I know about your ma, too, and

9

how she used to turn tricks over in East Saint Louis for a buck a tumble, and what happened to her four and a half years ago when that crazy cop turned his revolver on her and blew off her face. Don't think I don't pity you, boy, but you'll never get anywhere if you dodge the truth when you're dealing with me.'

'Okay, Mr Smarty Pants. If you've got all the answers, why waste your breath telling me things you already know?'

'Because you still don't believe a word I've said. You think this stuff about flying is a lot of hot air. You're going to work hard, Walt, harder than you've ever worked before, and you're going to want to quit on me almost every day, but if you stick with it and trust what I tell you, at the end of a few years you'll be able to fly. I swear it. You'll be able to lift yourself off the ground and fly through the air like a bird.'

'I'm from Missouri, remember? They don't call it the Show-Me-State for nothing.'

'Well, we're not in Missouri anymore, my little friend. We're in Kansas. And a flatter, more desolate place you've never seen in your life. When Coronado and his men marched through here in 1540 looking for the Cities of Gold, they got so lost that half of them went insane. There's nothing to tell you where you are. No mountains, no trees, no bumps in the road. It's flat as death out here, and once you've been around for a while, you'll understand there's nowhere to go but up – that the sky is the only friend you have.'

It was dark by the time we pulled into the station, so there was no way to vouch for the master's description of my new home. As far as I could tell, the town was no different from what you'd expect to see in a little town. A trifle colder, perhaps, and more than a trifle darker than what I was used to, but given that I had never been in a little town before, I had no idea what to expect. Everything was new to me: every smell was strange, every star in the sky seemed unfamiliar. If someone had told me I'd just entered the Land of Oz, I don't think I would have known the difference.

We walked through the station house and stood outside the door for a moment scanning the dark village. It was only seven o'clock in the evening, but the whole place was locked up, and except for a few lamps burning in the houses beyond, there was no sign of life anywhere. 'Don't worry,' Master Yehudi said, 'our ride will be along any minute.' He reached out and tried to take hold of my hand, but I yanked my arm away before he could get a firm grip. 'Keep your paws to yourself, Mr Master,' I said. 'You might think you own me now, but you don't own squat.'

About nine seconds after I uttered those words, a big gray horse appeared at the end of the street pulling a buckboard wagon. It looked like something from the Tom Mix western I'd seen that summer at the Picture Palace, but this was 1924, for Christ's sake, and when I caught sight of that antiquated vehicle rumbling down the street, I thought it was an apparition. But lo and behold, Master Yehudi waved when he saw it coming, and then that old gray horse stopped right in front of us, sidling up to the curb as gusts of steam poured from its nostrils. The driver was a round, chunky figure in a wide-brimmed hat whose body was wrapped in blankets, and at first I couldn't tell if it was a man, a woman, or a bear.

'Hello, Mother Sue,' the master said. 'Take a look at what I found.'

The woman gazed at me for a couple of seconds with blank, stone-cold eyes, and then, out of nowhere, flashed one of the warmest, friendliest smiles I've ever had the pleasure to receive. There couldn't have been more than two or three teeth jutting from her gums, and from the way her dark eyes glittered, I concluded that she was a Gypsy. She was Mother Sue, the Queen of the Gypsies, and Master Yehudi was her son, the Prince of Blackness. They were abducting me to the Castle of No Return, and if they didn't eat me for dinner that

11

night, they were going to turn me into a slavey boy, a groveling eunuch with an earring in my ear and a silk bandana wrapped around my head.

'Hop in, sonny,' Mother Sue said. Her voice was so deep and mannish, I would have been scared to death if I hadn't known she could smile. 'You'll see some blankets in the back. If you know what's good for you, you'll use 'em. We got a long cold ride ahead of us, and you don't want to get there with no frozen fanny.'

'His name is Walt,' the master said as he climbed up beside her. 'A pus-brained ragamuffin from honky-tonk row. If my hunch is correct, he's the one I've been looking for all these years.' Then, turning in my direction, he said brusquely, 'This is Mother Sue, kid. Treat her nice, and she'll give you only goodness in return. Cross her, and you'll regret the day you were born. She might be fat and toothless, but she's the closest thing to a mother you'll ever have.'

I don't know how long it took us to get to the house. It was out in the country somewhere, sixteen or seventeen miles from town, but I didn't learn that until later, for once I climbed in under the blankets and the wagon started down the road, I fell fast asleep. When I opened my eyes again, we were already there, and if the master hadn't roused me with a slap across the face, I probably would have slept until morning.

He led me into the house as Mother Sue unhitched the nag, and the first room we entered was the kitchen: a bare, dimly lit space with a wood stove in one corner and a kerosene lamp flickering in another. A black boy of about fifteen was sitting at the table reading a book. He wasn't brown like most of the colored folks I'd run across back home, he was the color of pitch, a black so black it was almost blue. He was a full-fledged Ethiopian, a pickaninny from the jungles of darkest Africa, and my heart just about stopped beating when I caught sight of him. He was a frail, scrawny fellow with bulging eyes and those enormous lips, and as soon as he stood up from his chair to greet us, I saw that his bones were all twisted and askew, that he had the jagged, hunchbacked body of a cripple.

'This is Aesop,' the master said to me, 'the finest boy who ever lived. Say hello to him, Walt, and shake his hand. He's going to be your new brother.'

'I ain't shaking hands with no nigger,' I said. 'You've got to be crazy if you'd think I'd do a thing like that.'

Master Yehudi let out a loud, prolonged sigh. It wasn't an expression of disgust so much as of sorrow, a monumental shudder from the depths of his soul. Then, with utmost deliberation and calm, he curled the index finger of his right hand into a frozen, beckoning hook and placed the tip of that hook directly under my chin, at the precise spot where the flesh meets the bone. Then he began to press, and all at once a horrific pain shot around the back of my neck and up into my skull. I had never felt pain like that before. I struggled to cry out, but my throat was blocked, and I could do no more than produce a sick gagging noise. The master continued to press with his finger, and presently I felt my feet lift off the ground. I was traveling upward, rising into the air like a feather, and the master seemed to be accomplishing this without the slightest effort, as if I were of no more consequence to him than a ladybug. Eventually, he had me up to where my face was on a level with his and I was looking directly into his eyes.

'We don't talk like that around here, boy,' he said. 'All men are brothers, and in this family everyone gets treated with respect. That's the law. If you don't like it, lump it. The law is the law, and whoever goes against it is turned into a slug and wallows in the earth for the rest of his days.'

They fed me and clothed me and gave me a room of my own. I wasn't spanked or paddled, I wasn't kicked around or punched or boxed on the ears, and yet tolerable as things were for me, I had never been more down at the mouth, more filled with bitterness and pent-up fury. For the first six months, I thought only about running away. I was a city boy who had grown up with jazz in his blood, a street kid with his eye on the main chance, and I loved the hurly-burly of crowds, the screech of trolley cars and the throb of neon, the stink of bootleg whiskey trickling in the gutters. I was a boogie-toed prankster, a midget scatman with a quick tongue and a hundred angles, and there I was stuck in the middle of nowhere, living under a sky that brought only weather – nearly all of it bad.

Master Yehudi's property consisted of thirty-seven acres of dirt, a two-story farmhouse, a chicken coop, a pigpen, and a barn. There were a dozen chickens in the coop, two cows and the gray horse in the barn, and six or seven pigs in the pen. There was no electricity, no plumbing, no telephone, no wireless, no phonograph, no nothing. The only source of entertainment was the piano in the parlor, but Aesop was the only one who could play it, and he made such a botch of even the simplest songs that I always left the room the moment he sat down and touched his fingers to the keys. The joint was a shit hole, the world capital of boredom, and I was already fed up with it after one day. They didn't even know about baseball in that house, and I had no one to talk to about my beloved Cardinals, which was about the only subject that interested me back then. I felt as if I'd fallen through a crack in time and landed in the stone age, a country where dinosaurs still roamed the earth. According to Mother Sue, Master

Yehudi had won the farm on a bet with some fellow in Chicago about seven years earlier. That must have been some bet, I said. The loser turns out to be the winner, and the winner's a chump who gets to rot away his future in Bungholeville USA.

I was a fiery little dunce back then, I'll admit it, but I'm not going to make any apologies for myself. I was who I was, a product of the people and places I'd come from, and there's no point in whining about that now. What impresses me most about those early months is how patient they were, how well they seemed to understand me and tolerate my antics. I ran away four times that first winter, once getting as far as Wichita, and each time they took me back, no questions asked. I was scarcely a hair's breadth greater than nothing, a molecule or two above the vanishing point of what constitutes a human being, and since the master reckoned that my soul was no loftier than an animal's, that's where he started me out: in the barn with the animals.

Much as I detested taking care of those chickens and pigs, I preferred their company to the people. It was difficult for me to decide which one I hated most, and every day I would reshuffle the order of my animosities. Mother Sue and Aesop came in for their fair share of inner scorn, but in the end it was the master who provoked my greatest ire and resentment. He was the scoundrel who had tricked me into going there, and if anyone was to blame for the fix I was in, he was the chief culprit. What galled me most was his sarcasm, the cracks and insults he hurled constantly in my direction, the way he would ride me and hound me for no reason but to prove how worthless I was. With the other two he was always polite, a model of decorum, but he rarely wasted an opportunity to say something mean-spirited on my account. It started the very first morning, and after that he never let up. Before long, I realized that he was no better than Uncle Slim. He might not have thrashed me the way Slim did, but the master's

15

words had power, and they hurt just as much as any blow to the head.

'Well, my fine-feathered rascal,' he said to me that first morning, 'give me the lowdown on what you know about the three R's.'

'Three?' I said, going for the quick, wise-guy retort. 'I ain't got but one arse, and I use it every time I sit down. Same as everybody else.'

'I mean school, you twerp. Have you ever set foot in a classroom – and if so, what did you learn there?'

'I don't need no school to teach me things. I've got better ways of spending my time than that.'

'Excellent. Spoken like a true scholar. But be more specific. What about the alphabet? Can you write the letters of the alphabet or not?'

'Some of them. The ones that serve my purpose. The others don't matter. They just give me a pain, so I don't worry about them.'

'And which ones serve your purpose?'

'Well, let's see. There's the *A*, I like that one, and the *W*. Then there's the whatchamacallit, the *L*, and the *E*, and the *R*, and the one that looks like a cross. The *T*. As in T-bone steak. Those letters are my buddies, and the rest can go fry in hell for all I care.'

'So you know how to write your name.'

'That's what I'm telling you, boss. I can write my name, I can count to kingdom come, and I know that the sun is a star in the sky. I also know that books are for girls and sissies, and if you're planning to teach me anything out of books, we can call off our arrangement right now.'

'Don't fret, kid. What you've just told me is music to my ears. The dumber you are, the better it is for both of us. There's less to undo that way, and that's going to save us a lot of time.'

16

'And what about the flying lessons? When do we start with them?'

'We've already started. From now on, everything we do is connected to your training. That won't always be apparent to you, so try to keep it in mind. If you don't forget, you'll be able to hang in there when the going gets rough. We're embarking on a long journey, son, and the first thing I have to do is break your spirit. I wish it could be some other way, but it can't. Considering the muck you spring from, that shouldn't be too hard a task.'

So I spent my days shoveling manure in the barn, freezing my eyebrows off as the others sat snug and cozy in the house. Mother Sue took care of the cooking and domestic chores, Aesop lounged around on the sofa reading books, and Master Yehudi did nothing at all. His principal occupation seemed to be sitting on a straight-backed wooden chair from sunrise to sundown and looking out the window. Except for his conversations with Aesop, that was the only thing I saw him do until spring. I sometimes listened in when the two of them talked, but I could never make sense of what they were saying. They used so many complicated words, it was as if they were communicating in their own private gibberish. Later on, when I settled into the swing of things a bit more, I learned that they were studying. Master Yehudi had taken it upon himself to educate Aesop in the liberal arts, and the books they read concerned any number of different subjects: history, science, literature, mathematics, Latin, French, and so on. He had his project of teaching me to fly, but he was also engaged in turning Aesop into a scholar, and as far as I could tell that second project meant a lot more to him than mine did. As the master put it to me one morning not long after my arrival: 'He was even worse off than you were, runt. When I found him twelve years ago, he was crawling through a cotton field in Georgia dressed in rags. He hadn't eaten in two days, and his mama, who was no more than a child herself, lay dead from TB in their shack fourteen miles down the road. That's how far the kid had wandered from home. He was delirious with hunger by then, and if I hadn't chanced upon him at that particular moment, there's no telling what would have happened. His body might be contorted into a tragic shape, but his mind is a glorious instrument, and he's already surpassed me in most fields. My plan is to send him to college in three years. He can continue his studies there, and once he graduates and goes out into the world, he'll become a leader of his race, a shining example to all the downtrodden black folks of this violent, hypocritical country.' I couldn't make head or tail of what the master was talking about, but the love in his voice burned through to me and impressed itself on my mind. For all my stupidity, I was able to understand that much. He loved Aesop as if he were his own son, and I was no better than a mutt, a mongrel beast to be spat on and left out in the rain.

Mother Sue was my companion in ignorance, my fellow illiterate and sluggard, and while that might have helped to create a bond between us, it did nothing of the sort. There was no overt hostility in her, but at the same time she gave me the willies, and I think it took me longer to adjust to her oddnesses than it did with the two others – who could hardly be called normal themselves. Even with the blankets removed from her body and the hat gone from her head, I had trouble determining which sex she belonged to. I found that distressing somehow, and even after I glimpsed her naked through the keyhole of her door and saw with my own eyes that she possessed a pair of titties and had no member dangling from her bush, I still wasn't entirely convinced. Her hands were tough like a man's, she had broad shoulders and muscles that bulged in her upper arms, and except when she flashed me one of her rare and beautiful smiles, her face was as remote and ungiving as a block of wood. That's closer to what unsettled me, perhaps: her silence, the way she seemed to look through me as if I wasn't there. In the pecking order of the household, I stood directly below her, which meant that I had more dealings with Mother Sue than with anyone else. She was the one who doled out my chores and checked up on me, who made sure I washed my face and brushed my teeth before going to bed, and yet for all the hours I spent in her company, she made me feel lonelier than if I had been truly alone. A hollowed-out sensation crept into my belly whenever she was around, as if just being near her would start to make me shrink. It didn't matter how I behaved. I could jump up and down or stand still, I could holler my head off or hold my tongue, and the results never varied. Mother Sue was a wall, and every time I approached that wall I was turned into a puff of smoke, a tiny cloud of ashes scattering in the wind.

The only one who showed me any genuine kindness was Aesop, but I was against him from the start, and there was nothing he could say or do that would ever change that. I couldn't help myself. It was in my blood to feel contempt for him, and given that he was the ugliest specimen of his kind I'd ever had the misfortune to see, it struck me as preposterous that we were living under the same roof. It went against the laws of nature, it transgressed everything that was holy and proper, and I wouldn't allow myself to accept it. When you threw in the fact that Aesop talked like no other colored boy on the face of the earth – more like an English lord than an American – and then threw in the additional fact that he was the master's favorite, I couldn't even think about him without succumbing to an onslaught of nerves. To make matters worse, I had to keep my mouth shut whenever he was around. A few choice remarks would have blown off some of my rage, I think, but I remembered the master's finger thrusting under my chin, and I was in no mood to submit to that torture again.

The worst part of it was that Aesop didn't seem to care

that I despised him so much. I perfected a whole repertoire of scowls and grimaces to use in his company, but whenever I shot one of those looks in his direction, he would just shake his head and smile to himself. It made me feel like an idiot. No matter how hard I tried to hurt him, he never let me get under his skin, never gave me the satisfaction of scoring a point against him. He wasn't simply winning the war between us, he was winning every damned battle of that war, and I figured that if I couldn't even beat a black devil in a fair exchange of insults, then the whole of that Kansas prairie must have been bewitched. I'd been shanghaied to a land of bad dreams, and the more I struggled to wake up, the scarier the nightmare became.

'You try too hard,' Aesop said to me one afternoon. 'You're so consumed with your own righteousness, it's made you blind to the things around you. And if you can't see what's in front of your nose, you'll never be able to look at yourself and know who you are.'

'I know who I am,' I said. 'There ain't nobody can steal that from me.'

'The master isn't stealing anything from you. He's giving you the gift of greatness.'

'Look, do me a favor, will you? Don't mention that buzzard's name when I'm around. He gives me the creeps, that master of yours, and the less I have to think about him, the better off I'm going to be.'

'He loves you, Walt. He believes in you with every ounce of his soul.'

'The hell he does. That faker don't give a rat's ass about nothing. He's the King of the Gypsies is what he is, and if he's got any soul at all – which I'm not saying he does – then it's packed with evil through and through.'

'King of the Gypsies?' Aesop's eyes bugged out in amazement. 'Is that what you think?' The idea must have bopped him on the funny bone, for a moment later he grabbed his stomach and started shaking in a fit of laughter. 'You sure know how to come up with some good ones,' he said, wiping the tears from his eyes. 'What on earth ever put that notion in your head?'

'Well,' I said, feeling my cheeks blush with embarrassment, 'if he ain't no Gypsy, what the hell is he, then?'

'A Hungarian.'

'A what?' I stammered. It was the first time I'd ever heard anyone use that word, and I was so flummoxed by it that I momentarily lost the power of speech.

'A Hungarian. He was born in Budapest and came to America as a young boy. He grew up in Brooklyn, New York, and both his father and grandfather were rabbis.'

'And what's that, some lesser form of rodent?'

'It's a Jewish teacher. Sort of like a minister or priest, only for Jews.'

'Well now,' I said, 'there you go. That explains everything, don't it? He's worse than a Gypsy, old Doctor Dark Brows – he's a kike. There ain't nothing worse than that on the whole miserable planet.'

'You'd better not let him hear you talking like that,' Aesop said.

'I know my rights,' I said. 'And no Jew man is going to shove me around, I swear it.'

'Easy does it, Walt. You're only asking for trouble.'

'And what about that witch, Mother Sue? Is she another one of them Hebes?'

Aesop shook his head and stared down at the ground. My voice was seething with such anger, he couldn't bring himself to look me in the eyes. 'No,' he said. 'She's an Oglala Sioux. Her grandfather was Sitting Bull's brother, and when she was young, she was the top bareback rider in Buffalo Bill's Wild West Show.'

'You're shitting me.'

'I wouldn't dream of it. What I'm telling you is the pure,

unvarnished truth. You're living in the same house with a Jew, a black man, and an Indian, and the sooner you accept the facts, the happier your life is going to be.'

I'd held on for three weeks until then, but after that conversation with Aesop I knew I couldn't stand it anymore. I lit out of there that same night – waiting until everyone was asleep and then crawling out of the covers, sneaking down the stairs, and tiptoeing into the frigid December darkness. There was no moon overhead, not even a star to shine down on me, and the moment I crossed the threshold, I was struck by a wind so fierce that it blew me straight back against the side of the house. My bones were no stronger than cotton in that wind. The night was aroar with clamor, and the air rushed and boomed as if it carried the voice of God, howling down its wrath on any creature foolish enough to rise against it. I became that fool, and time and again I picked myself off the ground and fought my way into the teeth of the maelstrom, spinning around like a pinwheel as I inched my body into the yard. After ten or twelve tries, I was all worn out, a spent and battered hulk. I had made it as far as the pigpen, and just as I was about to scramble to my knees once more, my eyes shut on me and I lost consciousness. Hours passed. I woke at the crack of dawn and found myself encircled by four slumbering pigs. If I hadn't landed among those swine, there's a good chance I would have frozen to death during the night. Thinking about it now, I suppose it was a miracle, but when I opened my eyes that morning and saw where I was, the first thing I did was jump to my feet and spit, cursing my rotten luck.

I had no doubt that Master Yehudi was responsible for what had happened. In that early stage of our history together, I attributed all sorts of supernatural powers to him, and I was fully convinced that he had brought forth that ferocious wind for no other reason than to stop me from running away. For several weeks after that, my head filled with a multitude of

22

wild theories and speculations. The scariest one had to do with Aesop – and my growing certainty that he had been born a white person. It was a terrible thing to contemplate, but all the evidence seemed to support my conclusion. He talked like a white person, didn't he? He acted a like a white person, he thought like a white person, he played the piano like a white person, and just because his skin was black, why should I believe my eyes when my gut told me something else? The only answer was that he had been born white. Years ago, the master had chosen him as his first student in the art of flying. He'd told Aesop to jump from the roof of the barn, and Aesop had jumped – but instead of catching the wind currents and soaring through the air, he'd fallen to the ground and broken every bone in his body. That accounted for his pitiful, lopsided frame, but then, to make matters even worse, Master Yehudi had punished him for his failure. Invoking the power of a hundred Jewish demons, he'd pointed his finger at his disciple and turned him into a ghastly nigger. Aesop's life had been destroyed, and I had no doubt that the same fate was in store for me. Not only would I wind up with black skin and a crippled body, but I would be forced to spend the rest of my days studying books.

I absconded for the second time in the middle of the afternoon. The night had thwarted me with its magic, so I countered with a new strategy and stole off in broad daylight, figuring that if I could see where I was going, there wouldn't be any goblins to menace my steps. For the first hour or two, everything went according to plan. I slipped out of the barn just after lunch and headed down the road to Cibola, intent on maintaining a brisk pace and reaching town before dark. From there I was going to hitch a ride on a freight train and wend my way back east. If I didn't mess up, in twenty-four hours I'd be strolling down the boulevards of dear old Saint Louis.

So there I was, jogging along that flat dusty highway with

the field mice and the crows, feeling more and more confident with each step I took, when all of a sudden I glanced up and saw a buckboard wagon approaching from the opposite direction. It looked surprisingly like the wagon that belonged to Master Yehudi, but since I'd just seen that one in the barn before I left, I shrugged it off as a coincidence and kept on walking. When I got to within about twelve yards of it, I glanced up again. My tongue froze to the roof of my mouth; my eyeballs dropped from their sockets and clattered at my feet. It was Master Yehudi's wagon all right, and sitting on top of that wagon was none other than the master himself, looking down at me with a big smile on his face. He eased the wagon to a halt and tipped his hat to me in a casual, friendly sort of way.

'Howdy, son. A bit nippy for a stroll this afternoon, don't you think?'

'The weather suits me fine,' I said. 'At least a fellow can breathe out here. You stay in one place too long, you start to choke on your own exhaust.'

'Sure, I know how it is. Every boy needs to stretch his legs. But the outing is over now, and it's time to go home. Hoist yourself aboard, Walt, and we'll see if we can't get there before the others notice we've been gone.'

I didn't have much choice, so I climbed up and sat myself beside him as he flicked the reins and got the horse going again. At least he wasn't treating me with his customary rudeness, and burned as I was that my escape had been foiled, I wasn't about to let him know what I'd been up to. He'd probably guessed that anyway, but rather than reveal how disappointed I was, I pretended to play along with the business about being out for a walk.

'It ain't good for a boy to be cooped up so much,' I said. 'It makes him sad and foul-tempered, and then he don't get down to his chores in the right spirit. If you give a guy a little fresh air, he's that much more willing to do his work.'

'I hear what you're saying, chum,' the master said, 'and I understand every word of it.'

'Well, what's it gonna be, captain? I know Cibola ain't much of a burg, but I'll bet they got a picture show or something. It might be nice to go there one evening. You know, a little jaunt to break the monotony. Or else maybe there's a ball club around here, one of them minor league outfits. When spring comes, why not let's take in a game or two? It don't have to be no big-time stuff like the Cards. I mean Class D is okay with me. Just as long as they use bats and balls, you won't hear a word of complaint from this corner. You never know, sir. If you give it half a chance, you might even take a shine to it yourself.'

'I'm sure I would. But there's a mountain of work still in front of us, and in the meantime the family has to lie low. The more invisible we make ourselves, the safer we're going to be. I don't want to scare you, but things aren't as dull in this neighborhood as they might seem. We have some powerful enemies around here, and they're not too thrilled by our presence in their county. A lot of them wouldn't mind if we suddenly stopped breathing, and we don't want to provoke them by strutting our motley selves in public.'

'As long as we mind our own business, who cares what other folks think?'

'That's just it. Some people think our business is their business, and I aim to keep a wide berth of those meddlers. Do you follow me, Walt?'

I told him I did, but the truth was I didn't follow him at all. The only thing I knew was that there were people who wanted to kill me and that I wasn't allowed to go to any ball games. Not even the sympathetic tone in the master's voice could make me understand that, and all during the ride home I kept telling myself to be strong and never say die. Sooner or later I'd find a way to get out of there, sooner or later I'd leave that Voodoo Man in the dust.

My third attempt failed just as miserably as the other two. I left in the morning that time, and even though I made it to the outskirts of Cibola, Master Yehudi was waiting for me again, perched on the buckboard wagon with that same self-satisfied grin spread across his face. I was utterly disarranged by that episode. Unlike the previous time, I could no longer dismiss his being there as a matter of chance. It was as if he had known I was going to run away before I knew it myself. The bastard was inside my head, sucking out the juices of my brain, and not even my innermost thoughts could be hidden from him.

Still, I didn't give up. I was just going to have to be more clever, more methodical in the way I went about it. After ample reflection, I concluded that the primary cause of my troubles was the farm itself. I couldn't get out of there because the place was so well-organized, so thoroughly self-sufficient. We had milk and butter from the cows, eggs from the chickens, meat from the pigs, vegetables from the root cellar, abundant stores of flour, salt, sugar, and cloth, and it was unnecessary for anyone to go to town to stock up on supplies. But what if we ran out of something, I told myself, what if there was a sudden shortage of some vital something we couldn't live without? The master would have to go off for more, wouldn't he? And as soon as he was gone, I'd sneak out of there and make my escape.

It was all so simple, I nearly gagged for joy when this idea came to me. It must have been February by then, and for the next month or so I thought of little else but sabotage. My mind churned with countless plots and schemes, conjuring up acts of untold terror and devastation. I figured I would start small – slashing a bag of flour or two, maybe pissing into the sugar barrel – but if those things failed to produce the desired result, I wasn't averse to more grandiose forms of vandalism: releasing the chickens from their coop, for example, or slitting the throats of the pigs. There wasn't anything I wasn't willing to do to get out of there, and if push came to shove, I was even prepared to set the straw on fire and burn down the barn.

None of it worked out as I imagined it would. I had my opportunities, but each time I was about to put a plan into operation, my nerve mysteriously failed me. Fear would well up in my lungs, my heart would begin to flutter, and just as my hand was poised to commit the deed, an invisible force would rob me of my strength. Nothing like that had ever happened before. I had always been a mischief-maker through and through, in full command of my impulses and desires. If I wanted to do something, I just went ahead and did it, plunging in with the recklessness of a born outlaw. Now I was stymied, blocked by a strange paralysis of will, and I despised myself for acting like such a coward, could not comprehend how a truant of my caliber could have sunk so low. Master Yehudi had beaten me to the punch again. He'd turned me into a puppet, and the more I struggled to defeat him, the tighter he pulled the strings.

I went through a month of hell before I found the courage to give it another shot. This time, luck seemed to be with me. Not ten minutes after hitting the road, I was picked up by a passing motorist, and he drove me all the way to Wichita. He was about the nicest fellow I'd ever met, a college boy on his way to see his fiancée, and we got along from the word go, regaling each other with stories for the whole two and a half hours. I wish I could remember his name. He was a sandy-haired lummox with freckles around his nose and a nifty little leather cap. For some reason, I remember that his girlfriend's name was Francine, but that must have been because he talked about her so much, going on at length about the rosy nipples on her breasts and the lacy trills attached to her undies. Leather Cap had a shiny new Ford roadster, and he sped down that empty highway as if there was no tomorrow. I got the giggles I felt so free and happy, and the more we

27

yacked about one thing and another, the freer and happier I felt. I'd really done it this time, I told myself. I'd really busted out of there, and from now on there'd be no stopping me.

I can't say precisely what I was expecting from Wichita, but it certainly wasn't the dreary little cow town I discovered that afternoon in 1925. The place was Podunk City, a pimple of yawns on a bare white butt. Where were the saloons and the gunslingers and the professional card sharks? Where was Wyatt Earp? Whatever Wichita had been in the past, its present incarnation was a sober, joyless muddle of shops and houses, a town built so low to the ground that your elbow knocked against the sky whenever you paused to scratch your head. I'd figured I'd get some scam going for myself, hang around for a few days while I built up my nest egg, and then travel back to Saint Louis in style. A quick tour of the streets convinced me to bag that notion, and half an hour after I'd arrived, I was already looking for a train to get me out of there.

I felt so glum and dejected, I didn't even notice that it had started to snow. March was the worst season for storms in that country, but the day had dawned so bright and clear, it hadn't even occurred to me to think the weather might change. It began with a small flurry, a few sprinkles of whiteness slithering through the clouds, but as I continued my walk across town in search of the rail depot, the flakes grew thicker and more intense, and when I stopped to check my bearings five or ten minutes later, I was already up to my ankles in the stuff. Snow was falling by the bucketful. Before I could say the word *blizzard*, the wind kicked up and started whirling the snow around in all directions at once. It was uncanny how fast it happened. One minute, I'd been walking through the streets of downtown Wichita, and the next minute I was lost, stumbling blindly through a white tempest. I had no clue as to where I was anymore. I was shivering under my wet clothes, the wind was in a frenzy, and I was smack in the middle of it, turning around in circles.

I'm not sure how long I blundered through that glop. No less than three hours, I would think, perhaps as many as five or six. I had reached town in the late afternoon, and I was still on my feet after nightfall, pushing my way through the mountainous drifts, hemmed in up to my knees, then up to my waist, then up to my neck, frantically looking for shelter before the snow swallowed my entire body. I had to keep moving. The slightest pause would bury me, and before I could fight my way out, I'd either freeze to death or suffocate. So I kept on struggling forward, even though I knew it was hopeless, even though I knew that each step was carrying me closer to my end. Where are the lights? I kept asking myself. I was wandering farther and farther away from town, out into the countryside where no one lived, and yet every time I shifted course, I found myself in the same darkness, surrounded by unbroken night and cold.

After a while, nothing felt real to me anymore. My mind had stopped working, and if my body was still dragging me along, it was only because it didn't know any better. When I saw the faint glow of light in the distance, it scarcely registered with me. I staggered toward it, no more conscious of what I was doing than a moth is when it zeroes in on a candle. At most I took it for a dream, an illusion cast before me by the shadows of death, and even though I kept it in front of me the whole time, I sensed it would be gone before I got there.

I don't remember crawling up the steps of the house or standing on the front porch, but I can still see my hand reaching out for the white porcelain doorknob, and I recall my surprise when I felt the knob turn and the latch clicked open. I stepped into the hallway, and everything was so bright in there, so intolerably radiant, that I was forced to shut my eyes. When I opened them again, a woman was standing in front of me – a beautiful woman with red hair. She was wearing a long white dress, and her blue eyes were looking at me with such wonder, such an expression of alarm, that I almost burst into tears. For a second or two, it crossed my mind that she was my mother, and then, when I remembered that my mother was dead, I realized that I must be dead myself and had just walked through the pearly gates.

'Look at you,' the woman said. 'You poor boy. Just look at you.'

'Forgive the intrusion, ma'am,' I said. 'My name is Walter Rawley, and I'm nine years old. I know this might sound strange, but I'd appreciate it if you told me where I am. I have a feeling this is heaven, and that don't seem right to me. After all the rotten things I done, I always figured I'd wind up in hell.'

'Oh dear,' the woman said. 'Just look at you. You're half frozen to death. Come into the parlor and warm yourself by the fire.'

Before I could repeat my question, she took me by the hand and led me around the staircase to the front room. Just as she opened the door, I heard her say, 'Darling, get this boy's clothes off him and sit him by the fire. I'm going upstairs to fetch some blankets.'

So I crossed the threshold by myself, stepping into the warmth of the parlor as clumps of snow dropped off me and started melting at my feet. A man was sitting at a small table in the corner, drinking coffee from a delicate china cup. He was nattily dressed in a pearl-gray suit, and his hair was slicked back with no part, glistening with brilliantine in the yellow lamplight. I was about to say something to him when he looked up and smiled, and right then and there I knew that I was dead and had gone straight to hell. Of all the shocks I've suffered in my long career, none was greater than the electrocution I received that night.

'Now you know,' the master said. 'Wherever you turn,

that's where I'm going to be. However far you run, I'll always be waiting for you at the other end. Master Yehudi is every-where, Walt, and it isn't possible to escape him.'

'You goddamn son-of-a-bitch,' I said. 'You double-crossing skunk. You shit-faced bag of garbage.'

'Watch your tongue, boy. This is Mrs Witherspoon's house, and she won't countenance any swearing here. If you don't want to get turned out into that storm, you'll strip off those clothes and behave yourself.'

'Make me, you big Jew turd,' I spat back at him. 'Just try and make me.'

But the master didn't have to do anything. A second after I gave him that answer, I felt a flood of hot, salty tears gush down my cheeks. I took a deep breath, gathering as much air into my lungs as I could, and then I let loose with a howl, a scream of pure, unbridled wretchedness. By the time it was halfway out of me, my throat felt all hoarse and choked up, and my head began to spin. I stopped to take another breath, and then, before I knew what was happening, I blacked out and fell to the floor.

I was sick for a long time after that. My body had caught fire, and as the fever burned within me, it looked more and more as though my next mailing address was going to be a wooden box. I spent the first days in Mrs Witherspoon's house, languishing in the upstairs guest room, but I remember none of that. Nor do I remember being taken back home, nor anything else for that matter until several weeks had passed. According to what they told me, I would have been a goner if not for Mother Sue – or Mother Sioux, as I eventually came to think of her. She sat by my bed around the clock, changing compresses and pouring spoonfuls of liquid down my throat, and three times a day she would get up from her chair and do a dance around my bed, beating out a special rhythm on her Oglala drum as she chanted prayers to the Great Spirit, imploring him to look down on me with sympathy and make me well again. I don't suppose it could have hurt the cause, for no professional doctor was ever called in to examine me, and considering that I did come round and make a full recovery, it's possible that her magic was what did the trick.

No one ever gave a medical name to my illness. My own thought was that it had been brought on by the hours I'd spent in the storm, but the master dismissed that explanation as of no account. It was the Ache of Being, he said, and it was bound to strike me down sooner or later. The poisons had to be purged from my system before I could advance to the next plateau of my training, and what might have dragged on for another six or nine months (with countless skirmishes between us) had been cut short by our fortuitous encounter in Wichita. I had been jolted into submission, he said, crushed by the knowledge that I would never triumph against him, and that mental blow had been the spark that triggered off the illness. After that, the rancor was cleansed out of me, and when I woke from the nightmare of my near death, the hatred festering inside me had been transformed into love.

I don't want to contradict the master's opinion, but it seems to me that my turnaround was a good deal simpler than that. It might have started just after my fever went down, when I woke up and saw Mother Sioux sitting beside me with one of those rapturous, beatific smiles on her face. 'Fancy that,' she said. 'My little Walnut's back in the land of the living.' There was such gladness in her voice, such an obvious concern for my well-being, that something inside me started to melt. 'No sweat, Sister Ma,' I said, barely conscious of what I was saying. 'I've just been snoozing is all.' I immediately shut my eyes and sank back into my torpor, but just as I was drifting off, I distinctly felt Mother Sioux's lips brush against my cheek. It was the first kiss anyone had given me since my mother died, and it brought on such a warm and welcoming glow, I realized that I didn't care where it had come from. If that chubby Indian squaw wanted to nuzzle with me like that, then by God let her, I wasn't going to stand in her way.

That was the first step, I think, but there were other incidents as well, not the least of which occurred a few days later, at a moment when my fever had shot back up again. I awoke in the early afternoon to find the room empty. I was about to crawl out of bed to make a stab at using the chamber pot, but once I disentangled my ears from the pillow, I heard whispering outside my door. Master Yehudi and Aesop were standing in the hall, engaged in a hushed conversation, and though I couldn't make out everything they said, I caught enough to determine the gist. Aesop was out there giving it to the master, standing up to the big man and telling him not to be so hard on me. I couldn't believe what I was hearing. After all the trouble and unpleasantness I had caused him, I felt mortally ashamed of myself to know that Aesop was on my side. 'You've crushed the soul out of him,' he whispered, 'and now he's in there lying on his deathbed. It's not fair, master. I know he's a hell-raiser and a scamp, but there's more than just rebellion in his heart. I've felt it, I've seen it with my own eyes. And even if I'm wrong, he still wouldn't deserve the kind of treatment you've given him. No one does.'

It felt extraordinary to have someone speak up for me like that, but even more extraordinary was that Aesop's harangue did not fall on deaf ears. That very night, as I lay tossing and turning in the dark, Master Yehudi himself crept into my room, sat down on the sweat-soaked bed, and took hold of my hand in his. I kept my eyes shut and didn't make a sound, pretending to be asleep the whole time he was there. 'Don't die on me, Walt,' he said softly, as if speaking to himself. 'You're a tough little bugger, and the time hasn't come for you to give up the ghost. We have great things in store for us, wondrous things you can't even imagine. You might think I'm against you, but I'm not. It's just that I know who you are, and I know you can handle the pressure. You've got the gift, son, and I'm going to take you farther than anyone has ever gone before. Do you hear me, Walt? I'm telling you not to die. I'm telling you I need you and that you mustn't die on me yet.'

I heard him all right. He was coming through to me loud and clear, and tempted as I was to say something in response, I beat back the urge and held my tongue. A long silence followed. Master Yehudi sat there in the darkness stroking my hand, and after a while, if I'm not mistaken, if I didn't doze off and dream what happened next, I heard, or at least I thought I heard, a series of broken-off sobs, an almost indiscernible rumbling that spilled out from the large man's chest and pierced the quiet of the room – once, twice, a dozen times.

It would be an exaggeration to say that I abandoned my suspicions all at once, but there's no question that my attitude started to change. I'd learned that escape was pointless, and now that I was stuck there whether I liked it or not, I decided to make the most of what I'd been given. Perhaps my brush with death had something to do with it, I don't know, but once I climbed out of my sickbed and got back on my feet, the chip I'd been carrying around on my shoulder was no longer there. I was so glad to be well again, it no longer bothered me that I was living with the outcasts of the universe. They were a curious, unsavoury lot, but in spite of my constant grumbling and bad behavior, each one of them had developed a certain affection for me, and I would have been a lout to ignore that. Perhaps it all boiled down to the fact that I was finally getting used to them. If you look into someone's face long enough, eventually you're going to feel that you're looking at yourself.

All that said, I don't mean to imply that my life became any easier. In the short run, it proved to be even rougher than before, and just because I'd throttled my resistance somewhat, that didn't make me any less of a wisenheimer, any less of the pugnacious little punk I'd always been. Spring was upon us, and within a week of my recovery I was out in the fields plowing up the ground and planting seeds, breaking my back like some grubby, bird-brained hick. I abhorred manual labor, and given that I had no knack for it whatsoever, I looked upon those days as a penance, an unending trial of blisters, bloody fingers, and stubbed toes. But at least I wasn't out there alone. The four of us worked together for approximately a month, suspending all other business as we hastened to get the crops in on time (corn, wheat, alfalfa, oats) and to prepare the soil for Mother Sioux's vegetable garden, which would keep our stomachs full throughout the summer. The work was too hard for us to stand around and chat, but I had an audience for my complaints now, and whenever I let forth with one of my caustic asides, I always managed to get a laugh out of someone. That was the big difference between the days before and after I fell sick. My mouth never stopped

35

working, but whereas previously my comments had been construed as vicious, ungrateful barbs, they were now looked upon as jokes, the rambunctious patter of a clever little clown.

Master Yehudi toiled like an ox, slogging away at his tasks as if he had been born to the land, and he never failed to accomplish more than the rest of us put together. Mother Sioux was steady, diligent, silent, advancing in a constant crouch as her vast rear end jutted up into the sky. She came from a race of hunters and warriors, and farming was as unnatural to her as it was to me. Inept as I might have been, however, Aesop was even worse, and it comforted me to know that he was not one bit more enthusiastic about wasting his time on that drudgery than I was. He wanted to be indoors reading his books, to be dreaming his dreams and hatching his ideas, and while he never openly confronted the master with his grievances, he was particularly responsive to my cracks, interrupting my jags of whimsy with spontaneous guffaws, and each time he laughed it was as if he were exhaling a loud *amen*, reassuring me that I'd hit the nail on the head. I had always thought of Aesop as a goody-goody, an inoffensive killjoy who never broke the rules, but after listening to his laughter out there in the fields, I began to form a new opinion of him. There was more spice in those crooked bones than I had imagined, and in spite of his earnestness and uppity ways, he was as much on the lookout for fun as any other fifteen-year-old. What I did was to provide him with some comic relief. My sharp tongue tickled him, my sass and pluck buoyed his spirits, and as time went on I understood that he was no longer a nuisance or a rival. He was a friend – the first real friend I'd ever had.

I don't mean to wax sentimental, but this is my childhood I'm talking about, the quiltwork of my earliest memories, and with so few attachments to talk about from later years, my friendship with Aesop deserves to be noted. As much as Master Yehudi himself, he marked me in ways that altered who I was, that changed the course and substance of my life. I'm not just referring to my prejudices, the old witchcraft of never looking past the color of a person's skin, but to the fact of friendship itself, to the bond that grew between us. Aesop became my comrade, my anchor in a sea of undifferentiated sky, and without him there to buck me up, I never would have found the courage to withstand the torments that engulfed me over the next twelve or fourteen months. The master had wept in the darkness of my sickroom, but once I was well again, he turned into a slave driver, subjecting me to agonies that no living soul should have to endure. When I look back on those days now, I'm astonished that I didn't die, that I'm actually still here to talk about them.

Once the planting season was over and our food was in the ground, the real work began. It was just after my tenth birthday, a pretty morning at the end of May. The master pulled me aside after breakfast and whispered into my ear, 'Brace yourself, kid. The fun is about to start.'

'You mean we ain't been having fun?' I said. 'Correct me if I'm wrong, but I thought that Four-H stuff was about the funnest whirl I've had since the last time I played Chinese checkers.'

'Working the land is one thing, a dull but necessary chore. But now we're going to turn our thoughts to the sky.'

'You mean like them birds you told me about?'

'That's it, Walt, just like the birds.'

'You're telling me you're still serious about that plan of yours?'

'Dead serious. We're about to advance to the thirteenth stage. If you do what I tell you, you'll be airborne a year from next Christmas.'

'Thirteenth stage? You mean I've already gone through twelve of them?'

'That's right, twelve. And you've passed each one with flying colors.'

37

'Well, shave my tonsils. And I never had no inkling. You've been holding out on me, boss.'

'I only tell you what you need to know. The rest is for me to worry about.'

'Twelve stages, huh? And how many more to go?'

'There are thirty-three in all.'

'If I get through the next twelve as fast as the first ones, I'll already be in the home stretch.'

'You won't, I promise you. However much you think you've suffered so far, it's nothing compared to what lies ahead.'

'The birds don't suffer. They just spread their wings and take off. If I got the gift like you say, I don't see why it shouldn't be a breeze.'

'Because, my little pumpkin-head, you're not a bird – you're a man. In order to lift you off the ground, we have to crack the heavens in two. We have to turn the whole bloody universe inside out.'

Once again, I didn't understand the tenth part of what the master was saying, but I nodded when he called me a man, feeling in that word a new tone of appreciation, an acknowledgment of the importance I had assumed in his eyes. He put his hand gently on my shoulder and led me out into the May morning. I felt nothing but trust for him at that moment, and though his face was set in a grim, inward-looking expression, it never crossed my mind that he would do anything to break that trust. That's probably how Isaac felt when Abraham took him up that mountain in Genesis, chapter twenty-two. If a man tells you he's your father, even if you know he's not, you let down your guard and get all stupid inside. You don't imagine that he's been conspiring against you with God, the Lord of Hosts. A boy's brain doesn't work that fast; it's not subtle enough to fathom such chicanery. All you know is that the big guy has placed his hand on your shoulder and given it a friendly squeeze. He tells you, Come with me, and so you turn yourself in that direction and follow him wherever he's going.

We walked out past the barn to the tool shed, a rickety little structure with a sagging roof and walls made of weathered, unpainted planks. Master Yehudi opened the door and stood there in silence for a long moment, gazing at the dark tangle of metal objects inside. At last he reached in and pulled out a shovel, a rusty lug of a thing that must have weighed fifteen or twenty pounds. He put the shovel in my hands, and I felt proud to be carrying it for him once we started walking again. We passed along the edge of the near cornfield, and it was a splendid morning, I remember, filled with darting robins and bluebirds, and my skin was tingling with a strange sense of aliveness, the blessing of the sun's warmth as it poured down upon me. By and by we came to a patch of untilled ground, a bare spot at the juncture of two fields, and the master turned to me and said, 'This is where we're going to put the hole. Do you want to do the digging, or would you rather leave it to me?'

I gave it my best shot, but my arms weren't up to it. I was too small to wield a shovel of that heft, and when the master saw me struggling just to pierce the soil, let alone slide the blade in under it, he told me to sit down and rest, he would finish the job himself. For the next two hours I watched him transform that patch of earth into an immense cavity, a hole as broad and deep as a giant's grave. He worked so fast that it seemed as if the earth was swallowing him up, and after a time he had burrowed down so low that I couldn't see his head anymore. I could hear his grunts, the locomotive huff and puff that accompanied each turn of the spade, and then a volley of loose dirt would come soaring up over the surface, hang for a second in midair, and then drop to the pile that was growing around the hole. He kept at it as if there were ten of him, an army of diggers bent on tunneling to Australia, and when he finally stopped and hoisted himself out of the pit, he was so smudged with filth and sweat that he looked like a man made of coal, a haggard vaudevillian about to die with his blackface on. I had never seen anyone pant so hard, had never witnessed a body so deprived of breath, and when he flung himself to the ground and didn't stir for the next ten minutes, I felt certain that his heart was about to give out on him.

I was too awed to speak. I studied the master's ribcage for signs of collapse, shuttling between joy and sorrow as his chest heaved up and down, up and down, swelling and shrinking against the long blue horizon. Halfway through my vigil, a cloud wandered in front of the sun and the sky turned ominously dark. I thought it was the angel of death passing overhead, but Master Yehudi's lungs kept on pumping as the air slowly brightened again, and a moment later he sat up and smiled, eagerly wiping the dirt from his face.

'Well,' he said, 'what do you think of our hole?'

'It's a grand hole,' I said, 'as deep and lovely a hole as there ever was.'

'I'm glad you like it, because you and that hole are going to be on intimate terms for the next twenty-four hours.'

'I don't mind. It looks like an interesting place to me. As long as it don't rain, it might be fun to sit in there for a while.'

'No need to worry about the rain, Walt.'

'You a weatherman or something? Maybe you haven't noticed, but conditions change around here about every fifteen minutes. When it comes to weather, this Kansas place is as fickle as it gets.'

'True enough. The skies in these parts can't be counted on. But I'm not saying it won't rain. Just that you don't have to worry if it does.'

'Sure, give me a cover, or one of them canvas thingamajigs – a tarp. That's good thinking. You can't go wrong if you plan for the worst.'

'I'm not putting you down there for fun and frolic. You'll

40

have a breath-hole, of course, a long tube to keep in your mouth for purposes of respiration, but otherwise it's going to be fairly dank and uncomfortable. A closed-in, wormy kind of discomfort, if you forgive my saying so. I doubt you'll forget the experience as long as you live.'

'I know I'm dumb, but if you don't stop talking in riddles, we'll be out here all day before I glom onto your drift.'

'I'm going to bury you, son.'

'Say what?'

'I'm going to put you down in that hole, cover you up with dirt, and bury you alive.'

'And you expect me to agree to that?'

'You don't have any choice. Either you go down there of your own volition or I strangle you with my two bare hands. One way, you get to live a long, prosperous life; the other way, your life ends in thirty seconds.'

So I let him bury me alive – an experience I would not recommend to anyone. Distasteful as the idea sounds, the actual incarceration is far worse, and once you've spent some time in the bowels of netherness as I did that day, the world can never look the same to you again. It becomes inexpressibly more beautiful, and yet that beauty is drenched in a light so transient, so unreal, that it never takes on any substance, and even though you can see it and touch it as you always did, a part of you understands that it is no more than a mirage. Feeling the dirt on top of you is one thing, the pressure and coldness of it, the panic of deathlike immobility, but the true terror doesn't begin until later, until after you've been unburied and can stand up and walk again. From then on, everything that happens to you on the surface is connected to those hours you spent underground. A little seed of craziness has been planted in your head, and even though you've won the struggle to survive, nearly everything else has been lost. Death lives inside you, eating away at your innocence and your hope, and in the end you're left with nothing but

41

the dirt, the solidity of the dirt, the everlasting power and triumph of the dirt.

That was how my initiation began. Over the weeks and months that followed, I lived through more of the same, an unremitting avalanche of wrongs. Each test was more terrible than the one before it, and if I managed not to back down, it was only from sheer reptilian stubbornness, a brainless passivity that lurked somewhere in the core of my soul. It had nothing to do with will or determination or courage. I had none of those qualities, and the farther I was pushed, the less pride I felt in my accomplishments. I was flogged with a bullwhip; I was thrown from a galloping horse; I was lashed to the roof of the barn for two days without food or water; I had my skin smeared with honey and then stood naked in the August heat as a thousand flies and wasps swarmed over me; I sat in a circle of fire for one whole night as my body became scorched with blisters; I was dunked repeatedly for six straight hours in a tubfull of vinegar; I was struck by lightning; I drank cow piss and ate horseshit; I took a knife and cut off the upper joint of my left pinky; I dangled for three days and three nights in a cocoon of ropes from the rafters in the attic. I did these things because Master Yehudi told me to do them, and if I could not bring myself to love him, neither did I hate him or resent him for the sufferings I endured. He no longer had to threaten me. I followed his commands with blind obedience, never bothering to question what his purpose might have been. He told me to jump, and I jumped. He told me to stop breathing, and I stopped breathing. This was the man who had promised to make me fly, and even though I never believed him, I let him use me as if I did. We had our bargain, after all, the pact we'd made that first night in Saint Louis, and I never forgot it. If he didn't come through for me by my thirteenth birthday, I was going to lop off his head with an axe. There was nothing personal about that arrangement – it was a simple matter of justice. If the son-of-a-bitch let me down, I was going to kill him, and he knew it as well as I did.

While these ordeals lasted, Aesop and Mother Sioux stuck by me as if I were their flesh and blood, the darling of their hearts. There were lulls between the various stages of my development, sometimes days, sometimes weeks, and more often than not Master Yehudi would vanish, leaving the farm altogether while my wounds mended and I recovered to face the next dumbfounding assault on my person. I had no idea where he went during those pauses, nor did I ask the others about it, since I always felt relieved when he was gone. Not only was I safe from further trials, but I was freed from the burden of the master's presence – his brooding silences and tormented looks, the enormity of the space he occupied – and that alone reassured me, gave me a chance to breathe again. The house was a happier place without him, and the three of us lived together in remarkable harmony. Plump Mother Sioux and her two skinny boys. Those were the days when Aesop and I became pals, and miserable as much of that time was for me, it also contains some good memories, perhaps the best memories of all. He was a great one for telling stories, Aesop was, and I liked nothing better than to listen to that sweet voice of his spinning out the wild tales that were crammed in his head. He knew hundreds of them, and whenever I asked him, lying in bed all bruised and sore from my latest pummeling, he would sit there for hours reciting one story after another. Jack the Giant Killer, Sinbad the Sailor, Ulysses the Wanderer, Billy the Kid, Lancelot and King Arthur, Paul Bunyan – I heard them all. The best ones, though, the stories he saved for when I was feeling particularly blue, were about my namesake, Sir Walter Raleigh. I remember how shocked I was when he told me I had a famous name, the name of a real-life adventurer and hero. To prove that he wasn't making it up, Aesop went to the book shelf and pulled down a thick volume with Sir Walter's

43

picture in it. I had never seen a more elegant face, and I soon fell into the habit of studying it for ten or fifteen minutes every day. I loved the pointy beard and razor-sharp eyes, the pearl earring fixed in his left lobe. It was the face of a pirate, a genuine swashbuckling knight, and from that day forth I carried Sir Walter inside me as a second self, an invisible brother to stand with me through thick and thin. Aesop recounted the stories of the cloak and the puddle, the search for El Dorado, the lost colony at Roanoke, the thirteen years in the Tower of London, the brave words he uttered at his beheading. He was the best poet of his day; he was a scholar, a scientist, and a freethinker; he was the number-one lover of women in all of England. 'Think of you and me put together,' Aesop said, 'and you begin to get an idea of who he was. A man with my brains and your guts, and tall and handsome as well – that's Sir Walter Raleigh, the most perfect man who ever lived.'

Every night, Mother Sioux would come into my room and tuck me in, sitting on my bed for however long it took me to fall asleep. I came to depend on this ritual, and though I was growing up fast and hard in every other way, I was still just a baby to her. I never let myself cry in front of Master Yehudi or Aesop, but with Mother Sioux I let the ducts give way on countless occasions, blubbering in her arms like some hapless mama's boy. Once, I remember, I even went so far as to touch on the subject of flying, and what she said was so unexpected, so calm in its assurance, that it pacified the turmoil within me for weeks to come – not because I believed it myself, but because she did, and she was the person I trusted most in the world.

'He's a wicked man,' I said, referring to the master, 'and by the time he's through with me, I'll be as hunched and crippled as Aesop.'

'No, sonny, it ain't so. You'll be dancing with the clouds in the sky.'

'With a harp in my hands and wings sprouting from my back.'

'In your own skin. In your own flesh and bones.'

'It's a bluff, Mother Sioux, a disgusting pack of lies. If he aims to teach me what he says, why don't he get down and do it? For one whole year, I've suffered every indignity known to man. I've been buried, I've been burned, I've been mutilated, and I'm still as bound to the earth as I ever was.'

'Those are the steps. It has to be done that way. But the worst is nearly behind you now.'

'So he's suckered you into believing it, too.'

'No one suckers Mother Sioux into anything. I'm too old and too fat to swallow what people say. False words are like chicken bones. They catch in my throat and I spit them out.'

'Men can't fly. It's as simple as that. Men can't fly because God don't want them to.'

'It can be done.'

'In some other world maybe. But not this one.'

'I saw it happen. When I was a little girl. I saw it with my own two eyes. And if it happened before, it can happen again.'

'You dreamed it. You thought you saw it, but it was only in your sleep.'

'My own father, Walt. My own father and my own brother. I saw them moving through the air like spirits. It wasn't flying the way you imagine it. Not like birds or moths, not with wings or anything like that. But they were up in the air, and they were moving. All slow and strange. As if they was swimming. Pushing their way through the air like swimmers, like spirits walking on the bottom of a lake.'

'Why didn't you tell me this before?'

'Because you wouldn't have believed me before. That's why I'm telling you now. Because the time is coming. If you listen to what the master tells you, it's coming sooner than you think.'

45

When spring rolled around for the second time, the farm work was like a holiday to me, and I threw myself into it with manic good cheer, welcoming the chance to live like a normal person again. Instead of lagging behind and grousing about my aches and pains, I surged along at top speed, daring myself to stick with it, reveling in my own exertions. I was still puny for my age, but I was older and stronger, and even though it was impossible, I did all I could to keep up with Master Yehudi himself. I was out to prove something, I suppose, to stun him into respecting me, to be noticed. This was a new way of fighting back, and every time the master told me to slow down, to ease off and not push so hard ('It's not an Olympic sport,' he would say, 'we're not out here competing for medals, kid'), I felt as if I had won a victory, as if I were gradually regaining possession of my soul.

My pinky joint had healed by then. What had once been a bloody mess of tissue and bone had smoothed over into an odd, nailless stump. I enjoyed looking at it now and running my thumb over the scar, touching that bit of me that was gone forever. I must have done it fifty or a hundred times a day, and every time I did, I would sound out the words *Saint Louis* in my head. I was struggling to hold on to my past, but by then the words had become just words, a ritual exercise in remembrance. They summoned forth no pictures, took me on no journeys back to where I had been. After eighteen months in Cibola, Saint Louis had been turned into a phantom city for me, and a little more of it was vanishing every day.

One afternoon that spring the weather became inordinately hot, boiling up to midsummer levels. The four of us were working out in the fields, and when the master removed his shirt for greater comfort, I saw that he was wearing something around his neck: a leather thong with a small, transparent globe hanging from it like a jewel or an ornament. When I approached him to have a better look – merely curious, with no ulterior motive – I saw that it was my missing pinky joint, encased in the pendant along with some kind of clear liquid. The master must have noticed my surprise, for he glanced down at his chest with an expression of alarm, as if he thought a spider might be crawling there. When he saw what it was, he took hold of the globe in his fingers and held it out to me, smiling with satisfaction. 'A pretty little widget, eh Walt?' he said.

'I don't know about pretty,' I said, 'but it looks awful familiar to me.'

'It should. It used to belong to you. For the first ten years of your life, it was part of who you were.'

'It still is. Just because it's detached from my body, that don't make it any less mine than before.'

'It's pickled in formaldehyde. Preserved like some dead fetus in a jar. It doesn't belong to you now, it belongs to science.'

'Yeah, then what's it doing around your neck? If it belongs to science, why not donate it to the wax museum?'

'Because it has special meaning for me, sport. I wear it to remind myself of the debt I owe you. Like a hangman's noose. This thing is the albatross of my conscience, and I can't let it fall into a stranger's hands.'

'What about my hands, then? Fair is fair, and I want my joint back. If anyone wears that necklace, it's got to be me.'

'I'll make a bargain with you. If you let me hold on to it a little longer, I'll think of it as yours. That's a promise. It's got your name on it, and once I get you off the ground, you can have it back.'

'For keeps?'

'For keeps. Of course for keeps.'

'And how long is this "little longer" going to be?'

47

'Not long. You're already standing on the brink.'

'The only brink I'm standing on is the brink of perdition. And if that's where I am, that's where you are, too. Ain't that so, master?'

'You catch on fast, son. United we stand, divided we fall. You for me and me for you, and where we stop nobody knows.'

This was the second time I had been given encouraging news about my progress. First from Mother Sioux, and now from the master himself. I won't deny that I felt flattered, but for all their confidence in my abilities, I failed to see that I was one jot closer to success. After that sweltering afternoon in May, we went through a period of epic heat, the hottest summer in living memory. The ground was a caldron, and every time you walked on it, you felt that the soles would melt right off your shoes. We prayed for rain at supper every evening, and for three months not a single drop fell from the sky. The air was so parched, so delirious in its desiccation, you could track the buzzing of a horsefly from a hundred yards away. Everything seemed to itch, to rasp like thistle rubbing against barbed wire, and the smell from the outhouse was so rank it singed the hairs in your nostrils. The corn wilted, drooped, and died; the lettuce bolted to grotesque, gargantuan heights, standing in the garden like mutant towers. By mid-August, you could drop a pebble down the well and count to six before you heard the water plink. No green beans, no corn on the cob, no succulent tomatoes like the year before. We subsisted on eggs and mush and smoked ham, and while there was enough to see us through the summer, our diminishing stores boded ill for the months that lay ahead. 'Tighten your belts, children,' the master would say to us at supper, 'tighten your belts and chew until you can't taste it anymore. If we don't stretch out what we have, it's going to be a long, hungry winter.'

For all the woes that assailed us during the drought, I was

happy, much happier than would have seemed possible. I had weathered the most gruesome parts of my initiation, and what stood before me now were the stages of mental struggle, the showdown between myself and myself. Master Yehudi was hardly an obstacle anymore. He would issue his commands and then disappear from my mind, leading me to places of such inwardness that I no longer remembered who I was. The physical stages had been a war, an act of defiance against the master's skull-denting cruelty, and he had never withdrawn from my sight, standing over me as he studied my reactions, watching my face for each microscopic shudder of pain. All that was finished now. He had turned into a gentle, munificent guide, talking in the soft voice of a seducer as he lured me into accepting one bizarre task after another. He had me go into the barn and count every blade of straw in the horse's stall. He had me stand on one leg for an entire night, then stand on the other leg for the whole of the next night. He tied me to a post in the midday sun and ordered me to repeat his name ten thousand times. He imposed a vow of silence on me, and for twenty-four days I did not speak to anyone, did not utter a sound even when I was alone. He had me roll my body across the yard, he had me hop, he had me jump through hoops. He taught me how to cry at will, and then he taught me how to laugh and cry at the same time. He made me teach myself how to juggle, and once I could juggle three stones, he made me juggle four. He blindfolded me for a week, then he plugged my ears for a week, then he bound my arms and legs together for a week and made me crawl on my belly like a worm.

The weather broke in early September. Downpours, lightning and thunder, high winds, a tornado that barely missed carrying away the house. Water levels rose again, but otherwise we were no better off than we'd been. The crops had failed, and with nothing to add to our long-term supplies, prospects for the future were bleak, touch and go at best. The

49

master reported that farmers all over the region had been similarly devastated, and the mood in town was turning ugly. Prices were down, credit was scarce, and talk of bank foreclosures was in the air. When pocketbooks are empty, the master said, brains fill with anger and smut. 'Those peckerwoods can rot for all I care,' he continued, 'but after a while they're going to look for someone to blame their troubles on, and when that happens, the four of us had better duck.' Throughout that strange autumn of storms and drenchings, Master Yehudi seemed distracted with worry, as if he were contemplating some unnameable disaster, a thing so black he dared not say it aloud. After coddling me all summer, urging me on through the rigors of my spiritual exercises, he suddenly seemed to have lost interest in me. His absences became more frequent, once or twice he stumbled in with what smelled like liquor on his breath, and he had all but abandoned his study sessions with Aesop. A new sadness had crept into his eyes, a look of wistfulness and foreboding. Much of this is dim to me now, but I remember that during the brief moments when he graced me with his company, he acted with surprising warmth. One incident stands out from the blur: an evening in early October when he walked into the house with a newspaper under his arm and a big grin on his face. 'I have good news for you,' he said to me, sitting down and spreading out the paper on the kitchen table. 'Your team won. I hope that makes you glad, because it says here it's been thirty-eight years since they came out on top.'

'My team?' I said.

'The Saint Louis Cardinals. That's your team, isn't it?'

'You bet it is. I'm with those Redbirds till the end of time.'

'Well, they've just won the World Series. According to what's printed here, the seventh game was the most breathless, riveting contest ever played.'

That was how I learned my boys had become the 1926 champions. Master Yehudi read me the account of the dramatic seventh inning, when Grover Cleveland Alexander came in to strike out Tony Lazzeri with the bases loaded. For the first few minutes, I thought he was making it up. The last I'd heard, Alexander was top dog on the Philly staff, and Lazzeri was a name that meant nothing to me. It sounded like a pile of foreign noodles smothered in garlic sauce, but then the master informed me that he was a rookie and that Grover had been traded to the Cards in mid-season. He'd hurled nine innings just the day before, shutting down the Yanks to knot the series at three games apiece, and here was Rogers Hornsby calling him in from the bullpen to snuff out a rally with the whole ball of wax on the line. And the old guy sauntered in, drunk as a skunk from last night's bender, and mowed down the young New York hotshot. If not for a couple of inches, it would have been another story. On the pitch before the third strike, Lazzeri drove one into the left field seats, a sure grand slam that hooked foul at the last second. It was enough to give you apoplexy. Alexander hung in there through the eighth and ninth to nail down the win, and to top it off, the game and the series ended when Babe Ruth, the one and only Sultan of Swat, was thrown out trying to steal second base. There had never been anything like it. It was the maddest, most infernal game in history, and my Redbirds were the champs, the best team in the world.

That was a watershed for me, a landmark event in my young life, but otherwise the fall was a somber stretch, a long interlude of boredom and quiet. After a while, I got so antsy that I asked Aesop if he wouldn't mind teaching me how to read. He was more than willing, but he had to clear it with Master Yehudi first, and when the master gave his approval, I confess that I was a little hurt. He'd always said how he wanted to keep me stupid – how it was an advantage as far as my training was concerned – and now he had blithely gone ahead and reversed himself without any explanation. For a time I thought it meant he had given up on me, and disappointment festered in my heart, a hangdog sorrow that dragged down all my bright dreams and turned them to dust. What had I done wrong, I asked myself, and why had he deserted me when I most needed him?

So I learned the letters and numbers with Aesop's help, and once I got started, they came so quickly that I wondered what all the fuss had been about. If I wasn't going to fly, at least I could convince the master that I wasn't a dolt, but so little effort was involved, it soon felt like a hollow victory. Spirits around the house picked up for a while in November when our food shortage was suddenly eliminated. Without telling anyone where he'd found the money to do such a thing, the master had secretly arranged for a delivery of canned goods. It felt like a miracle when it happened, an absolute bolt from the blue. A truck arrived at our door one morning and two burly men began unloading cartons from the back. There were hundreds of boxes, and each box contained two dozen cans of food: vegetables of every variety, meats and broths, puddings, preserved apricots and peaches, an outflow of unimaginable abundance. It took the men over an hour to haul the shipment into the house, and the whole time the master just stood there with his arms folded across his chest, grinning like a crafty old owl. Aesop and I both gawked, and after a while he called us over to him and put a hand on each of our shoulders. 'It can't hold a candle to Mother Sioux's cooking,' he said, 'but it's a damn sight better than mush, eh boys? When the chips are down, just remember who to count on. No matter how dark our troubles might be, I'll always find a way to pull us through.'

However he had managed it, the crisis was over. Our larder was full again, and we no longer stood up from meals craving more, no longer moaned about our gurgling bellies. You'd think this turnaround would have earned our undying gratitude, but the fact was that we quickly learned to take it for granted. Within ten days, it seemed perfectly normal that we

52

should be eating well, and by the end of the month it was hard to remember the days when we hadn't. That's how it is with want. As long as you lack something, you yearn for it without cease. If only I could have that one thing, you tell yourself, all my problems would be solved. But once you get it, once the object of your desires is thrust into your hands, it begins to lose its charm. Other wants assert themselves, other desires make themselves felt, and bit by bit you discover that you're right back where you started. So it was with my reading lessons; so it was with the newfound plenty jammed into the kitchen cupboards. I had thought those things would make a difference, but in the end they were no more than shadows, substitute longings for the one thing I really wanted – which was precisely the thing I couldn't have. I needed the master to love me again. That's what the story of those months came down to. I hungered for the master's affections, and no amount of food was ever going to satisfy me. After two years, I had learned that everything I was flowed directly from him. He had made me in his own image, and now he wasn't there for me anymore. For reasons I couldn't understand, I felt I had lost him forever.

It never occurred to me to think of Mrs Witherspoon. Not even when Mother Sioux dropped a hint one night about the master's 'widow lady' in Wichita did I put six and three together. I was backward in that regard, an eleven-year-old know-it-all who didn't understand the first thing that went on between men and women. I assumed it was all carnal, intermittent spasms of wayward lust, and when Aesop talked to me about planting his boners in a nice warm quim (he had just turned seventeen), I immediately thought of the whores I'd known in Saint Louis, the blowsy, wisecracking dolls who strutted up and down the alleys at two in the morning, peddling their bodies for cold, hard cash. I didn't know dirt about grown-up love or marriage or any of the so-called lofty sentiments. The only married couple I'd seen was Uncle Slim and Aunt Peg, and that was such a brutal combination, such a frenzy of spitting, cursing, and clamor, it probably made sense that I was so ignorant. When the master went away, I figured he was playing poker somewhere or belting back a bottle of rotgut in a Cibola speakeasy. It never dawned on me that he was in Wichita courting a high-class lady like Marion Witherspoon – and gradually getting his heart broken in the process. I had actually laid eyes on her myself, but I had been so sick and feverish at the time that I could scarcely remember her. She was a hallucination, a figment born in the throes of death, and even though her face flashed through me every now and then, I did not credit her as real. If anything, I thought she was my mother – but then I would grow scared, appalled that I couldn't recognize my own mother's ghost.

It took a couple of near disasters to set me straight. In early December, Aesop cut his finger opening a can of cling peaches. It seemed like nothing at first, a simple scratch that would heal in no time, but instead of scabbing over as it should have, it swelled up into a frightful bloat of pus and rawness, and by the third day poor Aesop was languishing in bed with a high fever. It was fortunate that Master Yehudi was home then, for in addition to his other talents, he had a fair knowledge of medicine, and when he went upstairs to Aesop's room the next morning to see how the patient was doing, he walked out two minutes later shaking his head and blinking back a rush of tears. 'There's no time to waste,' he said to me. 'Gangrene has set in, and unless we get rid of that finger now, it's liable to spread through his hand and up into his arm. Run outside and tell Mother Sioux to drop what's she's doing and put on two pots of water to boil. I'll go down to the kitchen and sharpen the knives. We have to operate within the hour.'

I did what I was told, and once I'd rounded up Mother Sioux from the barnyard, I dashed back into the house, climbed the stairs to the second floor, and parked myself beside my friend. Aesop looked dreadful. The lustrous black of his skin had turned to a chalky, mottled gray, and I could hear the phlegm rattling in his chest as his head lolled back and forth on the pillow.

'Hang on, buddy,' I said. 'It won't be long now. The master's going to fix you up, and before you know it you'll be downstairs at the ivories again, twiddling out one of your goofy rags.'

'Walt?' he said. 'Is that you, Walt?' He opened his bloodshot eyes and looked in the direction of my voice, but his pupils were so glazed over I wasn't sure he could see me.

'Of course it's me,' I answered. 'Who else do you think would be sitting here at a time like this?'

'He's going to cut off my finger, Walt. I'll be deformed for life, and no girl will ever want me.'

'You're already deformed for life, and that hasn't stopped you from hankering for twat, has it? He ain't going to cut off your dick, Aesop. Only a finger, and a finger on your left hand at that. As long as your willy's still attached, you can bang the broads till kingdom come.'

'I don't want to lose my finger,' he moaned. 'If I lose my finger, it means there's no justice. It means that God has turned his back on me.'

'I ain't got but nine and a half fingers myself, and it don't bother me hardly at all. Once you lose yours, we'll be just like twins. Bonafide members of the Nine Finger Club, brothers till the day we drop – just like the master always said.'

I did what I could to reassure him, but once the operation began, I was shunted aside and forgotten. I stood in the doorway with my hands over my face, peeking through the cracks every now and then as the master and Mother Sioux did their work. There was no ether or anaesthetic, and Aesop howled and howled, belting out a horrific, bloodcurdling noise that never slackened from start to finish. Sorry as I felt for him, those howls nearly undid me. They were inhuman, and the terror they expressed was so deep and so prolonged, it was all I could do not to begin screaming myself. Master Yehudi went about his business with the calm of a trained doctor, but the howls got to Mother Sioux just as badly as they got to me. That was the last thing I was expecting from her. I'd always thought that Indians hid their feelings, that they were braver and more stoical than white folks, but the truth was that Mother S. was unhinged, and as the blood continued to spurt and Aesop's pain continued to mount, she gasped and whimpered as if the knife was tearing into her own flesh. Master Yehudi told her to get a grip on herself. She apologized, but fifteen seconds later she started sobbing again. She was a pitiful nurse, and after a while her tearful interruptions so distracted the master that he had to send her out of the room. 'We need a fresh bucket of boiling water,' he said. 'Snap to it, woman. On the double.' It was just an excuse to get rid of her, and as she rushed past me into the hall, she buried her face in her hands and wept on blindly to the top of the stairs. I had a clear view of everything that happened after that: the way her foot snagged on the first step, the way her knee buckled as she tried to right her balance, and then the headlong fall down the stairs – the thumping, tumbling career of her huge bulk as it crashed to the bottom. She landed with a thud that shook the entire house. An instant later she let out a shriek, then grabbed hold of her left leg and started writhing around on the floor. 'You dumb old bitch,' she said to herself. 'You dumb old floozy bitch, now look what you done. You fell down the stairs and broke your goddamn leg.'

For the next couple of weeks, the house was as gloomy as a hospital. There were two invalids to be taken care of, and the master and I spent our days rushing up and down the stairs, serving them their meals, emptying their potties, and doing everything short of wiping their bedridden asses. Aesop was in a funk of self-pity and dejection, Mother Sioux rained down curses on herself from morning to night, and what with the animals to be looked after in the barn and the rooms to be cleaned and the beds to be made and the dishes to be washed and the stove to be fed, there wasn't so much as a minute left over for the master and me to do our work. Christmas was approaching, the time when I was supposed to be off the ground, and I was still as subject to the laws of gravity as I'd ever been. It was my darkest moment in over a year. I'd been turned into a regular citizen who did his chores and knew how to read and write, and if it went on any longer, I'd probably wind up taking elocution lessons and joining the Boy Scouts.

One morning, I woke up a little earlier than usual. I checked in on Aesop and Mother Sioux, saw that they were both still asleep, and tiptoed down the stairs, intending to surprise the master with my pre-dawn levee. Ordinarily, he would have been down in the kitchen at that hour, cooking breakfast and preparing to start the day. But there were no smells of coffee wafting up from the stove, no sounds of bacon crackling in the pan, and sure enough, when I entered the room it turned out to be empty. He's in the barn, I told myself, gathering eggs or milking one of the cows, but then I realized that the stove had not been lit. Starting the fire was the first order of business on winter mornings, and the temperature downstairs was frigid, cold enough for me to send forth a burst of vapor every time I exhaled. Well, I continued to myself, maybe the old guy is fagged out and wanted to catch up on his beauty sleep. That would certainly put a new twist on things, wouldn't it? For me to be the one to rouse him from bed instead of vice versa. So I went back upstairs and knocked on his bedroom door, and when there was no response after several tries, I opened the door and gingerly stepped across the threshold. Master Yehudi was nowhere to be found. Not only was he not in his bed, but the bed itself was neatly made and bore no signs of having been slept in that night. He's run out on us, I said to myself. He's upped and skedaddled, and that's the last we'll ever see of him.

For the next hour, my mind was a free-for-all of desperate thoughts. I spun from sorrow to anger, from belligerence to laughter, from snarling grief to vile self-mockery. The universe had gone up in smoke, and I was left to dwell among the ashes, alone forever among the smoldering ruins of betrayal.

Mother Sioux and Aesop slept on in their beds, oblivious to my rantings and my tears. Somehow or other (I can't remember how I got there), I was down in the kitchen again, lying on my stomach with my face pressed against the floor, rubbing my nose into the filthy wooden planks. There were no more tears to be gotten out of me – only a dry, choked heaving, an aftermath of hiccups and scorched, airless breaths. Presently I grew still, almost tranquil, and bit by bit a sense of calm spread through me, radiating out among my muscles and oozing toward the tips of my fingers and toes. There were no more thoughts in my head, no more feelings in my heart. I was weightless inside my own body, floating on a placid wave of nothingness, utterly detached and indifferent to the world around me. And that's when I did it for the first time – without warning, without the least notion that it was about to happen. Very slowly, I felt my body rise off the floor. The movement was so natural, so exquisite in its gentleness, it wasn't until I opened my eyes that I understood my limbs were touching only air. I was not far off the ground – no more than an inch or two – but I hung there without effort, suspended like the moon in the night sky, motionless and aloft, conscious only of the air fluttering in and out of my lungs. I can't say how long I hovered like that, but at a certain moment, with the same slowness and gentleness as before, I eased back to the ground. Everything had been drained out of me by then, and my eyes were already shut. Without so much as a single thought about what had just taken place, I fell into a deep, dreamless sleep, sinking like a stone to the bottom of the world.

I woke to the sound of voices, the shuffling of shoes against the bare wood floor. When I opened my eyes, I found myself looking directly into the blackness of Master Yehudi's left trouser leg. 'Greetings, kid,' he said, nudging me with his foot. 'Forty winks on the cold kitchen floor. Not the best place for a nap if you want to stay healthy.'

I tried to sit up, but my body felt so dull and turgid, it took all my strength just to lift myself onto one elbow. My head was a trembling mass of cobwebs, and no matter how hard I rubbed and blinked my eyes, I couldn't get them to focus properly.

'What's the trouble, Walt?' the master continued. 'You haven't been walking in your sleep, have you?'

'No, sir. Nothing like that.'

'Then why so glum? You look like you've been to a funeral.'

An immense sadness swept through me when he said that, and I suddenly felt myself on the verge of tears. 'Oh, master,' I said, grabbing hold of his leg with both arms and pressing my cheek against his shin. 'Oh, master, I thought you'd left me. I thought you'd left me, and were never coming back.'

The moment those words left my lips, I understood that I was wrong. It wasn't the master who had caused this feeling of vulnerability and despair, it was the thing I'd done just prior to falling asleep. It all came back in a vivid, nauseating rush: the moments I'd spent off the ground, the certainty that I had done what most certainly I could not have done. Rather than fill me with ecstasy or gladness, this breakthrough overpowered me with dread. I didn't know myself anymore. I was inhabited by something that wasn't me, and that thing was so terrible, so alien in its newness, I couldn't bring myself to talk about it. I let myself cry instead. I let the tears come pouring out of me, and once I started, I wasn't sure I'd ever be able to stop.

'Dear boy,' the master said, 'my dear, sweet boy.' He lowered himself to the ground and gathered me in his arms, patting my back and hugging me close to him as I went on weeping. Then, after a pause, I heard him speak again – but he was no longer addressing his words to me. For the first time since regaining consciousness, I understood that another person was in the room.

'He's the bravest lad who ever was,' the master said. 'He's worked so hard, he's worn himself out. A body can bear just so much, and I'm afraid the poor little fellow's all done in.'

That was when I finally looked up. I lifted my head off Master Yehudi's lap, cast my eyes about for a moment, and there was Mrs Witherspoon, standing in the light of the doorway. She was wearing a crimson overcoat and a black fur hat, I remember, and her cheeks were still flush from the winter cold. The instant our eyes met, she broke into a smile.

'Hello, Walt,' she said.

'And hello to you, ma'am,' I said, sniffing back the last of my tears.

'Meet your fairy godmother,' the master said. 'Mrs Witherspoon has come to rescue us, and she'll be staying in the house for a little while. Until things get back to normal.'

'You're the lady from Wichita, ain't you?' I said, realizing why her face looked so familiar to me.

'That's right,' she said. 'And you're the little boy who lost his way in the storm.'

'That was a long time ago,' I said, extricating myself from the master's arms and finally standing up. 'I can't say I remember much about it.'

'No,' she said, 'you probably don't. But I do.'

'Not only is Mrs Witherspoon a friend of the family,' the master said, 'she's our number-one champion and business partner. Just so you know the score, Walt. I want you to bear that in mind while she's here with us. The food that feeds you, the clothes that clothe you, the fire that warms you – all that comes courtesy of Mrs Witherspoon, and it would be a sad day if you ever forgot it.'

'Don't worry,' I said, suddenly feeling some spring in my soul again. 'I ain't no slob. When a handsome lady enters my house, I know how a gentleman is supposed to act.'

Without missing a beat, I turned my eyes in Mrs Witherspoon's direction, and with all the poise and bravura I could muster, flashed her the sexiest, most preposterous wink ever beheld by womankind. To her credit, Mrs Witherspoon neither blushed nor stammered. Giving as good as she got, she let out a brief laugh, and then, as cool and collected as an old bawd, tossed back a playful wink at me. It was a moment I still cherish, and the instant it happened, I knew we were going to be friends.

I had no idea what the master's arrangement with her was, and at the time I didn't give the matter much thought. What concerned me was that Mrs Witherspoon was there and that her presence relieved me of my job as nursemaid and bottle-washer. She took things in hand that first morning, and for the next three weeks the household ran as smoothly as a new pair of roller skates. To be honest, I didn't think she'd be capable of it, at least not when I saw her in that fancy coat and those expensive gloves. She looked like a woman who was used to having servants wait on her, and though she was pretty enough in a fragile sort of way, her skin was too pale for my taste and there was too little meat on her bones. It took me some time to adjust to her, since she didn't fit into any of the female categories I was familiar with. She wasn't a flapper or a hussy, she wasn't a meek housewifey blob, she wasn't a schoolmarm or a virgin battle-axe – but somehow a bit of all of them, which meant that you could never quite pin her down or predict what her next move was going to be. The only thing I felt certain about was that the master was in love with her. He always grew very still and soft-spoken when she entered the room, and more than once I caught him staring at her with a far-off look in his eyes when her head was turned the other way. Since they slept together in the same bed every night, and since I heard the mattress creak and bounce with a certain regularity, I took it for granted that she felt the same way about him. What I didn't know was that she had already turned him down in marriage three times – but even if I had known, I doubt it would have made much difference. I had other things on my mind just then, and they were a hell of a lot more important to me than the ups and downs of the master's love life.

I kept to myself as much as possible during those weeks, hiding out in my room as I explored the mysteries and terrors of my new gift. I did everything I could to tame it, to come to terms with it, to study its exact dimensions and accept it as a fundamental part of myself. That was the struggle: not just to master the skill, but to absorb its gruesome and shattering implications, to plunge into the maw of the beast. It had marked me with a special destiny, and I would be set apart from others for the rest of my life. Imagine waking up one morning to discover that you have a new face, and then imagine the hours you would have to spend in front of the mirror before you got used to it, before you could begin to feel comfortable with yourself again. Day after day, I would lock myself in my room, stretch out on the floor, and wish my body into the air. I practiced so much that it wasn't long before I could levitate at will, lifting myself off the ground in a matter of seconds. After a couple of weeks, I learned that it wasn't necessary to lie down on the floor. If I put myself in the proper trance, I was able to do it standing up, to float a good six inches into the air from a vertical position. Three days after that, I learned that I could begin the ascent with my eyes open. I could actually look down and see my feet rising off the floor, and still the spell would not be broken.

Meanwhile, the life of the others swirled around me. Aesop's bandages came off, Mother Sioux was fitted with a cane and began to hobble around again, the master and Mrs Witherspoon shook the bedsprings every night, filling the house with their groans. With so much hubbub to contend with, it wasn't always easy to come up with an excuse for shutting myself in my room. A couple of times, I felt certain that the master saw straight through me, that he understood my duplicity and was lenient only because he wanted me out of his hair. At any other moment, I would have been consumed with jealousy to be shunned like that, to know that he preferred the company of a woman to my own sterling, inimitable presence. Now that I was airborne, however, Master Yehudi was beginning to lose his godlike properties for me, and I no longer felt under the sway of his influence. I saw him as a man, a man no better or worse than other men, and if he wanted to spend his time cavorting with a skinny wench from Wichita, that was his affair. He had his affairs and I had mine, and that's how it was going to be from now on. I had taught myself how to fly, after all, or at least something that resembled flying, and I assumed that meant I was my own man now, that I was beholden to no one but myself. As it turned out, I had merely advanced to the next stage of my development. Devious and cunning as ever, the master was still far ahead of me, and I had a long road to travel before I became the hotshot I thought I was.

Aesop drooped in his nine-fingered state, a listless shadow of his former self, and though I spent as much time with him as I could, I was too busy with my experiments to give him the kind of attention he needed. He kept asking me why I spent so many hours alone in my room, and one morning (it must have been the fifteenth or sixteenth of December) I let forth with a small lie to help assuage his doubts about me. I didn't want him to think I'd stopped caring about him, and under the circumstances it seemed better to fib than to say nothing.

'It's in the nature of a surprise,' I said. 'If you promise not to breathe a word about it, I'll give you a hint.'

Aesop eyed me with suspicion. 'You're up to another one of your tricks, aren't you?'

'No tricks, I swear. What I'm telling you is on the level, the whole gob straight from the horse's mouth.'

'You don't have to hem and haw. If you have something to say, just come out and say it.'

'I will. But first you've got to promise.'

'This had better be good. I don't like giving my word for no reason, you know.'

'Oh, it's good all right, you can trust me on that.'

'Well,' he said, beginning to lose patience. 'What's the pitch, little brother?'

'Raise your right hand and swear you'll never tell. Swear on your mother's grave. Swear on the whites of your eyeballs. Swear on the pussy of every whore in Niggertown.'

Aesop sighed, grabbed hold of his balls with his left hand – which was how the two of us swore to sacred oaths – and lifted his right hand into the air. 'I promise,' he said, and then he repeated the things I'd told him to say.

'Well,' I said, improvising as I went along, 'it's like this. Christmas is coming up next week, and what with Mrs Witherspoon in the house and all, I've heard talk about a celebration on the twenty-fifth. Turkey and pudding, presents, maybe even a fir tree with baubles and popcorn on it. If this shindig comes off like I think it will, I don't want to be caught with my pants down. You know how it is. It ain't no fun to receive a present if you can't give one in return. So that's what I've been up to in my room all these days. I'm working on a present, concocting the biggest and best surprise my poor little brain can think of. I'll be unveiling it to you in just a few days, big brother, and I hope to hell you aren't disappointed.'

Everything I said about the Christmas party was true. I'd overheard the master and his lady talking about it one night through the walls, but until then it hadn't occurred to me to give anyone a present. Now that I'd planted the idea in my head, I saw it as a golden opportunity, the chance I'd been waiting for all along. If there was a Christmas dinner (and that same night the master announced there would be), I would use the occasion to show off my new talent. That would be my present to them. I would stand up and levitate before their eyes, and at last my secret would be known to the world.

I spent the next week and a half in a cold sweat. It was one thing to perform my stunts in private, but how could I be sure I wouldn't fall on my face when I walked out in front of them? If I didn't come through, I'd be turned into a laughing-stock, the butt of every joke for the next twenty-seven years. So began the longest, most tormented day of my life. From whatever angle you chose to look at it, the Yuletide bash was a triumph, a veritable banquet of laughter and gaiety, but I didn't enjoy myself one bit. I could barely chew the turkey for fear of choking on it, and the mashed turnips tasted like a mixture of library paste and mud. By the time we moved into the parlor to sing songs and exchange presents, I was ready to pass out. Mrs Witherspoon started off by giving me a blue sweater with red reindeer stitched across the front. Mother Sioux followed with a pair of hand-knit argyle socks, and then the master gave me a spanking new white baseball. Finally, Aesop gave me the portrait of Sir Walter Raleigh, which he'd cut out of the book and mounted in a sleek ebony frame. They were all generous gifts, but each time I unwrapped one, I could do no more than mumble a grim, inaudible thanks. Each present meant that I was drawing closer to the moment of truth, and each one sapped a little more of the spirit out of me. I sank down in my chair, and by the time I'd opened the last package, I had all but resolved to cancel the demonstration. I wasn't prepared, I told myself, I still needed more practice, and once I started in with those arguments, I had no trouble talking myself out of it. Then, just when I'd managed to glue my ass to the chair forever,

65

Aesop piped in with his two cents and the ceiling fell on top of me.

'Now it's Walt's turn,' he said in all innocence, thinking I was a man of my word. 'He's got something up his sleeve, and I can't wait for him to spring it on us.'

'That's right,' the master said, turning to me with one of his piercing, all-knowing looks. 'Young Mr Rawley has yet to be heard from.'

I was on the spot. I didn't have another present, and if I stalled any longer, they'd see me for the selfish ingrate I really was. So I stood up from my chair, my knee-bones knocking together, and said in a feeble little church-mouse voice: 'Here goes, ladies and gentlemen. If it don't work, you can't say it's from want of trying.'

The four of them were looking at me with such curiosity, such a raptness of puzzlement and attention, that I shut my eyes to block them out. I took a long slow breath and exhaled, spread my arms in the loose, slack-jointed way I'd worked on for so many hours, and went into my trance. I began to rise almost immediately, lifting off the ground in a smooth and gradual ascent, and when I reached a height of six or seven inches – the maximum I was capable of in those early months – I opened my eyes and looked out at my audience. Aesop and the two women were gaping in wonder, their three mouths formed into identical little o's. The master was smiling, however, smiling as the tears rolled down his cheeks, and even as I hovered before him, I saw that he was already reaching for the leather strap behind his collar. By the time I floated down again, he had slipped the necklace over his head and was holding it out to me in his extended palm. No one said a word. I started walking toward him, crossing the room with my eyes fixed on his eyes, not daring to look anywhere else. When I came to the place where Master Yehudi was sitting, I took my finger joint from him and fell to my knees, burying my face in his lap. I held on like that for close

66

to a minute, and when I finally found the courage to stand up again, I ran from the room, rushing to the kitchen and out into the cold night air – gasping for breath, gasping for life under the immensity of the winter stars.

We said good-bye to Mrs Witherspoon three days after that, waving to her from the kitchen door as she drove off in her emerald green Chrysler sedan. Then it was 1927, and for the first six months of that year I worked with savage concentration, pushing myself a little farther each week. Master Yehudi made it clear that levitation was only the beginning. It was a lovely accomplishment, of course, but nothing to set the world on fire with. Scores of people possessed the ability to lift themselves off the ground, and even after you subtracted the Indian fakirs and Tibetan monks and Congolese witch doctors, there were numerous examples from the so-called civilized nations, the white countries of Europe and North America. In Hungary alone, the master said, there had been five active levitators at the turn of the century, three of them right in his hometown of Budapest. It was a wonderful skill, but the public soon grew tired of it, and unless you could do more than hover just a few inches off the ground, there was no chance of turning it into a profitable career. The art of levitation had been sullied by tricksters and charlatans, the smoke-and-mirror boys out for a quick buck, and even the lamest, most tawdry magician on the vaudeville circuit could pull off the stunt of the floating girl: the bombshell in the scant, glittering costume who hangs in midair as a hoop is placed around her (Look: no strings, no wires) and travels the length of her outstretched body. That was standard procedure now, an established part of the repertoire, and it had put the real levitators out of business. Everyone knew it was a fake, and the fakery was so widespread that even when confronted with an act of genuine levitation, audiences insisted on believing it was a sham.

'There are only two ways of grabbing their attention,' the

master said. 'Either one will bring us a good life, but if you manage to combine the two of them into a single routine, there's no telling how far we might go. There isn't a bank in the world that could hold all the money we'd make then.'

'Two ways,' I said. 'Are they part of the thirty-three steps, or are we past that stuff now?'

'We're past it. You've gone as far as I did when I was your age, and beyond this point we're entering new territory, continents no one has ever seen before. I can help you with advice and instruction, I can steer you when you've gone off track, but all the essential things you'll have to discover for yourself. We've come to the crossroads, and from now on everything is up to you.'

'Tell me about the two ways. Give me the lowdown on the whole kaboodle, and we'll see if I've got it in me or not.'

'Loft and locomotion – those are the two ways. By loft I mean getting yourself up into the air. Not just half a foot, but three feet, six feet, twenty feet. The higher you go, the more spectacular the results will be. Three feet is nice, but it won't be enough to stun the crowds into amazement. That puts you just a little above eye-level for most adults, and that can't do the trick over the long haul. At six feet, you're hovering above their heads, and once you force them to look up, you'll be creating the kind of impression we want. At ten feet, the effect will be transcendent. At twenty feet, you'll be up there among the angels, Walt, a wondrous thing to behold, an apparition of light and beauty shining joy into the heart of every man, woman, and child who lifts his face up to you.'

'You're giving me goose bumps, master. When you talk like that, it sets my bones all atremble.'

'Loft is only the half of it, son. Before you get carried away, stop and consider locomotion. By that I mean moving yourself through the air. Forward or backward, as the case may be, but preferably both. Speed is of no consequence, but duration is vital, the very nub of the matter. Imagine the spectacle of gliding through the air for ten seconds. People will gasp. They'll point at you in disbelief, but before they can absorb the reality of what they're witnessing, the miracle will be over. Now stretch the performance to thirty seconds or a minute. It gets better, doesn't it? The soul begins to expand, the blood begins to flow more sweetly in your veins. Now stretch it to five minutes, to ten minutes, and imagine yourself turning figure eights and dancing pirouettes as you move, inexhaustible and free, with fifty thousand pairs of eyes trained on you as you float above the grass of the Polo Grounds in New York City. Try to imagine it, Walt, and you'll see what I've been seeing for all these months and years.'

'In the name of the Lord, Master Yehudi, I don't think I can stand it.'

'But wait, Walt, wait another second. Just suppose, for the sake of argument, just suppose that by some vast stroke of luck you were able to master both those things and perform them at the same time.'

'Loft and locomotion together?'

'That's it, Walt. Loft and locomotion together. What then?'

'I'd be flying, wouldn't I? I'd be flying through the air like a bird.'

'Not like a bird, my little man. Like a god. You'd be the wonder of wonders, Walt, the holy of holies. As long as men walked the earth, they'd worship you as the greatest man among them.'

I spent most of the winter working alone in the barn. The animals were there, but they paid no attention to me, watching my antigravitational feats with dumb indifference. Every now and then, the master would stop in to see how I was doing, but other than a few words of encouragement, he rarely said much. January proved to be the hardest month, and I made no progress at all. Levitation was almost as simple as breathing for me by then, but I was stuck at the same paltry height of six inches, and the idea of moving through the air seemed out of the question. It wasn't that I couldn't get the hang of those things, I couldn't even conceive of them, and work as I did to coax my body to express them, I couldn't find a way to begin. Nor was the master in any position to help. 'Trial and error,' he would say, 'trial and error, that's what it boils down to. You've come to the hard part now, and you can't expect to reach the heavens overnight.'

In early February, Aesop and Master Yehudi left the farm to go on a tour of colleges and universities back East. They wanted to make up their minds about where Aesop should be enrolled in September, and they were planning to be gone for a full month. I don't need to add that I begged to go along with them. They would be visiting cities like Boston and New York, giant metropolises with major league ball clubs and trolley cars and pinball machines, and the idea of being stuck in the boondocks was a bit hard to swallow. If I'd been making some headway on my loft and locomotion, it might not have been so awful to be left behind, but I wasn't getting anywhere, and I told the master that a change of scenery was just what I needed to get the juices flowing again. He laughed in that condescending way of his and said, 'Your time is coming, champ, but it's Aesop's turn now. The poor boy hasn't set eyes on a sidewalk or a traffic light for seven years, and it's my duty as a father to show him a little of the world. Books can only go so far, after all. A moment comes when you have to experience things in the flesh.'

'Talking about flesh,' I said, gulping back my disappointment, 'be sure to take care of Aesop's little pal. If there's one experience he's been craving, it's the chance to put it somewhere other than in his own hand.'

'Rest assured, Walt. It's on the agenda. Mrs Witherspoon gave me some extra cash for precisely that purpose.'

'That was thoughtful of her. Maybe she'll do the same for me one day.'

'I'm sure she would, but I doubt you're going to need her help.'

'We'll see about that. The way things stand now, I ain't interested anyway.'

'All the more reason to stay behind in Kansas and do your work. If you keep at it, there might be a surprise or two for me when I come back.'

So I spent the month of February alone with Mother Sioux, watching the snow fall and listening to the wind blow across the prairie. For the first couple of weeks, the weather was so cold that I couldn't bring myself to go out to the barn. I spent the better part of my time moping around the house, too dejected to think about practicing my stunts. Even with just the two of us, Mother Sioux had to keep up with her chores, and what with the extra effort required because of her bum leg, she tired more easily than she had before. Still, I pestered her to distraction, trying to get her to talk to me as she went about her work. For over two years I hadn't given much thought to anyone but myself, accepting the people around me more or less as they appeared on the surface. I had never bothered to probe into their pasts, had never really cared to know who they'd been before I entered their lives. Now, suddenly, I was gripped by a compulsion to learn everything I could about each one of them. I think it started because I missed them so much – the master and Aesop most of all, but Mrs Witherspoon as well. I'd liked having her around the house, and the place was a lot duller now that she was gone. Asking questions was a way to bring them back, and the more Mother Sioux talked about them, the less lonely I felt.

For all my insistence and nagging, I didn't get much out of her during the daytime. An occasional anecdote, a few dribs and drabs, suggestive hints. The evenings were more conducive to talk, and no matter how hard I pressed her, she rarely got going before we sat down to supper. Mother Sioux was a tight-lipped person, not given to idle chatter or shooting the breeze, but once she settled into the right mood, she wasn't half bad at telling stories. Her delivery was flat, and she didn't throw in many colorful details, but she had a knack for pausing every so often in the middle of a sentence or an idea, and those little breaks in the telling produced rather startling effects. They gave you a chance to think, to carry on with the story yourself, and by the time she started up again, you discovered that your head was filled with all kinds of vivid pictures that hadn't been there before.

One night, for no reason that I could understand, she took me up to her room on the second floor. She told me to sit on the bed, and once I'd made myself comfortable, she opened the lid of a battered old trunk that stood in the corner. I'd always thought it was a storage place for her sheets and blankets, but it turned out to be stuffed with objects from her past: photographs and beads, moccasins and rawhide dresses, arrowheads, newspaper clippings, and pressed flowers. One by one, she carried these mementoes over to the bed, sat down beside me, and explained what they meant. It was all true about her having worked for Buffalo Bill, I discovered, and the thing that got me when I looked through her old pictures was how pretty she'd been back then – pert and slim, with a full set of white teeth and two long, lovely braids. She'd been a regular Indian princess, a dream squaw like the girls in the movies, and it was hard to put that cute little package together with the roly-poly gimp who kept house for us, to accept the fact that they were one and the same person. It started when she was sixteen years old, she said, at the height of the Ghost Dance craze that swept through the Indian lands in the late 1880s. Those were the bad times, the years of the end of the world, and the red people believed that magic was the only thing that could save them from extinction. The cavalry was closing in from all sides, crowding them off the prairies onto small reservations, and the Blue-Coats had too many men to make a counterattack feasible. Dancing the Ghost Dance was the last line of resistance: to jiggle and shake yourself into a frenzy, to bounce and bob like the Holy Rollers and the screwballs who babble in tongues. You could fly out of your body then, and the white man's bullets would no longer touch you, no longer kill you, no longer empty your veins of blood. The Dance caught on everywhere, and eventually Sitting Bull himself threw in his lot with the shakers. The US Army got scared, fearing rebellion was in the works, and ordered Mother Sioux's great-uncle to stop. But the old boy told them to shove it, he could jitterbug in his own tepee if he wanted to, and who were they to meddle in his private business? So General Blue-Coat (I think his name was Miles, or Niles) called in Buffalo Bill to powwow with the chief. They were buddies from back when Sitting Bull had worked in the Wild West Show, and Cody was about the only paleface he trusted. So Bill trekked out to the reservation in South Dakota like a good soldier, but once he got there, the general changed his mind and wouldn't allow him to meet with Sitting Bull. Bill was understandably ticked off. Just as he was about to storm away, however, he caught sight of the young Mother Sioux (whose name back then was She Who Smiles like the Sun) and signed her on as a member of his troupe. At least the journey hadn't gone entirely for nought. For Mother Sioux, it probably meant the difference between life and death. A few days after her departure into the world of show business, Sitting Bull was murdered in a scuffle with some of the soldiers who were holding him prisoner, and not long after that, three hundred women, children, and old men were mowed down by a cavalry regiment at the so-called Battle of Wounded Knee, which wasn't a battle so much as a turkey shoot, a wholesale slaughter of the innocent.

There were tears in Mother Sioux's eyes when she spoke about this. 'Custer's revenge,' she muttered. 'I was two years old when Crazy Horse filled his body with arrows, and by the time I was sixteen, there was nothing left.'

'Aesop once explained it to me,' I said. 'It's a bit fuzzy now, but I recall him describing how there wouldn't have been no black slaves from Africa if the white folks had been given a free hand with the Indians. He said they wanted to turn the redskins into slaves, but the Catholic boss man in the old country put the nix on it. So the pirates went to Africa instead and rounded up a lot of darkies and hauled them off in chains. That's how Aesop told it, and I've never known him to lie about nothing. Indians were supposed to be treated good. Like that live-and-let-live stuff the master is always nattering about.'

'Supposed to,' Mother Sioux answered. 'But supposed to ain't the same as is.'

'You've got a point there, Ma. If you don't put your money where your mouth is, you can make all the promises you want, and it still don't add up to a mound of squash.'

She pulled out more photos after that, and then she started in on the theater programs, poster bills, and newspaper clippings. Mother Sioux had been just about everywhere, not just in America and Canada, but on the other side of the ocean as well. She had performed in front of the king and queen of England, she had signed her autograph for the tsar of Russia, she had drunk champagne with Sarah Bernhardt. After five or six years of touring with Buffalo Bill, she married an Irishman named Ted, a little jockey who rode steeplechase up and down the British Isles. They had a daughter named Daffodil, a stone cottage with blue morning glories and pink climbing roses in the garden, and for seven years her happiness knew no bounds. Then disaster struck. Ted and Daffodil were killed in a train wreck, and Mother Sioux returned to America with a broken heart. She married a pipe fitter whose name was also Ted, but unlike Ted One, Ted Two was a sot and a roughneck, and by and by Mother Sioux took to drink herself, so great was her sorrow whenever she compared her new life to her old. They wound up living together in a tar-paper shack on the outskirts of Memphis, Tennessee, and if not for the sudden, wholly chance appearance of Master Yehudi on their road one morning in the summer of 1912, Mother Sioux would have been a corpse before her time. He was walking along with the young Aesop in his arms (just two days after he'd rescued him in the cotton field) when he heard shrieks and howls rising from the broken-down hut that Mother Sioux called her home. Ted Two had just commenced pummeling her with his hairy fists, knocking out six or seven teeth with the first blows, and Master Yehudi, who was never one to walk away from trouble, entered the shack, gently placed his crippled child on the floor, and put an end to the donnybrook by sneaking up behind Ted Two, clamping his thumb and middle finger onto the crumbum's neck, and applying enough pressure to dispatch him to the land of dreams. The master then washed the blood from Mother Sioux's gums and lips, helped her to her feet, and glanced about at the squalor of the room. He didn't need more than twelve seconds to come to a decision. 'I have a proposal to make,' he said to the battered woman. 'Leave this louse on the floor and come with me. I have a rickets-plagued boy in want of a mother, and if you agree to take care of him, I'll agree to take care of you. I don't stay anywhere for very long, so you'll have to acquire a taste for travel, but I promise on my father's soul that I'll never let you and the child go hungry.'

The master was twenty-nine years old then, a radiant specimen of manhood sporting a waxed handlebar mustache and an impeccably knotted tie. Mother Sioux joined forces with him that morning, and for the next fifteen years she stuck with him through every twist and turn of his career, raising Aesop as if he were her own. I can't remember all the places she talked about, but the best stories always seemed to be centred around Chicago, a town they visited often. That was where Mrs Witherspoon hailed from, and once Mother Sioux got onto that subject, my head started to spin. She gave me only the sketchiest outline, but the bare facts were so curious, so weirdly theatrical, that it wasn't long before I had embroidered them into a full-blown drama. Marion Witherspoon had married her late husband when she was twenty or twenty-one. He himself had been raised in Kansas, the son of a wealthy family from Wichita who had run off to the big city the moment he came into his inheritance. Mother Sioux described him as a handsome, fun-loving rake, one of those mealy-mouthed charmers who could talk his way into a woman's skirt in less time than it took Jim Thorpe to tie his shoe. The young couple lived high on the hog for three or four years, but Mr Witherspoon had a weakness for the ponies, not to speak of a penchant for dabbling in a friendly game of cards some fifteen or twenty nights a month, and since he demonstrated more enthusiasm than skill at his chosen vices, his once vast fortune shrank to a pittance. Toward the end, the situation became so desperate that it looked as if he and his wife would have to move back to the family home in Wichita and that he, Charlie Witherspoon, the polo-playing gadabout and jokester of the North Side, would actually have to look for nine-to-five employment in some dreary grain-belt insurance company. That was where Master Yehudi entered the picture – in the back room of a Rush Street pool hall at four in the morning with said Mr Witherspoon and two or three anonymous others, all of them sitting around a green felt table holding cards in their hands. As they say in the funny papers, it wasn't Charlie's night, and there he was about to go belly-up, sitting on three Jacks and a pair of kings without a dime to throw in the pot. Master Yehudi was the only one left in the game, and since this was clearly the last good chance Charlie would ever have, he decided to go for broke. First he bet his property in Cibola, Kansas (which had once been his grandparents' farm), signing over the house and the land on a scrap of paper, and then, when Master

Yehudi hung in there and raised him, the gentleman signed another scrap of paper whereby he relinquished all claims to his own wife. Master Yehudi was holding four sevens, and since four of a kind always beats a full house, no matter how much royalty is crammed into that house, he won the farm and the woman, and poor, defeated Charlie Witherspoon, at last at his wits' end, wobbled home at dawn, entered the room where his wife lay asleep, and extracted a revolver from the bedside table, whereupon he blew his brains out right there on the bed.

That was how Master Yehudi came to pitch his tent in Kansas. After years of wandering, he finally had a place to call his own, and while it wasn't necessarily the place he'd had in mind, he wasn't about to spurn what those four sevens had given him. What puzzled me was how Mrs Witherspoon fit into the setup. If her husband had died broke, from whence had sprung the wherewithal for her to live so comfortably in her Wichita mansion, to pamper herself with fine clothes and emerald-green sedans and still have enough left over to fund Master Yehudi's projects? Mother Sioux had a ready answer for that one. Because she was smart. Once she caught on to the profligate ways of her husband, Mrs Witherspoon had begun fiddling with the books, stashing away bits of their monthly income in high-yield investments, stocks, corporate bonds, and other financial transactions. By the time she was widowed, this hanky-panky had produced some robust profits, multiplying her initial outlay by a factor of four, and with this tidy little fortune tucked into her purse, she was more than able to eat, drink, and make merry. But what about Master Yehudi? I asked. He'd won her fair and square in that poker game, and if Mrs Witherspoon belonged to him, why weren't they married? Why wasn't she here with us darning his socks and cooking his grub and carrying his babies in her womb?

Mother Sioux shook her head slowly back and forth. 'It's a

new world we're living in,' she said. 'Ain't nobody can own another's body no more. A woman ain't chattel to be bought and sold by men, least of all one of them new women like the master's lady. They love and hate, they grapple and spoon, they want and don't want, and as time goes on they each sink deeper under the other's skin. It's a real show, patty-cake, the follies and the circus all rolled into one, and dollars to doughnuts it's going to be like that till the day they die.'

These stories gave me a lot to chew on during the hours I spent alone, but the more I pondered what Mother Sioux had told me, the more twisted and confounding it became. My head grew weary from trying to parse the ins and outs of such complex doings, and at a certain point I just stopped, telling myself I'd short my brain wires if I kept up all that cogitation. Grown-ups were impenetrable creatures, and if I ever became one myself, I promised to write a letter back to my old self explaining how they got to be that way – but for now I'd had enough. It was a relief to let go like that, but once I abandoned those thoughts, I fell into a boredom so profound, so taxing in its bland and feathery sameness, that I finally went back to work. It wasn't because I wanted to, it's just that I couldn't think of any other way to fill the time.

I locked myself in my room again, and after three days of fruitless endeavor, I discovered what I had been doing wrong. The whole problem lay in my approach. I had somehow gotten it into my head that loft and locomotion could only be achieved through a two-step process. First levitate as high as I could, then push out and go. I had trained myself to do the one thing, and I figured I could accomplish the second thing by grafting it onto the first. But the truth was that the second thing canceled out what came before it. Again and again, I would lift myself into the air according to the old method, but as soon as I started to think about moving forward, I would flutter back to the ground, landing on my feet again

79

before I had a chance to get going. If I failed once, I failed a thousand times, and after a while I felt so disgusted, so bedeviled by my incompetence, that I took to throwing tantrums and pounding my fists on the floor. At last, in the full flush of anger and defeat, I picked myself up and jumped straight into the wall, hoping to smash myself into unconsciousness. I leapt, and for the briefest eyeblink of a second, just before my shoulder thudded against the plaster, I sensed that I was floating – that even as I rushed forward, I was losing touch with gravity, going up with a familiar buoyant surge as I lunged through the air. Before I could grasp what was happening, I had bounced off the wall and was crumpling onto the floor in pain. My whole left side throbbed from the impact, but I didn't care. I jumped to my feet and did a little dance around the room, laughing my head off for the next twenty minutes. I had cracked the secret. I understood. Forget right angles, I told myself. Think arc, think trajectory. It wasn't a matter of first going up and then going out, it was a matter of going up and out at the same time, of launching myself in one smooth, uninterrupted gesture into the arms of the great ambient nothingness.

I worked like a dog over the next eighteen or twenty days, practicing this new technique until it was embedded in my muscles and bones, a reflex action that no longer required the slightest pause for thought. Locomotion was a perfectible skill, a dreamlike walking through air that was essentially no different from walking on the ground, and just as a baby totters and falls with its first steps, I experienced a goodly dose of stumbles and spills when I began to spread my wings. Duration was the abiding issue for me at that point, the question of how long and how far I could keep myself going. The early results varied widely, ranging anywhere from three to fifteen seconds, and since the speed at which I moved was achingly slow, the best I could manage was seven or eight feet, not even the distance from one wall of my room to another. It wasn't a vigorous, smart-stepping amble, but a kind of shuffling ghost-walk, the way an aerialist advances along a high wire. Still, I kept on working with confidence, no longer subject to swoons of discouragement as I'd been before. I was inching forward now, and nothing was going to stop me. Even if I hadn't risen higher than my standard six or seven inches, I figured it was best to concentrate on locomotion for the time being. Once I'd achieved some mastery in that area, I would turn my attention to loft and tackle that problem as well. It made sense, and even if I had it to do all over again, I wouldn't budge from that plan. How could I have known that time was already running short, that fewer days were left than any of us had imagined?

After Master Yehudi and Aesop returned, spirits in the household percolated as never before. It was the end of an era, and we were all looking ahead to the future now, anticipating the new lives that waited for us beyond the boundaries of the farm. Aesop would be the first to go – off to Yale in September – but if things went according to schedule, the rest of us would be following suit by the turn of the year. Now that I had passed to the next stage of my training, the master calculated that I'd be ready to perform in public in roughly nine months. It was still a long way to go for someone my age, but he talked about it as something real now, and what with his use of words like *bookings, venues,* and *box office net,* he kept me humming in a state of permanent excitement. I wasn't Walt Rawley anymore, the white trash nobody without a pot to piss in, I was Walt the Wonder Boy, the diminutive daredevil who defied the laws of gravity, the one and only ace of the air. Once we hit the road and let the world see what I could do, I was going to be a sensation, the most talked-about personality in America.

As for Aesop, his tour back East had been an unqualified success. They'd given him special exams, they'd interviewed him, they'd picked and probed the contents of his wooly skull, and to hear the master tell it, he'd knocked the socks off the lot of them. Not a single college had turned him down, but Yale was offering a four-year scholarship – along with food and lodging and a small living allowance – and that had tipped the balance in their favor. Boola, boola, bulldogs of the world unite. Recalling these facts now, I understand what an achievement it was for a self-taught black youngster to have scaled the ramparts of those cold-hearted institutions. I knew nothing about books, had no yardstick to measure my friend's abilities against anyone else's, but I took it on blind faith that he was a genius, and the idea that a bunch of sourpusses and stuffed shirts at Yale College should want him as a student struck me as natural, the most fitting thing in the world.

If I was too dumb to grasp the significance of Aesop's triumph, I was more than bowled over by the new clothes he brought back from his trip. He returned in a raccoon coat and a blue-and-white beanie, and he looked so strange in that getup that I couldn't help laughing when he walked through the door. The master had had him fitted for two brown tweed suits in Boston, and now that he was home, he took to wearing them around the house instead of his old farm duds, complete with white shirt, stiff collar, necktie, and a pair of gleaming, dung-hued brogans. It was altogether impressive how he carried himself in those threads – as if they made him more erect, more dignified, more aware of his own importance. Even though he didn't have to, he started shaving every morning, and I would keep him company in the kitchen as he lathered up his mug and dipped his straight-edged razor into the chilly bucket, holding a little mirror for him as he told me about the things he'd seen and done in the big cities along the Atlantic coast. The master had done more than just get him into college, he'd shown him the time of his life, and Aesop remembered every minute of it: the high spots, the low spots, and all the spots in between. He talked about the skyscrapers, the museums, the variety shows, the restaurants, the libraries, the sidewalks thronged with people of every color and description. 'Kansas is an illusion,' he said one morning as he scraped away at his invisible beard, 'a stopping place on the road to reality.'

'You don't have to tell me,' I said. 'This hole is so backward, the state went dry before they even heard of Prohibition in the rest of the country.'

'I drank a beer in New York City, Walt.'

'Well, I figured you must have done.'

'In a speakeasy. An illegal establishment on MacDougal Street, right in the heart of Greenwich Village. I wish you could have been there with me.'

'I can't stand the taste of them suds, Aesop. Give me a good stiff bourbon, though, and I'll drink any man under the table.'

'I'm not saying it tasted good. But it was exciting to be there with all those people, quaffing my drink in a crowded place like that.'

'I'll bet it wasn't the only exciting thing you did.'

'No, not by a long shot. It was just one of many.'

'I'll bet your pecker got some good workouts, too. I'm just making a wild guess, of course, so correct me if I'm wrong.'

Aesop paused with the razor in midair, grew thoughtful for a moment, and then started grinning into the mirror. 'Let's just say it wasn't neglected, little brother, and we'll leave it at that.'

'Can you tell me her name? I don't mean to be pushy, but I'm curious to find out who the lucky girl was.'

'Well, if you must know, her name was Mabel.'

'Mabel. Not bad, all things considered. She sounds like a dolly with some flesh on her bones. Was she old or young?'

'She wasn't old, and she wasn't young. But you hit it right about the flesh. Mabel was the fattest, blackest mama you'd ever hope to sink your teeth into. She was so big, I couldn't tell where she started and where she ended. It was like wrestling with a hippo, Walt. But once you get into the swing of it, the anatomy takes care of itself. You creep into her bed as a boy, and half an hour later you walk out as a man.'

Now that he had graduated to manhood, Aesop decided the moment had come to sit down and write his autobiography. That was how he planned to spend the months before he left home – telling the story of his life so far, from his birth in a rural shack in Georgia to his deflowering in a Harlem bordello, wrapped in the blubbery arms of Mabel the whore. The words began to flow, but the title vexed him, and I remember how he dithered back and forth about it. One day he was going to call the book *Confessions of a Negro Foundling*; the next day he changed it to *Aesop's Adventures: The True History and Unvarnished Opinions of a Lost Boy*; the day after that it was going to be *The Road to Yale: The Life of a Negro Scholar from His Humble Origins to the Present*. Those were just some of them, and for as long as he worked on that book, he kept trying out different ones, shuffling and reshuffling his ideas until he'd built up a stack of title pages every bit as tall as the manuscript itself. He must have toiled eight or ten hours a day on his opus, and I can remember peeking through the door as he sat there hunched over his desk, marvelling at how a person could sit still for so long, engaged in no other activity than guiding the nib of a pen across a leaf of white foolscap. It was my first experience with the making of books, and even when Aesop called me into his room to read selected passages of his work aloud, I found it hard to tally all that silence and concentration with the stories that came tumbling from his lips. We were all in the book – Master Yehudi, Mother Sioux, myself – and to my clumsy, untutored ear, the thing had every intention of becoming a masterpiece. I laughed at some parts, I cried at others, and what more can a person want from a book than to feel the prick of such delights and sorrows? Now that I'm writing a book of my own, not a day goes by when I don't think about Aesop up there in his room.

That was sixty-five springs ago, and I can still see him sitting at his desk, scribbling away at his youthful memoirs as the light poured through the window, catching the dust particles that danced around him. If I concentrate hard enough, I can still hear the breath going in and out of his lungs, I can still hear the point of his pen scratching across the paper.

While Aesop worked indoors, Master Yehudi and I spent our days in the fields, toiling untold hours on my act. In a fit of optimism after his return, he'd announced to us at dinner that there wouldn't be any planting that year. 'To hell with the crops,' he said. 'There's enough food to last through the winter, and by the time spring comes again, we'll be long gone from this place. The way I look at it, it would be a sin to grow things we'll never need.' There was general rejoicing over this new policy, and for once the early spring was free of drudge work and plowing, the interminable weeks of bent backs and slogging through mud. My locomotion breakthrough had turned the tide, and Master Yehudi was so confident now that he was willing to let the farm go to pot. It was the only sane decision a man could make. We'd all done our time, and why eat dirt when we'd soon be counting our gold?

That doesn't mean we didn't bust our asses out there – particularly myself – but I enjoyed the work, and no matter how hard the master pushed me, I never wanted to quit. Once the weather turned warm, we usually kept going until after dark, working by torchlight in the far meadows as the moon rose into the sky. I was inexhaustible, consumed by a happiness that swept me along from one challenge to the next. By May first, I was able to walk from ten to twelve yards as a matter of routine. By May fifth, I had extended it to twenty yards, and less than a week after that I had pushed it to forty: a hundred and twenty feet of airborne locomotion, nearly ten uninterrupted minutes of pure magic. That was when the master hit upon the idea of having me practice over water. There was a pond in the northeast corner of the property, and from then on we did all our work over there, riding out in the buckboard wagon every morning after breakfast to a point where we could no longer see the house – alone together in the silent fields, barely saying a word to each other for hours on end. The water intimidated me at first, and since I didn't know how to swim, it was no laughing matter to test my prowess over that element. The pond must have been sixty feet across, and the water level in at least half of it was over my head. I fell in sixteen or twenty times the first day, and on four of those occasions the master had to jump in and fish me out. After that, we came equipped with towels and several changes of clothes, but by the end of the week they were no longer necessary. I conquered my fear of the water by pretending it wasn't there. If I didn't look down, I discovered I could propel my body across the surface without getting wet. It was as simple as that, and by the last days of May 1927, I was walking on water with the same skill as Jesus himself.

Somewhere in the middle of that time, Lindbergh made his solo flight across the Atlantic, traveling nonstop from New York City to Paris in thirty-three hours. We heard about it from Mrs Witherspoon, who drove out from Wichita one day with a pile of newspapers in the back seat of her car. The farm was so cut off from the world, even big stories like that one escaped our notice. If it hadn't been for her wanting to come all that way, we never would have heard a peep about it. I've always found it strange that Lindbergh's stunt coincided so exactly with my own efforts, that at the precise moment he was making his way across the ocean, I was traversing my little pond in Kansas – the two of us in the air together, each one accomplishing his feat at the same time. It was as if the sky had suddenly opened itself up to man, and we were the first pioneers, the Columbus and Magellan of human flight. I didn't know the Lone Eagle from a hole in the wall, but I felt linked to him after that, as if we shared some dark fraternal bond. It couldn't have been a coincidence that his plane was called the *Spirit of St Louis*. That was my town, too, the town of champions and twentieth-century heroes, and without even knowing it, Lindbergh had named his plane in my honor.

Mrs Witherspoon hung around for a couple of days and nights. After she left, the master and I got back to business, shifting the focus of our attention from locomotion to loft. I had done what I could do with horizontal travel; now it was time to attempt the vertical. Lindbergh was an inspiration to me, I freely confess it, but I wanted to do him one better: to do with my body what he'd done with a machine. It would be on a smaller scale, perhaps, but it would be infinitely more stupendous, a thing that would dwarf his fame overnight. Try as I did, however, I couldn't make an inch of headway. For a week and a half, the master and I struggled out by the pond, equally daunted by the task we'd set for ourselves, and at the end of that time I was still no higher than I'd been before. Then, on the evening of June fifth, Master Yehudi made a suggestion that began to turn things around.

'I'm just speculating,' he said, 'but it occurs to me that your necklace might have something to do with it. It can't weigh more than an ounce or two, but given the mathematics of what you're attempting, that could be enough. For each millimeter you rise into the air, the weight of the object increases in geometric proportion to the height – meaning that once you're six inches off the ground, you're carrying the equivalent of forty extra pounds. That comes to half your total weight. If my calculations are correct, it's no wonder you've been having such a rough time of it.'

'I've worn that thing since Christmas,' I said. 'It's my lucky charm, and I can't do nothing without it.'

'Yes you can, Walt. The first time you got yourself off the ground, it was slung around my neck, remember? I'm not

87

saying you don't have a sentimental attachment to it, but we're intruding on deep spiritual matters here, and it could be that you can't be whole to do what you have to do, that you have to leave a part of yourself behind before you can attain the full magnitude of your gift.'

'That's just double-talk. I'm wearing clothes, ain't I? I'm wearing shoes and socks, ain't I? If the necklace is bogging me down, then those things are doing it too. And I sure as hell ain't going to flaunt my stuff in public without no clothes on.'

'It can't hurt to try. There's nothing to lose, Walt, and everything to gain. If I'm wrong, so be it. If I'm not, it would be an awful pity if we never had a chance to find out.'

He had me there, so with much skepticism and reluctance I removed the good luck charm and placed it in the master's hand. 'All right,' I said, 'we'll give it a whirl. But if it don't turn out like you say, that's the last we'll ever talk about it.'

Over the course of the next hour, I managed to double my previous record, ascending to heights of twelve to fourteen inches. By nightfall, I had raised myself a good two and a half feet off the ground, demonstrating that Master Yehudi's hunch had been correct, a prophetic insight into the causes and consequences of the levitation arts. The thrill was spectacular – to feel myself hovering at such a distance from the ground, to be literally on the verge of flying – but above two feet it was difficult for me to maintain a vertical position without beginning to totter and grow dizzy. It was all so new to me up there, I wasn't able to find my natural equilibrium. I felt long to myself, as if I were composed of segments and not made of a continuous piece, and my head and shoulders responded in one way while my shins and ankles responded in another. So as not to tip over, I found myself easing into a prone position when I got up there, instinctively knowing it would be safer and more comfortable to have my entire body stretched over the ground than just the soles of my feet. I was still too nervous to think about moving forward in that position, but late that night, just before we knocked off and went home to bed, I tucked my head under my chest and managed to do a slow somersault in the air, completing a full, unbroken circle without once grazing the earth.

The master and I rode back to the house that night drunk with joy. Everything seemed possible to us now: the conquest of both loft and locomotion, the ascension into actual flight, the dream of dreams. That was our greatest moment together, I think, the moment when our whole future fell into place at last. On June sixth, however, just one night after reaching that pinnacle, my training ground to an abrupt and irrevocable halt. The thing that Master Yehudi had been dreading for so long finally came to pass, and when it did, it happened with such violence, caused such havoc and upheaval in our hearts, that neither one of us was ever the same again.

I had worked well all day, and as was our habit throughout that miraculous spring, we decided to linger on into the night. At seven thirty, we ate a supper of sandwiches that Mother Sioux had packed for us that morning and then resumed our labors as darkness gathered in the surrounding fields. It must have been close to ten o'clock when we heard the sound of horses. It was no more than a faint rumbling at first, a disturbance in the ground that made me think of distant thunder, as if a lightning storm were brewing somewhere in the next county. I had just completed a double somersault at the edge of the pond and was waiting for the master's comments, but instead of speaking in his normal calm voice, he grabbed hold of my arm in a sudden, panic-stricken gesture. 'Listen,' he said. And then he said it again: 'Listen to that. They're coming. The bastards are coming.' I pricked up my ears, and sure enough, the sound was getting louder. A couple of seconds passed, and then I understood that it was the sound of horses, a stampeding clatter of hooves charging in our direction.

'Don't move,' the master said. 'Stay where you are and don't move a muscle until I come back.'

Then, without a word of explanation, he started running toward the house, tearing through the fields like a sprinter. I ignored his command and took off after him, racing along as fast as my legs could carry me. We were a good quarter mile from the house, but before we'd traveled a hundred yards, flames were already visible, a glowing surge of red and yellow pulsing against the black sky. We heard whoops and war yodels, a volley of shots rang out, and then we heard the unmistakable sound of human screams. The master kept running, steadily increasing the distance between us, but once he came to the stand of oaks on the far side of the barn, he stopped. I pushed on to the verge of the trees myself, intent on continuing all the way to the house, but the master saw me out of the corner of his eye and wrestled me to the ground before I could go any farther. 'We're too late,' he said. 'If we go in there now, we're only going to get ourselves killed. There's twelve of them and two of us, and they've all got rifles and guns. Pray to God they don't find us, Walt, but there's not a damned thing we can do for the others.'

So we stood there helplessly behind the trees, watching the Ku Klux Klan do its work. A dozen men on a dozen horses pranced about the yard, a mob of yelping murderers with white sheets over their heads, and we were powerless to thwart them. They dragged Aesop and Mother Sioux out of the burning house, put ropes around their necks, and strung them up to the elm tree by the side of the road, each one to a different branch. Aesop howled, Mother Sioux said nothing, and within minutes they were both dead. My two best friends were murdered before my eyes, and all I could do was watch, fighting back tears as Master Yehudi clamped his palm over my mouth. Once the killing was over, a couple of the Klansmen stuck a wooden cross in the ground, doused it with gasoline, and set it on fire. The cross burned as the house burned, the men whooped it up a little more, firing rounds of buckshot into the air, and then they all climbed onto their horses and rode off in the direction of Cibola. The house was incandescent by then, a fireball of heat and roaring timbers, and by the time the last of the men was gone, the roof had already given way, collapsing to the ground in a shower of sparks and meteors. I felt as if I had seen the sun explode. I felt as if I had just witnessed the end of the world.

II

We buried them on the property that night, lowering their bodies into two unmarked graves beside the barn. We should have said some prayers, but our lungs were too full of sobbing for that, so we just covered them up with dirt and said nothing, working in silence as the salt water trickled down our cheeks. Then, without returning to the smoldering house, without even bothering to see if any of our belongings were still intact, we hitched the mare to the wagon and drove off into the darkness, leaving Cibola behind us for good.

It took all night and half the next morning before we made it to Mrs Witherspoon's house in Wichita, and for the rest of that summer the master's grief was so bad I thought he might be in danger of dying himself. He scarcely stirred from his bed, he scarcely ate, he scarcely talked. Except for the tears that dropped from his eyes every three or four hours, there was no way to tell if you were looking at a man or a block of stone. The big fella was all done in, ravaged by sorrow and self-recrimination, and no matter how hard I wished he'd snap out of it, he only got worse as the weeks went by. 'I saw it coming,' he'd sometimes mutter to himself. 'I saw it coming, and I didn't lift a finger to stop it. It's my fault. It's my fault they're dead. I couldn't have done a better job if I'd killed them with my own two hands, and a man who kills deserves no mercy. He doesn't deserve to live.'

I shuddered to see him like that, all useless and inert, and in the long run it scared me every bit as much as what had happened to Aesop and Mother Sioux – maybe even more. I don't mean to sound coldhearted about it, but life is for the living, and shocked as I was by the massacre of my friends, I was still just a kid, a little jumping bean with ants in my pants and rubber in my knees, and I didn't have it in me to

95

walk around mewling and mourning for very long. I shed my tears, I cursed God, I banged my head against the floor, but after carrying on like that for a few days, I was ready to put it behind me and get on to other things. I don't suppose that speaks too well of me as a person, but there's no point in pretending I felt what I didn't feel. I missed Aesop and Mother Sioux, I ached to be with them again – but they were gone, and no amount of begging was going to bring them back. As far as I was concerned, it was time to shake our toes and get cracking. My head was still stuffed with dreams about my new career, and piggish as those dreams might have been, I couldn't wait to get started, to launch myself into the firmament and dazzle the world with my greatness.

Imagine my disappointment, then, as I watched June turn into July and Master Yehudi still languished; imagine how my spirits sank when July became August and he still showed no signs of rebounding from the tragedy. Not only did it put a crimp in my plans, but I felt let down, bollixed, left in the lurch. An essential flaw in the master's character had been revealed to me, and I resented him for his lack of inner toughness, his refusal to face up to the shittiness of life. I had depended on him for so many years, had drawn so much strength from his strength, and now he was acting like any other blithering optimist, another one of those guys who welcomed the good when it came but couldn't accept the bad. It turned my stomach to see him fall apart like that, and as his grief dragged on, I couldn't help but lose some faith in him. If not for Mrs Witherspoon, there's a chance I would have thrown in the towel and split. 'Your master is a big man,' she said to me one morning, 'and big men have big feelings. They feel more than other men – bigger joys, bigger angers, bigger sorrows. He's in pain now, and it's going to last longer for him than it would for someone else. Don't let it frighten you, Walt. He'll get over it eventually. You just have to be patient.'

That's what she said, but deep down I'm not so sure she

believed those words herself. As time went on, I sensed that she was growing just as disgusted with him as I was, and I liked it that we saw eye to eye on such an important matter. She was one salty broad, Mrs W., and now that I was living in her house and spending every day in her company, I understood that we had much more in common than I had previously suspected. She'd been on her best behavior when she visited the farm, all prim and fusty so as not to offend Aesop and Mother Sioux, but now that she was on her own turf, she was free to let go and unfurl her true nature. For the first couple of weeks, nearly everything about that nature surprised me, riddled as it was with bad habits and unchecked bouts of self-indulgence. I'm not just talking about her penchant for booze (no less than six or seven gin and tonics per day), nor her passion for cigarettes (puffing on bygone brands like Picayunes and Sweet Caporals from morning to night), but a certain overall laxness, as if lurking behind her ladylike exterior there was a loose, slattern's soul struggling to break free. The tipoff was her mouth, and once she'd imbibed a round or two of her favorite beverage, she'd lapse into some of the coarsest, most vulgar language I've ever heard from the lips of a woman, zinging out the pungent one-liners as fast as a tommy gun burps bullets. After all the clean living I'd done on the farm, I found it refreshing to mingle with someone who wasn't bound by a high moral purpose, whose only aim in life was to enjoy herself and make as much money as she could. So we became friends, leaving Master Yehudi to his anguish as we sweated out the dog days and boredom of the hot Wichita summer.

I knew she was fond of me, but I don't want to exaggerate the depth of her affections, at least not at that early stage. Mrs Witherspoon had a definite reason for keeping me happy, and while I'd like to flatter myself it was because she found me such a sterling companion, such a witty, devil-may-care fellow, the truth was that she was thinking about the future

97

health of her bank account. Why else would a woman of her gumption and sex appeal bother to pal around with a stump-dicked brat like myself? She saw me as a business opportunity, a dollar sign in the shape of a boy, and she knew that if my career was handled with the proper care and acumen, it was going to make her the richest woman in thirteen counties. I'm not saying that we didn't have some fun times together, but it was always in the service of her own interests, and she sucked up to me and won me over as a way to keep me in the fold, to make sure I didn't sneak away before she'd cashed in on my talent.

So be it. I don't blame her for acting like that, and if I'd been in her shoes, I probably would have done the same thing. Still, I won't deny that it sometimes bugged me to see how little an impression my magic made on her. Throughout those dreary weeks and months, I kept my hand in by practicing my routine no less than one or two hours a day. So as not to spook the people who drove past the house, I confined myself to the indoors, working in the upstairs parlor with the shades drawn. Not only did Mrs Witherspoon rarely bother to watch these sessions, but on the few occasions when she did enter the room, she would observe the spectacle of my levitations without twitching a muscle, studying me with the blank-eyed objectivity of a butcher inspecting a slab of beef. No matter how extraordinary the stunts I performed, she accepted them as part of the natural order of things, no more strange or inexplicable than the waxing of the moon or the noise of the wind. Maybe she was too drunk to notice the difference between a miracle and an everyday event, or maybe the mystery of it just left her cold, but when it came to entertainment, she'd have sooner driven through a rain-storm to see some third-rate picture show than watch me float above the goddamn tables and chairs in her living room. My act was no more than a means to an end for her. As long as the end was assured, she couldn't have cared less about the means.

But she was good to me, I won't take that away from her. Whatever her motives might have been, she didn't stint on the amusements, and not once did she hesitate to fork out dough on my behalf. Two days after my arrival, she took me on a shopping spree in downtown Wichita, outfitting me with a whole new set of clothes. After that there was the ice cream parlor, the candy shop, the penny arcade. She was always one step ahead of me, and before I even knew I wanted something, she'd already be offering it to me, thrusting it into my hands with a wink and a little pat on the head. After all the hard times I'd been through, I can't say I objected to whiling away my days in the lap of luxury. I slept in a soft bed with embroidered sheets and down pillows, I ate the gigantic meals cooked for us by Nelly Boggs the colored maid, I never had to put on the same pair of underpants two mornings in a row. Most afternoons, we'd escape the heat by taking a spin through the countryside in the emerald sedan, whizzing down the empty roads with the windows open and the air rushing in on us from all sides. Mrs Witherspoon loved speed, and I don't think I ever saw her happier than when she was pressing her foot on the gas pedal: laughing between snorts from her silver flask, her bobbed red hair fluttering like the legs of an overturned caterpillar. The woman had no fear, no sense that a car traveling at seventy or eighty miles an hour can actually kill someone. I did my best to hide my fear when she floored it like that, but once we got to sixty-five or seventy I couldn't help myself. The panic welling up inside me would do something to my stomach, and before long I'd be letting out one fart after another, a whole chain of stink bombs accompanied by loud staccato butt music. I needn't add that I almost died of shame, for Mrs Witherspoon was not someone to let indiscretions like that pass without comment. The first time it happened, she burst out laughing

99

so hard I thought her head was going to fly off her shoulders. Then, without warning, she slammed her foot on the brakes and brought the car to a skidding, heart-pounding stop.

'A few more corkers like those,' she said, 'and we'll have to drive around in gas masks.'

'I don't smell nothing,' I said, giving the only answer that seemed possible.

Mrs Witherspoon sniffed loudly, then screwed up her nose and made a face. 'Smell again, sport. The whole bean brigade's been traveling with us, tooting Dixie from your rear end.'

'Just a little gas,' I said, subtly changing tactics. 'If I'm not mistaken, a car won't run if you don't fill it with gas.'

'Depends on the octane, honey. The kind of chemistry experiment we're discussing here, it's liable to get us both blown up.'

'Yeah, well, at least that's a better way to die than crashing into a tree.'

'Don't worry, snookums,' she said, unexpectedly softening her tone. She reached out and touched my head, gently running her fingertips through my hair. 'I'm a hell of a driver. No matter how fast we're going, you're always safe with Lady Marion at the controls.'

'That sounds good,' I said, enjoying the pressure of her hand against my scalp, 'but I'd feel a lot better if you'd put that in writing.'

She let out a short, throaty guffaw and smiled. 'Here's a tip for the future,' she said. 'If you think I'm going too fast, just close your eyes and yell. The louder you yell, the more fun it's going to be for both of us.'

So that's what I did, or at least what I tried to do. On subsequent outings I always made a point of shutting my eyes when the speedometer reached seventy-five, but a few times the farts came sneaking out at seventy, once even as low as sixty-five (when it looked like we were about to plow into an oncoming truck and veered away at the last second). Those lapses did nothing for my self-respect, but none was worse than the trauma that occurred in early August when my bunghole went for broke and I wound up crapping my pants. It was a brutally hot day. No rain had fallen in over two weeks, and every leaf on every tree in the whole flat countryside was covered with dust. Mrs Witherspoon was a little more plastered than usual, I think, and by the time we left the city limits she'd worked herself into one of those charged-up, fuck-the-world moods. She pushed her buggy past fifty on the first turn, and after that there was no stopping her. Dust flew everywhere. It showered down on the windshield, it danced inside our clothes, it battered our teeth, and all she did was laugh, pressing down on the accelerator as if she meant to break the Mokey Dugway speed record. I shut my eyes and howled for all I was worth, clutching the dashboard as the car shimmied and roared along the dry, divot-scarred turnpike. After twenty or thirty seconds of mounting terror, I knew that my number was up. I was going to die on that stupid road, and these were my last moments on earth. That was when the turd slid out of my crack: a loose and slippery cigar that thudded against my drawers with a warm, sickening wetness, then started sliding down my leg. When I realized what had happened, I couldn't think of any better response than to burst into tears.

Meanwhile, the ride continued, and by the time the car came to a halt some ten or twelve minutes later, I was soaked through and through – with sweat, with shit, with tears. My entire being was awash in body fluids and misery.

'Well, buckaroo,' Mrs Witherspoon announced, lighting up a cigarette to savor her triumph. 'We did it. We broke the century mark. I'll bet you I'm the first woman in this whole tight-assed state who ever did that. What do you think? Pretty good for an old bag like me, no?'

'You ain't no old bag, ma'am,' I said.

'Ah, that's nice. I appreciate that one. You've got a soft touch with the ladies, kid. In a few more years, you'll be knocking them dead with that kind of talk.'

I wanted to go on chatting with her like that, all calm and easy as if nothing had happened, but now that the car had stopped, the smell from my pants was getting more noticeable, and I knew it was only a matter of seconds before my secret came out. Humiliation stung me again, and before I could say another word, I was sobbing into my hands beside her.

'Jesus, Walt,' I heard her say. 'Jesus Christ almighty. You've really done it this time, haven't you?'

'I'm sorry,' I said, not daring to look at her. 'I couldn't help it.'

'It's probably all that candy I've been feeding you. Your belly isn't used to it.'

'Maybe. Or maybe I just don't have no guts.'

'Don't be dumb, boy. You had a little accident is all. It happens to everyone.'

'Sure. As long as you're in diapers it does. I ain't never been so embarrassed in all my life.'

'Forget it. This is no time to feel sorry for yourself. We've got to clean up that little backside of yours before any gunk oozes onto the upholstery. Are you listening to me, Walt? I don't care about your bloody bowel movements, I just don't want my car to bear the brunt. There's a pond behind those trees over there, and that's where I'm taking you now. We'll scrub off the mustard and relish, and then you'll be as good as new.'

I didn't have much choice but to go along with her. It was pretty awful having to stand up and walk, what with all the sloshing and slithering taking place inside my pants, and since I still hadn't quelled my sobs, my chest went on heaving and shuddering, letting forth a whole range of weird, half-stifled sounds. Mrs Witherspoon walked ahead of me, leading the way to the pond. It was about a hundred feet back from the road, set off from its surroundings by a barrier of scrawny trees and shrubs, a little oasis in the middle of the prairie. When we came to the edge of the water, she told me to strip off my clothes, urging me on in a matter-of-fact tone of voice. I didn't want to do it, at least not with her looking at me, but once I realized she wasn't going to turn her back, I fixed my eyes on the ground and submitted to the ordeal. First she undid my shoes and pulled off my socks; then, without the slightest pause, she unbuckled my belt, unbuttoned my fly, and tugged. Pants and undies fell to my ankles in one swoop, and there I was standing with my dick in the breeze before a grown woman, my white legs stained with brown mush and my asshole reeking like yesterday's garbage. It was surely one of the low points of my life, but to Mrs Wither-spoon's immense credit (and this is a thing I've never forgotten), she didn't make a sound. Not one groan of disgust, not one gasp. With all the tenderness of a mother washing her newborn baby, she dipped her hands into the water and began cleaning me off, splashing and rubbing my naked skin until every sign of my disgrace had been removed.

'There,' she said, patting me dry with a handkerchief she'd pulled from her red beaded purse. 'Out of sight, out of mind.'

'Fair enough,' I said, 'but what do we do with them fouled-up undies?'

'We leave them for the birds, that's what, and that goes for the pants, too.'

'And you expect me to ride home like that? Without no stitch on my nether bottom?'

'Why not? Your shirttails hang down to your knees, and it's not as though there's much to hide anyway. We're talking microscopes, kid, the crown jewels of Lilliput.'

'Don't cast aspersions on my privates, ma'am. They may be trifles to you, but I'm proud of them just the same.'

'Of course you are. And a cute little dicky-bird it is, Walt,

103

with those bald nuts and smooth, babydoll thighs. You've got everything it takes to be a man' – and here, to my great astonishment, she gathered up the whole package in her palm and gave it a good healthy shake – 'but you're not quite there yet. Besides, no one's going to see you in the car. We'll skip the ice cream parlor today and drive straight home. If it makes you feel any better, I'll smuggle you into the house through the back door. How's that? I'm the only one who's going to know about it, and you can bet your bottom dollar I'll never tell.'

'Not even the master?'

'Least of all the master. What happened out here today is strictly between you and me.'

She could be a good egg, that woman, and whenever it really counted, she was about the best there was. At other times, though, I couldn't make heads or tails of her. Just when you thought she was your bosom buddy, she'd turn around and do something unexpected – tease you, for instance, or snub you, or go silent on you – and the beautiful little world you'd been living in would suddenly go sour. There was a lot I didn't understand, grown-up things that were still over my head, but little by little I began to catch on that she was pining for Master Yehudi. She was bingeing herself into the blues as she waited for him to come round, and if things had gone on much longer, I don't doubt that she would have jumped off the deep end.

The turning point came about two nights after the shit episode. We were sitting on lawn chairs in the backyard, watching the fireflies dart in and out of the bushes and listening to the crickets chirp their tinny songs. That passed for big-time entertainment in those days, even in the so-called Roaring Twenties. I hate to debunk popular legends, but there wasn't a hell of a lot that roared in Wichita, and after two months of scouring that sleepy burg for noise and diversion, we'd more than used up the available resources. We'd seen every motion picture, slurped down every ice cream, played every pinball machine, taken a spin on every merry-go-round. It wasn't worth the effort to go out anymore, and for several nights running we'd just stayed put, letting the torpor spread through our bones like some fatal disease. I was sucking on a glass of tepid lemonade that night, I recall, Mrs W. was off on another bender, and neither one of us had punctured the silence in over forty minutes.

'I used to think,' she finally said, following some secret train of thought, 'I used to think he was the most dashing stud ever to trot out of the fucking stable.'

I took a sip of my drink, looked up at the stars in the night sky, and yawned. 'Who's that?' I said, not bothering to conceal my boredom.

'Who do you think, pisshead?' Her speech was slurred and barely comprehensible. If I hadn't known her better, I would have taken her for a stumblebum with water on the brain.

'Oh,' I said, suddenly realizing where the conversation was headed.

'Yeah, that one, Mr Birdman, that's the one I'm talking about.'

'Well, he's in a bad way, ma'am, you know that, and all we can do is hope his soul mends before it's too late.'

'I'm not talking about his soul, nitwit. I'm talking about his pecker. He's still got one, doesn't he?'

'I guess so. It's not as if I'm in the habit of asking him about it.'

'Well, a man has to do his duty. He can't leave a girl high and dry for two months and expect to get away with it. That's not how it works. A pussy needs love. It needs to be stroked and fed, just like any other animal.'

Even in the darkness with no one looking, I could feel myself blush. 'Are you sure you want to be telling me this, Mrs Witherspoon?'

'There's no one else, sweetheart. And besides, you're old

enough to know about these things. You don't want to walk through life like all those other numbskulls, do you?'

'I always figured I'd let nature take care of itself.'

'That's where you're wrong. A man's got to tend his honey pot. He's got to make sure the stopper's in and it doesn't run out of juice. Do you hear what I'm saying?'

'I think so.'

'Think so? What kind of bullshit answer is that?'

'Yeah, I hear you.'

'It's not as if I haven't had other offers, you know. I'm a young, healthy girl, and I'm sick and tired of waiting around like this. I've been diddling my own twat all summer, and it just won't wash anymore. I can't make it any clearer than that, can I?'

'The way I heard it, you've already turned down the master three times.'

'Well, things change, don't they, Mr Know-It-All?'

'Maybe they do, maybe they don't. It's not for me to say.'

It was on the point of turning ugly, and I wanted no part of it – to sit there listening to her blather on about her disappointed cunt. I wasn't equipped to handle that kind of stuff, and peeved as I was at the master myself, I didn't have the heart to join in and attack his manhood. I could have stood up and walked away, I guess, but then she would have started screaming at me, and nine minutes later every cop in Wichita would have been out there in the yard with us, hauling us off to jail for disturbing the peace.

As it was, I needn't have worried. Before she could get in another word, a loud noise suddenly exploded from within the house. It was more of a boom than a crash, I suppose, a kind of long, hollow detonation that immediately gave way to several resounding thuds: *thwack, thwack, thwack,* as if the walls were about to tumble down. For some reason, Mrs Witherspoon found this funny. She threw back her head in a fit of laughter, and for the next fifteen seconds the air rippled out of her windpipe like a swarm of flying grasshoppers. I'd never heard laughter like that before. It sounded like one of the ten plagues, like two-hundred-proof gin, like four hundred hyenas stalking the streets of Crazytown. Then, even as the thuds continued, she started raving at the top of her voice. 'Do you hear that?' she shouted. 'Do you hear that, Walt! That's me! That's the sound of my thoughts, the sound of the thoughts bouncing in my brain! Just like popcorn, Walt! My skull's about to crack in two! Ha, ha! My whole head's going to burst to bits!'

Just then, the thuds were replaced by the noise of shattering glass. First one thing broke, then another: cups, mirrors, bottles, a deafening barrage. It was hard to tell what was what, but each thing shattered differently, and it went on for a long time, more than a minute, I would say, and after the first few seconds the din was everywhere, the whole night was screeching with the sound of splintering glass. Without even thinking, I jumped to my feet and ran toward the house. Mrs Witherspoon made a stab at following me, but she was too drunk to get very far. The last thing I remember is looking back and seeing her slip – flat on her face, just like a sot in the funnies. She let out a yelp. Then, realizing there was no point in trying to get up, she started in on another giggling jag. That was how I left her: rolling around on the ground and laughing, laughing her poor potted guts all over the lawn.

The only idea that flashed through my head was that someone had broken into the house and was attacking Master Yehudi. By the time I got through the back door and started climbing the stairs, however, all was quiet again. That seemed strange, yet even stranger was what happened next. I walked down the hall to the master's room, knocked tentatively on the door, and heard him call out to me in a clear, perfectly normal voice: 'Come in.' So I went in, and there was Master Yehudi himself, standing in his bathrobe and slippers in the middle of the room, hands in his pockets and a curious little smile on his face. Everything was destruction around him. The bed was in a dozen pieces, the walls were gouged, a million white feathers floated in the air. Broken picture frames, broken glasses, broken chairs, broken bits of nameless things – they were all strewn about the floor like so much rubble. He allowed me a couple of seconds to take in what I was seeing, and then he spoke, addressing me with all the calm of a man who's just stepped out of a warm bath. 'Good evening, Walt,' he said. 'And what brings you up here at this late hour?'

'Master Yehudi,' I said. 'Are you all right?'

'All right? Of course I'm all right. Don't I look all right?'

'I don't know. Yes, well, maybe you do. But this,' I said, gesturing to the ruins at my feet, 'what about this? I don't get it. The place is a shambles, it's all in smithereens.'

'An exercise in catharsis, son.'

'An exercise in what?'

'No matter. It's a kind of heart medicine, a balm for ailing spirits.'

'You mean to tell me you done all this yourself?'

'It had to be done. I'm sorry about all the commotion, but sooner or later it had to be done.'

From the way he was looking at me, I sensed he was back to his old snappy self. His voice had regained its haughty timbre, and he seemed to be mixing kindness and sarcasm with the old familiar cunning. 'Does that mean,' I said, still not daring to hope, 'does that mean things are going to be different around here now?'

'We have an obligation to remember the dead. That's the fundamental law. If we didn't remember them, we'd lose the right to call ourselves human. Do you follow me, Walt?'

'Yes, sir, I follow. There ain't a day that goes by when I don't think about our dear darlings and what was done to them. It's just . . .'

'Just what, Walt?'

'It's just that time is wasting, and we'd be doing the world an injustice if we didn't think about ourselves, too.'

'You have a quick mind, son. Maybe there's hope for you yet.'

'It's not just me, you understand. There's Mrs Witherspoon, too. These last couple of weeks, she's worked herself into quite a conniption. If my eyes didn't fool me just now, I believe she's passed out on the lawn, snoring in a puddle of her own barf.'

'I'm not going to apologize for things that need no apology. I did what I had to do, and it took as long as it had to take. Now a new chapter begins. The demons have fled, and the dark night of the soul is over.' He took a deep breath, removed his hands from his pockets, and clasped me firmly on the shoulder. 'What do you say, little man? Are you ready to show them your stuff?'

'I'm ready, boss. You bet your boots I'm ready. Just rig up a place for me to do it, and I'm your boy till death do us part.'

I gave my first public performance on August 25, 1927, appearing as Walt the Wonder Boy for a one-show booking at the Pawnee County Fair in Larned, Kansas. It would be hard to imagine a more modest debut, but as things turned out, it came within an inch of being my swan song. It wasn't that I flubbed up the act, but the crowd was so raucous and mean-spirited, so filled with drunks and hooters, that if not for some quick thinking on the master's part, I might not have lived to see another day.

They'd roped off a field on the other side of the horticultural exhibits, out past the stalls with the prize-winning ears of corn and the two-headed cow and the six-hundred pound pig, and I remember traveling for what seemed like half a mile before coming to a little pond with murky green water and white scum floating on top. It struck me as a woeful site for such a historic occasion, but the master wanted me to start small, with as little fuss and fanfare as possible. 'Even Ty Cobb played in the bush leagues,' he said, as we climbed out of Mrs Witherspoon's car. 'You have to get some performances under your belt. Do well here, and we'll start talking about the big time in a few months.'

Unfortunately, there was no grandstand for the spectators, which made for a lot of tired legs and surly complaints, and with tickets going at ten cents a pop, the crowd was already feeling chiseled before I made my entrance. There couldn't have been more than sixty or seventy of them, a bunch of thick-necked hayseeds milling around in their overalls and flannel shirts – delegates from the First International Congress of Bumpkins. Half of them were guzzling bathtub hootch from little brown cough-syrup bottles and the other half had just finished theirs and were itching for more. When Master

Yehudi stepped forward in his black tuxedo and silk hat to announce the world premiere of Walt the Wonder Boy, the wisecracks and heckling began. Maybe they didn't like his clothes, or maybe they objected to his Brooklyn-Budapest accent, but I'm certain it didn't help that I was wearing the worst costume in the annals of show business: a long white robe that made me look like some midget John the Baptist, complete with leather sandals and a hemp sash tied around my waist. The master had insisted on what he called an 'otherworldly look', but I felt like a twit in that getup, and when I heard some clown yell at the top of his voice – 'Walt the Wonder Girl' – I realized I wasn't alone in my sentiments.

If I found the courage to begin, it was only because of Aesop. I knew he was looking down on me from wherever he was, and I wasn't going to let myself fail him. He was counting on me to shine, and whatever that soused-up mob of fools might have thought of me, I owed it to my brother to give it the best shot I could. So I walked to the edge of the pond and went into my spread-arms-and-trance routine, struggling to shut out the catcalls and insults. I heard some oohs and ahs when my body rose off the ground – but dimly, only dimly, for I was already in a separate world by then, walled off from friend and foe alike in the glory of my ascent. It was the first performance I had ever given, but I already had the makings of a trouper, and I'm certain I would have won over the crowd if not for some birdbrain who took it upon himself to hurl a bottle in my direction. Nineteen times out of twenty, the projectile sails past me and no harm is done, but this was a day for flukes and longshots, and the damned thing clunked me square in the noggin. The blow addled my concentration (not to speak of rendering me unconscious), and before I knew which end was up, I was sinking like a bag of pennies to the bottom of the water. If the master hadn't been on his toes, diving in after me without bothering to shed his coat and tails, I probably would have

111

drowned in that crummy mudhole, and that would have been the first and last bow I ever took.

So we left Larned in disgrace, hightailing it out of there as those bloodthirsty hicks pelted us with eggs and stones and watermelons. No one seemed to care that I'd almost died from that blow on the head, and they went on laughing as the good master rescued me from the drink and carried me to the safety of Mrs W.'s car. I was still semidelirious from my visit to Davy Jones's locker, and I coughed and puked all over the master's shirt as he ran across the field with my wet body bouncing in his arms. I couldn't hear everything that was said, but enough reached my ears for me to gather that opinions about us were sharply divided. Some people took the religious view, boldly asserting that we were in league with the devil. Others called us fakes and charlatans, and still others had no opinion at all. They yelled for the pure pleasure of yelling, just glad to be part of the mayhem as they let forth with angry, wordless howls. Fortunately, the car was waiting for us on the other side of the roped-off area, and we managed to get inside before the rowdies caught up with us. A few eggs thudded against the rear window as we drove off, but no glass shattered, no shots rang out, and all in all I suppose we were lucky to escape with our hides intact.

We must have traveled two miles before either one of us found the courage to speak. We were out among the farms and pastures by then, tooling along a bumpy byway in our drenched and sopping clothes. With each jolt of the car, another spurt of pond water gushed from us and sank into Mrs Witherspoon's deluxe suede upholstery. It sounds funny as I tell it now, but I wasn't the least bit tempted to laugh at the time. I just sat there stewing in the front seat, trying to control my temper and figure out what had gone wrong. In spite of his errors and miscalculations, it didn't seem fair to blame the master. He'd been through a lot, and I knew his judgment wasn't all it should have been, but it was my fault

112

for going along with him. I never should have allowed myself to get sucked into such a half-assed, poorly planned operation. It was my butt on the line out there, and when all was said and done, it was my job to protect it.

'Well, partner,' the master said, doing his best to crack a smile, 'welcome to show biz.'

'That wasn't no show biz,' I said. 'What happened back there was assault and battery. It was like walking into an ambush and getting scalped.'

'That's the rough and tumble, kid, the give and take of crowds. Once the curtain goes up, you never know what's going to happen.'

'I don't mean to be disrespectful, sir, but that kind of talk ain't nothing but wind.'

'Oh, ho,' he said, amused by my plucky rejoinder. 'The little lad's in a huff. And what kind of talk do you propose we engage in, Mr Rawley?'

'Practical talk, sir. The kind of talk that'll stop us from repeating our mistakes.'

'We didn't make any mistakes. We just drew a bum audience, that's all. Sometimes you get lucky, sometimes you don't.'

'Luck's got nothing to do with it. We did a lot of dumb things today, and we wound up paying the price.'

'I thought you were brilliant. If not for that flying bottle, it would have been a four-star success.'

'Well, for one thing, I'd sincerely like to ditch this costume. It's about the awfulest piece of hokum I ever saw. We don't need no otherworldy trappings. The act's got enough of that already, and we don't want to confuse folks by dressing me up like some nancy-boy angel. It puts them off. It makes me look like I'm supposed to be better than they are.'

'You *are* better, Walt. Don't ever forget that.'

'Maybe so. But once we let them know that, we're sunk. They were against me before I even started.'

'The costume had nothing to do with it. That crowd was stoned, pickled to the toe jam in their socks. They were so crosseyed, not one of them even saw what you had on.'

'You're the best teacher there is, master, and I'm truly grateful to you for saving my life today, but on this particular point, you're as wrong as any mortal man can be. The costume stinks. I'm sorry to be so blunt, but no matter how hard you yell at me, I ain't never wearing it again.'

'Why would I yell at you? We're in this together, son, and you're free to express your opinions. If you want to dress another way, all you have to do is tell me.'

'On the level?'

'It's a long trip back to Wichita, and there's no reason why we shouldn't discuss these things now.'

'I don't mean to grumble,' I said, jumping through the door he'd just opened for me, 'but the way I see it, we ain't got a prayer unless we win them over from the get-go. These rubes don't like no fancy stuff. They didn't take to your penguin suit, and they didn't take to my sissy robes. And all that high-flown talk you pitched them at the start – it went right over their heads.'

'It was nothing but gibberish. Just to get them in the mood.'

'Whatever you say. But how's about we skip it in the future? Just keep it simple and folksy. You know, something like "Ladies and gentlemen, I'm proud to present," and then back off and let me come on. If you wear a plain old seersucker suit and a nice straw hat, no one will take offense. They'll think you're a friendly, good-hearted Joe out to make an honest buck. That's the key, the whole sack of onions. I stroll out before them like a little know-nothing, a wide-eyed farm boy dressed in denim overalls and a plaid shirt. No shoes, no socks, a barefoot nobody with the same geek mug as their own sons and nephews. They take one look at me and relax. It's like I'm a member of the family. And then, the moment I start rising into the air, their hearts fail them. It's that simple.

Soften them up, then hit them with the whammy. It's bound to be good. Two minutes into the act, they'll be eating out of our hands like squirrels.'

It took almost three hours to get home, and all during the ride I talked, speaking my mind to the master in a way I'd never done before. I covered everything I could think of – from costumes to venues, from ticket-taking to music, from show times to publicity – and he let me have my say. There's no question that he was impressed, maybe even a little startled by my thoroughness and strong opinions, but I was fighting for my life that afternoon, and it wouldn't have helped the cause to hold back and mince words. Master Yehudi had launched a ship that was full of holes, and rather than try to plug those holes as the water rushed in and sank us, I wanted to drag the thing back to port and rebuild it from the bottom up. The master listened to my ideas without interrupting or making fun of me, and in the end he gave in on most of the points I raised. It couldn't have been easy for him to accept his failure as a showman, but Master Yehudi wanted things to work as much as I did, and he was big enough to admit that he'd gotten us off on the wrong track. It wasn't that he didn't have a method, but that method was out of date, more suited to the corny prewar style he'd grown up with than to the jump and jangle of the new age. I was after something modern, something sleek and savvy and direct, and little by little I managed to talk him into it, to bring him around to a different approach.

Still, on certain issues he refused to fall in line. I was keen on taking the act to Saint Louis and showing off in front of my old hometown, but he nipped that proposition in the bud. 'That's the most dangerous spot on earth for you,' he said, 'and the minute you go back there, you'll be signing your own death warrant. Mark my words. Saint Louis is bad medicine. It's a poison place, and you'll never get out of there alive.' I couldn't understand his vehemence, but he talked like someone whose mind was set, and there was no way I could go against him. As it turned out, his words proved to be dead on the mark. Just one month after he spoke them to me, Saint Louis was hit by the worst tornado of the century. The twister shot through town like a cannonball from hell, and by the time it left five minutes later, a thousand buildings had been flattened, a hundred people were dead, and two thousand others lay writhing in the wreckage with broken bones and blood pouring from their wounds. We were on our way to Vernon, Oklahoma, by then, on the fifth leg of a fourteen-stop tour, and when I picked up the morning edition of the local rag and saw the pictures on the front page, I almost regurgitated my breakfast. I'd thought the master had lost his touch, but once again I'd sold him short. He knew things I would never know, he heard things no one else could hear, and not a man in the world could match him. If I ever doubt his words again, I told myself, may the Lord strike me down and scatter my corpse to the pigs.

But I'm going too fast. The tornado didn't come until late September, and for the time being it's still August twenty-fifth. Master Yehudi and I are still sitting in our clammy clothes, and we're still driving back to Mrs Witherspoon's house in Wichita. After our long conversation about revamping the act, I was beginning to feel a little better about our prospects, but I wouldn't go so far as to say that my mind was totally at ease. Putting the lid on Saint Louis was one thing, a minor difference of opinion, but there were other matters that troubled me more deeply. Essential flaws in the arrangement, you might call them, and now that I had bared my soul about so much, I figured I should go for the brass ring. So I plunged in and brought up the subject of Mrs Witherspoon. I had never dared to speak about her before, and I hoped the master wasn't going to haul off and belt me in the snout.

'Maybe it's none of my business,' I said, stepping as

gingerly as I could, 'but I still don't see why Mrs Witherspoon didn't come with us.'

'She didn't want to be in the way,' the master said. 'She thought she might jinx us.'

'But she's our backer, ain't she? She's the one who's footing the bill. You'd think she'd want to stick around and keep a close eye on her investment.'

'She's what they call a silent partner.'

'Silent? You're funning me, boss. That missus is about the unsilentest frail this side of a car factory. Why, she'll chew off your ear and spit out the pieces before you can get a word in.'

'In life, yes. But I'm talking about business. In life, there's no question she's got a tongue on her. I'm not going to argue with you about that.'

'I don't know what her problem is, but all those days when you were out of commission there, she did some awfully strange things. I'm not saying she ain't a good sport and all that, but there were times, let me tell you, there were times when it gave me the creeps to see her carry on the way she did.'

'She's been distraught. You can't blame her, Walt. She's had some rough things to swallow these past months, and she's a lot more fragile than you think she is. You just have to be patient with her.'

'That's pretty much the same thing she said about you.'

'She's a smart woman. A little high-strung, perhaps, but she's got a good head on her shoulders, and her heart's in the right place.'

'Mother Sioux, may her soul rest in peace, once told me you were fixing to marry her.'

'I was. Then I wasn't anymore. Then I was. Then I wasn't. Now who knows. If the years have taught me anything, kid, it's that anything can happen. When it comes to men and women, all bets are off.'

'Yeah, she's a frisky one, I'll grant you that. Just when you think you've roped her in, she slips the knot and bolts to the next pasture.'

'Exactly. Which explains why it's sometimes best to do nothing. If you just stand there and wait, there's a chance the thing you're hoping for will come right to you.'

'It's all too deep for me, sir.'

'You're not the only one, Walt.'

'But if and ever you do get hitched, I'll lay odds it won't be a very smooth ride.'

'Don't worry yourself about that. Just concentrate on your work and leave the love business to me. I don't need any advice from the peanut gallery. It's my song, and I'll sing it in my own way.'

I didn't have the balls to push it any farther than that. Master Yehudi was a genius and a wizard, but it was growing abundantly clear to me that he didn't understand the first thing about women. I'd been privy to Mrs Witherspoon's innermost thoughts, I'd listened to her drunken, bawdy confidences on many an occasion, and I knew the master was never going to get anywhere with her unless he took the bull by the horns. She didn't want to be deferred to, she wanted to be stormed and conquered, and the longer he shilly-shallied around, the worse his chances would be. But how to tell him that? I couldn't do it. Not if I valued my own skin I couldn't, so I kept my mouth shut and let the matter ride. It was his damned goose, I told myself, and if he was so bent on cooking it, who was I to stand in his way?

So we returned to Wichita and got busy making plans for a fresh start. Mrs W. said nary a word about the water stains on the seats, but I suppose she thought of them as a business expense, part of the risk you take when you set your sights on making big money. It took about three weeks to wrap up the preparations – scheduling performances, printing hand-bills and posters, rehearsing the new routine – and during that time the master and Mrs Witherspoon were pretty cozy with each other, a lot more lovey-dovey than I'd expected them to be. Maybe I was all wrong, I thought, and the master knew exactly what he was doing. But then, on the day of our departure, he committed an error, a tactical blunder that showed up the weakness of his overall strategy. I saw it with my own eyes, standing on the porch as the master and the missus said their farewells, and it was a painful thing to behold, a sad little chapter in the history of heartbreak.

He said: 'So long, sister. We'll see you in a month and three days.' And she said: 'Off you go, boys – into the wild blue yonder.' There was an awkward silence after that, and since it made me feel uncomfortable, I opened my big mouth and said: 'What do you say, ma'am? Why not hop in the car and come with us?'

I could see her eyes light up when I said that, and sure as *dog* and *god* are the same word spelled backwards and forwards, she would have given six years off her life to chuck everything and climb aboard. She turned to the master and said: 'Well, what do you think? Should I go with you or not?' And he, pompous oaf that he was, patted her on the shoulder and said: 'It's up to you, my dear.' Her eyes clouded over for a second, but even then all was not lost. Still hopeful of hearing the right words from him, she gave it another shot and said: 'No, you decide. I wouldn't want to be in the way.' And he said: 'You're a free agent, Marion. It's not for me to tell you what to do.' And that was that. I saw the light go out in her eyes; her face closed up into a taut, quizzical expression; and then she shrugged. 'Never mind,' she said. 'There's too much to do here anyway.' Then, forcing a brave little smile to her lips, she added: 'Drop me a postcard when you get a chance. The last I heard, they still go for a penny apiece.'

And there it was, folks. The opportunity of a lifetime – lost forever. The master let it slip right through his fingers, and the worst part of it was, I don't even think he realized what he'd done.

We traveled in a different car this time – a black, secondhand Ford that Mrs Witherspoon had picked out for us after our return from Larned. She'd dubbed it the Wondermobile, and though it couldn't match the size and smoothness of the Chrysler, it did everything it was asked to do. We set off on a rainy morning in mid-September, and one hour out of Wichita I'd already forgotten about the hearts-and-flowers fumble I'd witnessed on the porch. My mental beams were fixed on Oklahoma, the first state booked for the tour, and when we pulled into Redbird two days later, I was as keyed up as a jack-in-the-box and crazier than a monkey. It's going to work this time, I told myself. Yes sir, this is where it all begins. Even the name of the town struck me as a good omen, and since I was nothing if not superstitious in those days, it had a powerful effect on my spirits. Redbird. Just like my ball club in Saint Louis, my dear old chums the Cardinals.

It was the same act in a new set of clothes, but everything felt different somehow, and the audience took a shine to me the moment I came on – which was half the battle right there. Master Yehudi did his cornpone spiel to the hilt, my Huck Finn costume was the last word in understatement, and all in all we knocked them dead. Six or seven women fainted, children screamed, grown men gasped in awe and disbelief. For thirty minutes I kept them spellbound, prancing and tumbling in midair, gliding my little body over the surface of a broad and sparkling lake, and then, at the end, pushing myself to a record height of four and a half feet before floating back to the ground and taking my bow. The applause was thunderous, ecstatic. They whooped and cried, they banged pots and pans, they tossed confetti into the air. This was my first taste of success, and I loved it, I loved it in a way I've never loved anything before or since.

Dunbar and Battiest. Jumbo and Plunketsville. Pickens, Muse, and Bethel. Wapanucka. Boggy Depot and Kingfisher. Gerty, Ringling, and Marble City. If this were a movie, here's where the calendar pages would start flying off the wall. We'd see them fluttering against a background of country roads and tumbleweed, and then the names of those towns would flash by as we followed the progress of the black Ford across a map of eastern Oklahoma. The music would be jaunty and full of bounce, a syncopated chug-chug to ape the noise of ringing cash registers. Shot would follow shot, each one melting into the other. Bushel baskets brimming with coins, roadside bungalows, clapping hands and stomping feet, open mouths, bug-eyed faces turned to the sky. The whole sequence would take about ten seconds, and by the time it was over, the story of that month would be known to every person in the theater. Ah, the old Hollywood razzmatazz. There's nothing like it for hustling things along. It may not be subtle, but it gets the job done.

So much for the quirks of memory. If I'm suddenly thinking about movies now, it's probably because I saw so many of them in the months that followed. After the Oklahoma triumph, bookings ceased to be a problem, and the master and I spent most of our time on the road, moving around from one backwater to another. We played Texas, Arkansas, and Louisiana, dipping farther and farther south as winter came on, and I tended to fill in the dead time between performances by visiting the local Bijou for a peek at the latest flick. The master generally had business to take care of – talking to fair managers and ticket sellers, distributing handbills and posters around town, adjusting nuts and bolts for the upcoming performance – which meant he seldom had time to go with me. More often than not, I'd come back to find him alone in the room, sitting in a chair reading his book. It was always the same book – a battered little green volume that he carried with him on all our travels – and it became as familiar to me as the lines and contours of his face. It was written in Latin, of all things, and the author's name was Spinoza, a detail I've never forgotten, even after so many years. When I asked the master why he kept studying that one book over and over again, he told me it was because you could never get to the bottom of it. The deeper you go, he said, the more there is, and the more there is, the longer it takes to read it.

'A magic book,' I said. 'It can't never use itself up.'

'That's it, squirt. It's inexhaustible. You drink down the wine, put the glass back on the table, and lo and behold, you reach for the glass again and discover it's still full.'

'And there you are, drunk as a skunk for the price of one drink.'

'I couldn't have put it better myself,' he said, suddenly turning from me and gazing out the window. 'You get drunk on the world, boy. Drunk on the mystery of the world.'

Christ but I was happy out there on the road with him. Just moving from place to place was enough to keep my spirits up, but when you added in all the other ingredients – the crowds, the performances, the money we made – those first months were hands down the best months I'd ever lived. Even after the initial excitement wore off and I grew accustomed to the routine, I still didn't want it to stop. Lumpy beds, flat tires, bad food, all the rainouts and lulls and boring stretches were as nothing to me, mere pebbles bouncing off the skin of a rhinoceros. We'd climb into the Ford and blow out of town, another seventy or hundred bucks stashed away in the trunk, and then mosey on to the next whistle-stop, watching the landscape roll by as we chewed over the finer points of the last performance. The master was a prince to me, always encouraging and counseling and listening to what I said, and he never made me feel that I was one bit less important than he was. So many things had changed between us since the summer, it was as if we were on a new footing now, as if we'd reached some kind of permanent equilibrium. He did his job and I did mine, and together we made the thing work.

The stock market didn't crash until two years later, but the Depression had already started in the hinterlands, and farmers and rural folks throughout the region were feeling the pinch. We came across a lot of desperate people on our travels, and Master Yehudi taught me never to look down on them. They needed Walt the Wonder Boy, he said, and I must never forget the responsibility that need entailed. To watch a twelve-year-old do what only saints and prophets had done before him was like a jolt from heaven, and my performances could bring spiritual uplift to thousands of suffering souls. That didn't mean I shouldn't make a bundle doing it, but unless I understood that I had to touch people's hearts, I'd never gain the following I deserved. I think that's why the master started my career in such out-of-the-way places, such a rinky-dink collection of forgotten corners and crevices on the map. He wanted the word about me to spread slowly, for support to begin from the ground up. It wasn't just a matter of breaking me in, it was a way of controlling things, of making sure I didn't turn out to be a flash in the pan.

Who was I to object? The bookings were organized in a systematic way, the turnouts were good, and we always had a roof over our heads when we went to sleep at night. I was doing what I wanted to do, and the feeling it gave me was so good, so exhilarating, I couldn't have cared less if the people who saw me perform were from Paris, France, or Paris, Texas. Every now and then, of course, we encountered a bump in the road, but Master Yehudi seemed to be prepared for any and all situations. Once, for example, a truant officer came knocking on the door of our rooming house in Dublin, Mississippi. Why isn't this lad in school? he said to the master, pointing his long bony finger at me. There are laws against

124

this, you know, statutes, regulations, and so on and so forth. I figured we were sunk, but the master only smiled, asked the gentleman to step in, and then pulled a piece of paper from the breast pocket of his coat. It was covered with official-looking stamps and seals, and once the truant officer read it through, he tipped his hat in an embarrassed sort of way, apologized for the mixup, and left. God knows what was written on that paper, but it did the trick in one fast hurry. Before I could make out any of the words, the master had already folded up the letter and slipped it back into his coat pocket. 'What does it say?' I asked, but even though I asked again, he never answered me. He just patted his pocket and grinned, looking awfully smug and pleased with himself. He reminded me of a cat who'd just polished off the family bird, and he wasn't about to tell me how he'd opened the cage.

From the latter part of 1927 through the first half of 1928, I lived in a cocoon of total concentration. I never thought about the past, I never thought about the future – only about what was happening now, the thing I was doing at this or that moment. On the average, we didn't spend more than three or four days a month in Wichita, and the rest of the time we were on the road, bee-lining hither and yon in the black Wondermobile. The first real pause didn't come until the middle of May. My thirteenth birthday was approaching, and the master thought it might be a good idea to take a couple of weeks off. We'd go back to Mrs Witherspoon's, he said, and eat some home cooking for a change. We'd relax and celebrate and count our money, and then, after we were done playing pasha, we'd pack up our bags and take off again. That sounded fine with me, but once we got there and settled in for our holiday, I sensed that something was wrong. It wasn't the master or Mrs Witherspoon. They were both lovely to me, and relations between them were particularly harmonious just then. Nor was it anything connected to the house. Nelly Boggs's cooking was in top form, the bed was still comfortable, the spring weather was superb. Yet the moment we walked through the door, an inexplicable heaviness invaded my heart, a murky sort of sadness and disquiet. I assumed I'd feel better after a night's sleep, but the feeling didn't go away; it just sat inside me like a lump of undigested stew, and no matter what I said to myself, I couldn't get rid of it. If anything, it seemed to be growing, to be taking on a life of its own, and to such an extent that by the third night, just after I put on my pajamas and crawled into bed, I was overcome by an irresistible urge to cry. It seemed crazy, and yet half a minute later I was sobbing into the pillow, weeping my blinkers out in an onrush of misery and remorse.

When I sat down to breakfast with Master Yehudi early the next morning, I couldn't hold myself back, the words came out before I even knew I was going to say them. Mrs Witherspoon was still upstairs in bed, and it was just the two of us at the table, waiting for Nelly Boggs to come out of the kitchen and serve us our sausages and scrambled eggs.

'Remember that law you told me about?' I said.

The master, whose nose was buried in the paper, glanced up from the headlines and gave me a long blank stare. 'Law?' he said. 'What law is that?'

'You remember. The one about duties and such. How we wouldn't be human no more if we forgot the dead.'

'Of course I remember.'

'Well, it seems to me we've been breaking that law left and right.'

'How so, Walt? Aesop and Mother Sioux are inside us. We carry them in our hearts wherever we go. Nothing's ever going to change that.'

'But we just walked away, didn't we? They was murdered by a pack of devils and demons, and we never did nothing about it.'

'We couldn't. If we'd gone after them, they would have killed us, too.'

126

'That night, maybe. But what about now? If we're supposed to remember the dead, then we don't have no choice but to hunt down the bastards and see they get what's coming to them. I mean, hell, we're having a fine old time, ain't we? Barnstorming around the country in our motor car, raking in the dough, strutting before the world like a pair of hotshots. But what about my pal Aesop? What about funny old Mother Sioux? They're moldering in their graves is what, and the trash that hung them's still running free.'

'Get a grip on yourself,' the master said, studying me closely as the tears sprang forth again and started running down my cheeks. His voice was stern, almost on the point of anger. 'Sure, we could go after them,' he said. 'We could track them down and bring them to justice, but that's the only job we'd have for the rest of our lives. The cops won't help us, I'll guarantee you that, and if you think a jury would convict them, think again. The Klan is everywhere, Walt, they own the whole rotten charade. They're the same nice smiling folks you used to see on the streets of Cibola – Tom Skinner, Judd McNally, Harold Dowd – they're all part of it, every last one of them. The butcher, the baker, the candlestick maker. We'd have to kill them ourselves, and once we went after them, they'd go after us. A lot of blood would be shed, Walt, and most of it would be ours.'

'It ain't fair,' I said, sniffling through another rush of tears. 'It ain't fair, and it ain't right.'

'You know that, and I know that, and as long as we both know it, Aesop and Mother Sioux are taken care of.'

'They're writhing in torment, master, and their souls won't never be at peace until we do what we've got to do.'

'No, Walt, you're wrong. They're both at peace already.'

'Yeah? And what makes you such an expert on what the dead are doing in their graves?'

'Because I've been with them. I've been with them and spoken to them, and they're not suffering anymore. They want us to go on with our work. That's what they told me. They want us to remember them by keeping up with the work we've started.'

'What?' I said, suddenly feeling my skin crawl. 'What the hell are you talking about?'

'They come to me, Walt. Almost every night for the past six months. They come to me and sit down on my bed, singing songs and stroking my face. They're happier than they were in this world, believe me. Aesop and Mother Sioux are angels now, and nothing can hurt them anymore.'

It was about the strangest, most fantastical thing I'd ever heard, and yet Master Yehudi told it with such conviction, such straightforward sincerity and calm, I never doubted that he was telling the truth. Even if it wasn't true in an absolute sense, there was no question that he believed it – and even if he didn't believe it, then he'd just turned in one of the most powerful acting performances of all time. I sat there in a kind of feverish immobility, letting the vision linger in my head, trying to hold on to the picture of Aesop and Mother Sioux singing to the master in the middle of the night. It doesn't really matter if it happened or not, for the fact was that it changed everything for me. The pain began to subside, the black clouds began to disperse, and by the time I stood up from the table that morning, the worst of the grief was gone. In the end, that's the only thing that matters. If the master lied, then he did it for a reason. And if he didn't lie, then the story stands as told, and there's no cause to defend him. One way or the other, he saved me. One way or the other, he rescued my soul from the jaws of the beast.

Ten days later, we picked up where we had left off, driving away from Wichita in yet another new car. Our earnings were such that we could afford something better now, so we traded in the Ford for Wondermobile II, a silver-gray Pierce Arrow with leather seats and running boards the size of sofas. We'd been in the black since early spring, which meant that Mrs

Witherspoon had been reimbursed for her initial expenditures, there was money in the bank for the master and myself, and we no longer had to pinch pennies as we had before. The whole operation had moved up a notch or two: larger towns for the performances, small hotels instead of rooming houses and guest cottages to flop our bones in, more stylish transportation. I was back on the beam by the time we left, all charged up and ready to roll, and for the next few months I pulled out one stop after another, adding new wrinkles and flourishes to the act almost every week. I had grown so accustomed to the crowds by then, felt so at ease during my performances, that I was able to improvise as I went along, actually to invent and discover new turns in the middle of a show. In the beginning I had always stuck to the routine, rigidly following the steps the master and I had worked out in advance, but I was past that now, I had hit my stride, and I was no longer afraid to experiment. Locomotion had always been my strength. It was the heart of my act, the thing that separated me from every levitator who had come before me, but my loft was no better than average, a fair to middling five feet. I wanted to improve on that, to double or even triple that mark if I could, but I no longer had the luxury of all-day practice sessions, the old freedom of working under Master Yehudi's supervision for ten or twelve hours at a stretch. I was a pro now, with all the burdens and scheduling constraints of a pro, and the only place I could practice was in front of a live audience.

So that's what I did, especially after that little holiday in Wichita, and to my immense wonderment I found that the pressure inspired me. Some of my finest tricks date from that period, and without the eyes of the crowd to spur me on, I doubt that I would have mustered the courage to try half the things I did. It all started with the staircase number, which was the first time I ever made use of an 'invisible prop' – the term I later coined for my invention. We were in upper

Michigan then, and smack in the middle of the performance, just as I rose to begin my crossing of the lake, I caught sight of a building in the distance. It was a large brick structure, probably a warehouse or an old factory, and it had a fire escape running down one of the walls. I couldn't help but notice those metal stairs. The sunlight was bouncing off of them at just that moment, and they were gleaming with a frantic kind of brightness in the late afternoon sun. Without giving the matter any thought, I lifted one foot into the air, as if I were about to climb a real staircase, and put it down on an invisible step; then I lifted the other foot and put it down on the next step. It wasn't that I felt anything solid in the air, but I was nevertheless going up, gradually ascending a staircase that stretched from one end of the lake to the other. Even though I couldn't see it, I had a definite picture of it in my mind. To the best of my recollection, it looked something like this:

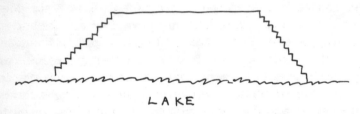

L A KE

At its highest point – the platform in the middle – it was roughly nine and a half feet above the surface of the water – a good four feet higher than I'd ever been before. The eerie thing was that I didn't hesitate. Once I had that picture clearly in my mind, I knew I could depend on it to get me across. All I had to do was follow the shape of the imaginary bridge, and it would support me as if it were real. A few moments later, I was gliding across the lake with nary a hitch or a stumble. Twelve steps up, fifty-two steps across, and then twelve steps down. The results were nothing less than perfect.

After that breakthrough, I discovered that I could use other props just as effectively. As long as I could imagine the thing I wanted, as long as I could visualize it with a high degree of clarity and definition, it would be available to me for the performance. That was how I developed some of the most memorable portions of my act: the rope-ladder routine, the slide routine, the seesaw routine, the high-wire routine, the countless innovations I was heralded for. Not only did these turns enhance the audience's pleasure, but they thrust me into an entirely new relationship with my work. I wasn't just a robot anymore, a wind-up baboon who did the same set of tricks for every show – I was evolving into an artist, a true creator who performed as much for his own sake as for the sake of others. It was the unpredictability that excited me, the adventure of never knowing what was going to happen from one show to the next. If your only motive is to be loved, to ingratiate yourself with the crowd, you're bound to fall into bad habits, and eventually the public will grow tired of you. You have to keep testing yourself, pushing your talent as hard as you can. You do it for yourself, but in the end it's this struggle to do better that most endears you to your fans. That's the paradox. People begin to sense that you're out there taking risks for them. They're allowed to share in the mystery, to participate in whatever nameless thing is driving you to do it, and once that happens, you're no longer just a performer, you're on the way to becoming a star. In the fall of 1928, that's exactly where I was: on the brink of becoming a star.

By mid October we found ourselves in central Illinois, playing out a last few gigs before we headed back to Wichita for a well-earned breather. If I remember correctly, we'd just finished up a show in Gibson City, one of those lost little towns with a Buck Rogers skyline of water towers and grain elevators. From a distance you think you're approaching a hefty burg, and then you get there and discover those grain elevators are all they've got. We'd already checked out of the

131

hotel and were sitting in a diner on the main drag, slurping down some liquid refreshments before we jumped into the car and took off. It was a dead hour of the day, somewhere between breakfast and lunch, and Master Yehudi and I were the only customers. I had just downed the last bits of foam from my hot chocolate, I remember, when the bell on the door jangled and a third customer walked in. Out of idle curiosity, I glanced up to take a gander at the new arrival, and who should it turn out to be but my Uncle Slim, the old chinless wonder himself? It couldn't have been warmer than thirty-five degrees that day, but he was dressed in a threadbare summer suit. The collar was turned up against his neck, and he was clutching the two halves of the jacket in his right hand. He shivered as he crossed the threshold, looking like a chihuahua blown in by the north wind, and if I hadn't been so stunned, I probably would have laughed at the sight.

Master Yehudi's back was turned to the door. When he saw the expression on my face (I must have gone white), he wheeled around to have a look at what had so discombobulated me. Slim was still standing in the entrance, rubbing his hands together and surveying the joint with his squinty eyes, and the moment he zoomed in on us, he broke into one of those snaggletoothed grins I'd always dreaded as a boy. This meeting was no accident. He'd come to Gibson City because he wanted to talk, and sure as six and seven made thirteen, the unluckiest number there was, we were staring at a mess of trouble.

'Well, well,' he said, oozing false amiability as he sauntered over to our table. 'Fancy that. I come to the back of beyond on personal business, drop in at the local beanery for a cup of java, and who should I run into but my long-lost nephew? Little Walt, the apple of my eye, the freckle-faced boy wonder. It's like destiny is what it is. Like finding a needle in a haystack.' Without a word from either the master or myself, he parked himself in the empty chair beside me. 'You don't mind if I sit down, do you?' he said. 'I'm just so bowled over by this joyful occasion, I have to get off my pins before I pass out.' Then he banged me on the back and tousled my hair, still pretending how happy he was to see me – which maybe he was, but not for any of the reasons a normal person would be. It gave me the chills to be touched by him like that. I squirmed away from his hand, but he paid no attention to the rebuff, chattering on in that slimy way of his and baring his crooked brown teeth at every opportunity. 'Well, old bean,' he continued, 'it looks like the world's been treating you pretty good these days, don't it? From what the papers tell me, you're the cat's pajamas, the greatest thing since rye bread. Your mentor here must be flush with pride – not to speak of just plain flush, since his wallet can't have suffered none in the process. I can't tell you the good it does me, Walt, seeing my kin make a name for himself in the big world.'

'State your business, friend,' the master said, finally breaking in on Slim's monologue. 'The kid and I were just on our way out, and we don't have time to sit around shooting the breeze.'

'Hell,' Slim said, doing his best to look offended, 'can't a guy catch up on the news with his own sister's son? What's the rush? From the looks of that machine you got parked at the curb, you'll get where you're going in no time.'

'Walt's got nothing to say to you,' the master said, 'and as far as I'm concerned, you've got nothing to say to him.'

'I wouldn't be so sure about that,' Slim said, reaching for the crumpled cheroot in his pocket and lighting up. 'He's got a right to know about his poor Aunt Peg, and I've got the right to tell him.'

'What about her?' I said, barely getting my voice above a whisper.

'Hey, the kid can talk!' Slim said, pinching my cheek with mock enthusiasm. 'For a moment there, I thought he'd cut out your tongue, Walt.'

133

'What about her?' I repeated.

'She's dead, son, that's what. She got took by that tornado that demolished Saint Louis last year. The whole house fell on top of her, and that was the end of sweet old Peg. It happened just like that.'

'And you escaped,' I said.

'It was the Lord's will,' Slim said. 'As chance would have it, I was on the other side of town, doing an honest day's work.'

'Too bad it wasn't the other way around,' I said. 'Aunt Peg was no great shakes, but at least she didn't sock me around like you did.'

'Hey, now,' Slim said, 'that's no way to talk to your uncle. I'm your own flesh and blood, Walt, and you don't have to tell no fibs about me. Not when I'm here on such a vital errand. Mr Yehudi and me got things to talk about, and I don't need no cracks from you gumming up the works.'

'I believe you're mistaken,' the master said. 'You and I have nothing to talk about. Walt and I are running late now, and I'm afraid you'll have to excuse us.'

'Not so fast, mister,' Slim said, suddenly forgetting his fake charm. His voice was seething with petulance and anger, just as I'd always remembered it. 'You and I made a deal, and you're not going to worm out on me now.'

'Deal?' the master said. 'What deal was that?'

'The one we made in Saint Louis four years ago. Did you think I'd forget or something? I'm not stupid, you know. You promised me a cut of the profits, and I'm here to claim my fair share. Twenty-five percent. That's what you promised, and that's what I want.'

'As I recall, Mr Sparks,' the master said, trying to control his temper, 'you just about kissed my feet when I told you I'd take the boy off your hands. You were slobbering all over me, telling me how glad you were to be rid of him. That was the deal, Mr Sparks. I asked for the boy, and you gave him to me.'

'I had my conditions. I spelled them out for you, and you agreed. Twenty-five percent. You're not going to tell me there's no deal. You promised me, and I took you at your word.'

'Dream on, laddie. If you think there's a deal, then show me the contract. Show me the piece of paper where it says you have one dime coming to you.'

'We shook hands on it. It was a gentlemen's agreement, all on the up and up.'

'You have a splendid imagination, Mr Sparks, but you're a liar and a crook. If you have a complaint against me, take it to a lawyer, and we'll see how well your case stands up in court. But until that happens, kindly have the decency to remove your ugly face from my sight.' Then the master turned to me and said, 'Come on, Walt, let's go. They're waiting for us in Urbana, and we don't have a minute to lose.'

The master threw a dollar on the table and stood up, and I stood up with him. But Slim wasn't finished having his say, and he managed to get in the last word, delivering a few parting shots as we left the diner. 'You think you're smart, mister,' he said, 'but you ain't done with me yet. Nobody calls Edward J. Sparks a liar and gets away with it, you hear? That's right, keep on walking out the door – it don't matter. But that's the last time you'll ever turn your back on me. Be warned, pal. I'm coming after you. I'm coming after you and that scummy kid, and once I get to you, you'll be sorry you ever talked to me like that. You'll be sorry till the day you die.'

He pursued us to the door of the restaurant, showering us with his deranged threats as we climbed into the Pierce Arrow and the master started up the engine. The noise drowned out my uncle's words, but his lips were still moving, and I could see the veins bulging in his scrawny neck. That was how we left him: beside himself with fury as he watched us pull away, shaking his fist at us and mouthing his inaudible vengeance. My uncle had been wandering in the desert for forty years, and all he had to show for it was a history of stumbles and wrong turns, an endless string of failures. Watching his face through the rear window of the car, I understood that he had a purpose now, that the fucker had finally found a mission in life.

Once we were out of town, the master turned to me and said, 'That bigmouth doesn't have a leg to stand on. It's all a bluff, jive and nonsense from start to finish. The guy's a born loser, and if he ever so much as lays a hand on you, Walt, I'll kill him. I swear it. I'll chop that grifter into so many pieces, they'll still be finding bits of him in Canada twenty years from now.'

I was proud of the way the master had handled himself in the diner, but that didn't mean I wasn't worried. My mother's older brother was a slippery customer, and now that he'd set his mind on something, he wasn't likely to be distracted from his goal. Personally speaking, I had no wish to consider his side of the dispute. Maybe the master had promised him twenty-five percent and maybe he hadn't, but that was all water down the toilet now, and the only thing I wanted was to have that son-of-a-bitch out of my life for good. He'd bounced me off the walls too many times for me to feel anything but hatred for him, and whether he had a rightful claim to the money or not, the truth was he didn't deserve a penny. But alas, what I felt didn't count for a damn. Nor what the master felt. It was all up to Slim, and I knew in my bones that he was coming, that he'd keep on coming until his hands were pressed around my throat.

These fears and premonitions didn't leave me. They cast a pall over everything that happened in the days and months that followed, affecting my mood to the point where even the joy of my growing success was contaminated. It was particularly bad in the beginning. Everywhere we went, every

136

town we traveled to, I kept expecting Slim to pop up again. Sitting in a restaurant, walking into the hotel lobby, stepping out of the car: my uncle was liable to appear at any humdrum moment, bursting through the fabric of my life with no warning. That was what made the situation so hard to bear. It was the uncertainty, the thought that all my happiness could be smashed in the blink of an eye. The only spot that felt safe to me anymore was standing before a crowd and doing my act. Slim wouldn't dare to make a move in public, at least not when I was the center of attention like that, and given all the anxiety I carried around with me the rest of the time, performing became a kind of mental repose, a respite from the terror that stalked my heart. I threw myself into my work as never before, exulting in the freedom and protection it gave me. Something had shifted inside my soul, and I understood that this was who I was now: not Walter Rawley, the kid who turned into Walt the Wonder Boy for one hour a day, but Walt the Wonder Boy through and through, a person who did not exist except when he was in the air. The ground was an illusion, a no-man's land mined with traps and shadows, and everything that happened down there was false. Only the air was real now, and for twenty-three hours a day I lived as a stranger to myself, cut off from my old pleasures and habits, a cowering bundle of desperation and fright.

The work kept me going, and fortunately there was lots of it, an endless parade of winter bookings. After our return to Wichita, the master worked out an elaborate tour, with a record number of weekly performances. Of all the smart moves he made, his cleverest stroke was getting us to Florida for the worst of the cold weather. We were there from mid-January to the end of March, covering the peninsula from top to bottom, and for this one extended trip – the first and only time it ever happened – Mrs Witherspoon tagged along with us. Contrary to all that garbage about being a jinx, she brought me nothing but good luck. Luck not only as far as Slim was concerned (we saw neither hide nor tail of him), but luck in terms of packed audiences, large box-office receipts, and good companionship (she liked going to the movies as much as I did). Those were the days of the Florida land boom, and rich people had begun flocking down there in their white suits and diamond necklaces to dance away the winter under the palm trees. It was my first experience going out in front of swells. I did my act at country clubs, golf courses, and dude ranches, and for all their polish and sophistication, those blue-bloods took to me with the same gusto as the wretched of the earth. It made no difference. My act was universal, and it floored everyone in the same way, rich and poor alike.

By the time we returned to Kansas, I was beginning to feel more like myself again. Slim hadn't shown his face in over five months, and I figured that if he was planning any sur-prises, he would have sprung them on us by now. When we took off again for the upper Midwest at the end of April, I had more or less stopped thinking about him. That scary scene in Gibson City was so far in the past, it sometimes felt as if it had never happened. I was relaxed and confident, and if there was anything on my mind beside the act, it was the hair that had started growing in my armpits and around my crotch, all that late-sprouting stuff that announced my entrance into the land of wet dreams and dirty thoughts. My guard was down, and just as I'd always known it would, just as I'd feared when the whole business started, the blade fell at the very moment I was least expecting it. The master and I were in Northfield, Minnesota, a little town about forty miles south of Saint Paul, and as was my custom prior to evening performances, I went to the local movie house to fritter away a couple of hours. The talkies were in full swing by then, and I couldn't get enough of them, I went every chance I had, sometimes seeing the same picture three or four times. On that particular day, the feature show was *Cocoanuts*, the new Marx Brothers comedy set in Florida. I'd already seen it before, but I was crazy about those clowns, especially Harpo, the mute one with the nutty wig and the loud honker, and I hopped to when I heard it was playing that afternoon. The theater was a fair-size establishment, with seats for two or three hundred people, but owing to the good spring weather, there couldn't have been more than half a dozen folks in attendance with me. Not that I cared, of course. I settled in with a bag of popcorn and proceeded to laugh my head off, oblivious to the other bodies scattered in the dark. About twenty or thirty minutes into it, I sniffed something strange, a curiously sweet medicinal odor wafting up from behind me. It was a strong smell, and it was getting stronger by the second. Before I could turn around to see what it was, a rag drenched in that pungent concoction was clamped over my face. I bucked and struggled to break free of it, but a hand pushed me back, and then, before I could gather my strength for a second effort, the fight suddenly went out of me. My muscles went limp; my skin melted into a buttery ooze; my head detached itself from my body. Wherever I was from then on, it wasn't any place I'd been to before.

I had imagined all kinds of battles and confrontations with Slim – fistfights, holdups, guns going off in dark alleys – but not once did it enter my mind that he'd kidnap me. It wasn't in my uncle's M.O. to do something that required such long-term planning. He was a hothead, a banjo-brain who jumped into things on the spur of the moment, and if he broke the mold on my account, it only shows how bitter he was, how deeply my success had rankled him. I was the one big chance he'd ever have, and he wasn't going to blow it by flying off the handle. Not this time. He was going to act like a proper gangster, a slick professional who thought of all the angles, and he'd end up putting the screws to us but good. He wasn't in it just for the money, and he wasn't in it just for revenge – he wanted both, and snatching me for ransom was the magic combination, the way to kill those two birds with one stone.

He had a partner this time, a corpulent yegg by the name of Fritz, and considering what mental lightweights they were, they did a pretty thorough job of keeping me hidden. First they stashed me in a cave on the outskirts of Northfield, a dank, filthy hole where I spent three days and nights, my legs bound in thick ropes and a gag tied around my mouth; then they gave me a second dose of ether and took me somewhere else, a basement in what must have been an apartment building in Minneapolis or Saint Paul. That lasted only a day, and from there we drove to the country again, settling into an abandoned prospector's house in what I later learned was South Dakota. It looked more like the moon than the earth out there, all treeless and desolate and still, and we were so far back from any road that even if I'd managed to run away from them, it would have taken me hours to find help. They'd stocked the place with a couple of months' worth of canned food, and all signs pointed to a long, nerve-racking siege. That was how Slim had chosen to play it: as slowly as he could. He wanted to make the master squirm, and if that meant dragging things out a little bit, so much the better. He wasn't in any rush. It was all so delicious for him, why put a stop to it before he'd had his fun?

I had never seen him so cocky, so buoyed up and satisfied with himself. He strutted around that cabin like a four-star general, barking out orders and laughing at his own jokes, a whirlwind of lunatic bravado. It disgusted me to see him like that, but at the same time it spared me from the full impact of his cruelty. With everything coming up aces for him, Slim could afford to be generous, and he never went at me with quite the savagery I was expecting. That isn't to say he didn't slap me around from time to time, zinging me across the mouth or twisting my ears when it struck his fancy, but most of his abuse came in the form of taunts and verbal digs. He never wearied of telling me how he'd 'turned the tables on that lousy Jew', or of making fun of the acne eruptions that mottled my face ('Look, boy, another pus-gusher'; 'Whoa there, pal, get a load of them volcanoes stitched across your brow'), or of reminding me how my fate now rested in his hands. To emphasize this last point, he'd sometimes saunter over to me twirling a gun on his finger and press the tip of the barrel against my skull. 'See what I mean, fella?' he'd say, and then burst out laughing. 'A little squeeze on this trigger here, and your brains go splat against the wall.' Once or twice, he went ahead and pulled the trigger, but that was only to scare me. As long as he hadn't pocketed the ransom money, I knew he wouldn't have the guts to load that gun with live ammunition.

It was no picnic, but I found I could handle that stuff. Sticks and stones, as they say, and I realized it was a lot better to listen to his yammering than get my bones broken in two. As long as I kept my mouth shut and didn't provoke him, he usually ran out of steam after fifteen or twenty minutes. Since they kept the gag on me most of the time, I didn't have much choice in the matter anyway. But even when my lips were free, I did everything I could to ignore his cracks. I came up with scores of juicy rebuttals and insults, but I generally kept them to myself, knowing full well that the less I wrangled with the bastard, the less he would get under my skin. Beyond that, I didn't have much to cling to. Slim was too crazy to be trusted, and there was nothing to guarantee he wouldn't find a way to kill me once he collected the money. I couldn't know what he had in mind, and that not knowing was the thing that tortured me most. I could endure the hardships of incarceration, but my head was never free of visions of what was to come: having my throat cut, having a bullet fired through my heart, having the skin peeled off my bones.

Fritz did nothing to assuage these torments. He was little more than a yes-man, a blundering fatso who wheezed and shuffled his way through the various minor tasks that Slim doled out to him. He cooked the beans on the wood stove, he swept the floors, he emptied the shit buckets, he adjusted and tightened the ropes around my arms and legs. God knows where Slim had dug up that bovine gumball, but I don't suppose he could have asked for a more willing henchman. Fritz was maid, butler, and errand boy, the stalwart ninny who never spoke a word of complaint. He sat through those long days and nights as if the Badlands were the finest vacation spot in America, perfectly content to bide his time and do nothing, to stare out the window, to breathe. For ten or twelve days he didn't say much of anything to me, but then, after the first ransom note was sent to Master Yehudi, Slim started driving off to town every morning, presumably to post letters or make telephone calls or communicate his demands by some other means, and Fritz and I started spending a portion of every day alone together. I wouldn't go so far as to say that we developed an understanding, but at least he didn't scare me the way Slim did. Fritz had nothing personal against me. He was just doing his job, and it wasn't long before I realized that he was as much in the dark about the future as I was.

'He's going to kill me, ain't he?' I said to him once, sitting in a chair as he fed me my midday meal of baked beans and crackers. Slim was so intimidated by the thought that I'd fly away, he never let the ropes come off, not even when I was eating or sleeping or taking a shit. So Fritz spoon-fed me my grub, shoveling it into my mouth as if I were a baby.

'Huh?' Fritz said, responding in that bright, rapid-fire way of his. His eyes looked blank, as if his brain had stalled in traffic somewhere between Pittsburgh and the Allegheny Mountains. 'You just say somethin'?'

'He's going to bump me off, ain't he?' I repeated. 'I mean, there ain't a chance in hell I'll ever walk out of here alive.'

'Dunno about that, bub. Your uncle don't tell me nothin' about what he's going to do. He just goes and does it.'

'And you don't mind that he doesn't let you in on things?'

'Nope, I don't mind. As long as I get my cut, why should I mind? What he does with you is none of my beeswax.'

'And what makes you so sure he'll pay up what he owes you?'

'Nothin'. But if he don't do what he's supposed to do, I'll bust his ass.'

'It's never going to work, Fritz. All those letters Slim's been mailing from the post office in town – why, they'll trace you turtles to this shack in no time, no time at all.'

'Ha, that's a good one. You think we're stupid, don't you?'

'Yeah, that's what I think. Pretty stupid.'

'Ha. And what if I told you we got another partner? And what if that partner happens to be the guy those letters was goin' to?'

'Well, what if you did?'

'Yeah, as if I just didn't. See what I'm drivin' at, bub? This

143

other party passes on the notes and such to the folks with the cash. There ain't no way they'll find us here.'

'And what about him, the guy you're in cahoots with? He invisible or something?

'Yeah, that's right. He took one of them vanishin' powders and went up in a puff of smoke.'

That was about the longest conversation I ever had with him: Fritz at his most eloquent and long-winded. It wasn't that he was mean to me, but he had ice in his veins and crackerjacks wadded in his skull, and I could never get through to him. I couldn't turn him against Uncle Slim, I couldn't persuade him to untie the ropes ('Sorry, bub, no can do'), I couldn't shake his loyalty and steadfastness by one jot. Any other person would have answered my question in one of two ways: by telling me it was true or telling me it was false. Yes, he would have said, Slim was planning to cut my throat, or else he would have patted me on the head and assured me that my fears were groundless. Even if the person lied when he said those things (for any number of reasons, both good and bad), I would have been given a straight answer. But not with Fritz. Fritz was honest to a fault, and since he couldn't answer my question, he said he didn't know, forgetting that normal human decency requires a person to give a firm answer to a question as monumental as that one. But Fritz hadn't learned the rules of human behavior. He was a nobodaddy and a clod, and any pimple-faced boy could see that talking to him was a waste of breath.

Oh, I had a jolly time in South Dakota, all right, a regular laughathon of nonstop fun and entertainment. Bound and gagged for more than a month, left alone in a locked room with twelve rusty shovels and pitchforks to keep me company, certain that I would die a brutal, pulverizing death. My only hope was that the master would rescue me, and again and again I dreamed of how he and a posse of men would swoop down on the hut, plug Fritz and Slim full of lead, and carry me back to the land of the living. But the weeks passed, and nothing ever changed. And then, when things did change, it was only for the worse. Once the ransom notes and negotiations started, I thought I detected a gradual hardening of Slim's mood, an ever-so-slight ebbing of his confidence. The game had turned serious now. The first rush of enthusiasm had subsided, and little by little his jocularity was losing out to his old snappish, foul-tempered self. He nagged at Fritz, he groused about the dull food, he broke some plates against the wall. Those were the earliest signs, and eventually they were followed by others: kicking me off my chair, poking fun at Fritz's blimpy torso, tightening the ropes around my limbs. It seemed clear that the pressure was getting to him, but why this should have been so I couldn't say. I wasn't privy to the discussions that went on in the other room, I didn't read the ransom notes or see the newspaper articles that were written about me, and the little I heard through the door was so muffled and fragmented, I could never fit the pieces together. All I knew was that Slim was acting more and more like Slim. The trend was unmistakable, and once he got back to being who he was, I knew that everything that had happened so far would feel like a holiday, a cruise to the Lesser Antilles on a goddamn luxury yacht.

By early June, he'd pushed himself close to the snapping point. Even Fritz, the ever placid and unbudgeable Fritz, was beginning to show symptoms of wear and tear, and I could see in his eyes that Slim's razzing could only go so far before his fellow dunderhead took offense. That became the most fervent object of my prayers – an out-and-out brawl – but even if it didn't come to that, it gave me no small comfort to see how often their conversations were erupting into minor squabbles, which mostly consisted of Slim needling Fritz and Fritz sulking in the corner, staring down at the floor and muttering curses under his breath. If nothing else, it took some of the burden off me, and with so many dangers lurking in the air, to be forgotten for even five or ten minutes was a blessing, an unimaginable boon.

Each day, the weather grew a little hotter, bore down a little more heavily on my skin. The sun never seemed to set anymore, and I itched almost constantly from the ropes. With the coming of the heat, spiders had infested the back room where I spent most of my time. They ran up and down my legs, covered my face, hatched their eggs in my hair. No sooner would I shake one off than another would find me. Mosquitoes dive-bombed into my ears, flies wriggled and buzzed in sixteen different webs, I excreted a never-ending flow of sweat. If it wasn't the creepy-crawlies that got me, it was the dryness in my throat. And if it wasn't thirst, it was sadness, a relentless crumbling of my will and resolve. I was turning into porridge, a moondog boiling in a pot of spit and ragged fur, and no matter how hard I struggled to be brave and strong, there were moments when I couldn't help myself anymore, when the tears just fell from my eyes and wouldn't stop.

One afternoon, Slim burst into my little hideaway and caught me in the middle of one of these crying fits. 'Why so glum, pal?' he said. 'Don't you know that tomorrow is your big day?'

It mortified me for him to see me like that, so I turned away my head without responding. I didn't have any idea what he was talking about, and since I could only speak with my eyes, there was no way I could find out. By then, it hardly seemed to matter anymore.

'Pay day, chum. Tomorrow we get the dough, and a pretty little bundle it's going to be. Fifty thousand dancing girls lying cheek to jowl in a battered straw suitcase. Just what the doctor ordered, eh kid? It's a hell of a retirement plan, let me tell you, and when you throw in the fact that them bills is unmarked, I can spend them all the way to Mexico and the feds won't be none the wiser.'

I didn't have any reason to doubt him. He was talking so fast, and his nerves were so jangled, it seemed clear that something was up. Still, I didn't respond. I didn't want to give him the satisfaction, so I continued looking away. After a moment, Slim sat down on the bed opposite my chair. When I still didn't respond, he leaned forward, untied the gag, and pulled it away from my mouth.

'Look at me when I'm talking to you,' he said.

But still, I kept my eyes fixed on the floor, refusing to return his gaze. Without any warning, he sprang forward and slapped me across the cheek – once, very hard. I looked up.

'That's better,' he said. Normally, he would have smiled over his little victory, but he was beyond such petty antics today. His expression turned grim, and for the next few seconds he stared at me so hard, I thought I'd shrivel up in my clothes. 'You're a lucky boy,' he continued. 'Fifty thousand bucks, nephew. Do you think you're worth that kind of dough? I never thought they'd go that high, but the price just kept climbing, and they never even flinched. Shit, boy, there ain't nobody in the world who'd cough up them apples for me. On the open market I wouldn't fetch no more than a nickel or two – and that's on a good day, when I'm at my sweetest and most lovable. And here you got that Jew crud willing to fork over fifty grand to get you back. I suppose that makes you kind of special, don't it? Or do you think he's just bluffing? Is that what he's up to, nephew? Making more promises he don't intend to keep?'

I was looking at him now, but that didn't mean I had any intention of answering his questions. Uncle Slim was nearly on top of me, coiled like an infielder on the edge of the bed, thrusting his face right against mine. He was so close, I could see every bloodshot vein in his eyes, every craterlike pore of his skin. His pupils were dilated, he was short of breath, and any second now it looked as if he was going to lunge forward and bite off my nose.

147

'Walt the Wonder Boy,' he said, lowering his voice to a whisper. 'It's got a nice ring to it, don't it? Walt . . . the . . . Wonder . . . Boy. Everybody's heard about you, kid, you're the talk of the whole fucking country. I've seen you perform myself, you know. Not once, but several times – six or seven times in the past year. There ain't nothing like it, is there? A runt who walks on water. It's the damnedest trick I ever saw, the slickest bit of hocus-pocus since the radio. No wires, no mirrors, no trapdoors. What's the gimmick, Walt? How in hell do you get yourself off the ground like that?'

I wasn't going to talk, I wasn't going to say a word to him, but after staring him down through the silence for ten or fifteen seconds, he jumped up and whacked me in the temple with the heel of his hand, then slapped me across the jaw with the other hand.

'There's no gimmick,' I said.

'Ho, ho,' he said. 'Ho, ho, ho.'

'The act's on the level. What you see is what there is.'

'And you expect me to believe that?'

'I don't care what you believe. I'm telling you there's no trick.'

'Lying's a sin, Walt, you know that. Especially to your elders. Liars burn in hell, and if you don't stop feeding me this bullshit, that's exactly where you're going. Into the fires of hell. Count on it, boy. I want the truth, and I want it now.'

'And that's what I'm giving you. The whole truth and nothing but the truth, so help me God.'

'All right,' he said, slapping his knees in frustration. 'If that's how you want to play it, that's how we'll play it.' He bounced up from the bed and grabbed me by the collar, yanking me out of my chair with one swift jerk of his arm. 'If you're so goddamn sure of yourself, then show me. We'll step outside and have a little demonstration. But you better deliver the goods, wise guy. I don't truck with no fibbers. You hear me, Walt? It's put up or shut up. You get yourself off the ground, or your ass is fucking grass.'

He dragged me into the other room, yelling and haranguing as my head thumped against the floor and splinters jabbed into my scalp. There was nothing I could do to fight back. The ropes were still fastened around my arms and legs, and the best I could do was writhe and scream, begging for mercy as the blood trickled through my hair.

'Untie him,' he ordered Fritz. 'The squirt says he can fly, and we're going to hold him to his word. No ifs, ands, or buts. It's show time, gents. Little Walt's going to spread his wings and dance in the air for us.'

I could see Fritz's face from my position on the floor, and he was looking at Slim with a mixture of horror and confusion. The fat man was so stunned, he didn't even try to speak.

'Well?' Slim said. 'What are you waiting for? Untie him!'

'But Slim,' Fritz stammered. 'It don't make no sense. We let him fly into the air, and he'll fly clear away from us. Just like you always said.'

'Forget what I said. Just undo the ropes, and we'll see what kind of bullshitter he really is. I'm betting he don't get a foot off the ground. Not one measly inch. And even if he does, who the fuck cares? I've got my gun, don't I? One shot in the leg, and he'll fall down faster than a goddamn duck.'

This cockeyed argument seemed to persuade Fritz. He shrugged, walked to the center of the room where Slim had deposited me, and bent down to do what he'd been told. The moment he loosened the first knot, however, I felt a surge of fear and revulsion wash through me.

'I ain't going to do it,' I said.

'Oh, you'll do it,' Slim said. My hands were free by then, and Fritz had turned his attention to the ropes around my legs. 'You'll do it all day if I tell you to.'

'You can shoot me dead,' I blubbered. 'You can slit my

throat or burn me to ashes, but there ain't no way I'm going to do it.'

Slim chuckled briefly, then sent the point of his shoe flying into my back. The breath burst out of me like a rocket, and I hit the floor in pain.

'Aw, lay off him, Slim,' Fritz said, working on the last knot around my ankles. 'He ain't in the mood. Any dope can see that.'

'And who asked your opinion, tubby?' Slim said, turning his anger on a man who weighed twice what he did and was three times as strong.

'Cut it out,' Fritz said, grunting from the effort as he raised himself off the floor. 'You know I don't like it when you call me them names.'

'Names?' Slim shouted. 'What names are you talking about, fatso?'

'You know. All that tubby and fatso stuff. It ain't nice to mock a fella like that.'

'Getting sensitive, are we? And what am I supposed to call you, then? Just take a look in the mirror and tell me what you see. A mountain of flesh, that's what. I calls 'em as I sees 'em, fatso. You want another name, then start shedding a few pounds.'

Fritz had about the longest, slowest fuse of any man I'd ever met, but this time Slim had pushed him too far. I could feel it, I could taste it, and even as I lay there gasping for air and trying to recover from the blow to my back, I understood that this was the one opening I'd ever have. My arms and legs were free, a hostile hubbub was brewing above me, and all I had to do was pick my moment. It came when Fritz took a step toward Slim and poked him in the chest. 'You got no call to go on like that,' he said. 'Not when I asked you to stop.'

Without making a sound, I began crawling in the direction of the door, inching forward as smoothly and unhurriedly as

I could. I heard a thud behind me. Then there was another thud, followed by the noise of scuffling shoes on the bare wood floor. Shouts and grunts and foul words punctuated the sandpaper tango, but by then I was pushing my hand against the screen door, which luckily was too warped to fit into the jam. I opened it with one shove, crept forward another half foot or so, and then tumbled out into the sunlight, landing shoulder-first on the hard South Dakota dirt.

My muscles felt all strange and spongy. When I tried to stand up, I scarcely recognized them anymore. They'd gone stupid on me, and I couldn't get them to work. After so much confinement and inactivity, I'd been turned into a spastic clown. I battled my way to my feet, but no sooner did I take a step than I began to stumble. I fell, picked myself up, lurched forward another yard or two, then fell again. I didn't have a second to waste, and there I was wobbling around like a wino, belly-flopping between every third and fourth step. By sheer persistence, I finally made it to Slim's car, a dented old jalopy parked around the side of the house. The sun had turned the thing into an oven, and when I touched the door handle, the metal was so hot I almost let out a scream. Fortunately, I knew my way around cars. The master had taught me how to drive, and I had no trouble releasing the hand brake, pulling out the choke, and turning the key in the ignition. There was no time to adjust the seat, however. My legs were too short, and the only way I could get my foot on the gas pedal was to slide down, hanging onto the steering wheel for dear life. The first cough of the motor halted the fight inside the cabin, and by the time I got the car in gear, Slim was already bolting out the door and racing toward me with his gun in his hand. I spun out in an arc, trying to keep as much distance between us as I could, but the bastard was gaining on me and I couldn't take my hand off the wheel to shift into second. I saw Slim lift the gun and take aim. Instead of swerving right, I swerved left, barreling straight into him with the fender. It caught him just above the knee, and he bounced off and fell to the ground. That gave me a few seconds to work with. Before Slim could stand up, I'd straightened out the wheel and pointed myself in the right direction. I threw the car into second and pressed the pedal to the floor. A bullet went crashing through the rear window, shattering the glass behind me. Another bullet thumped into the dashboard, opening up a hole in the glove-compartment door. I groped for the clutch with my left foot, shifted into third, and then I was off. I pushed the car up to thirty, forty miles an hour, bouncing over the rough terrain like a bronco buster as I waited for the next bullet to come tearing through my back. But there were no more bullets. I'd left that shitbag in the dust, and when I came upon the road a few minutes later, I was home free.

Was I happy to see the master again? You bet your life I was. Did my heart pound with joy when he opened his arms and smothered me in a long embrace? Yes, my heart pounded with joy. Did we weep over our good fortune? Of course we did. Did we laugh and celebrate and dance a hundred jigs? We did all that and more.

Master Yehudi said: 'I'll never let you out of my sight again.'

And I said: 'I'll never go nowhere without you, not for the rest of my days.'

There's an old adage about not appreciating what you have until you've lost it. Accurate as that wisdom is, I can't say it ever applied to me. I knew what I'd lost all along: from the moment I was carried out of that movie theater in Northfield, Minnesota, to the moment I laid eyes on the master again in Rapid City, South Dakota. For five and a half weeks I mourned the loss of everything that was good and precious to me, and I stand before the world now to testify that nothing can compare to the sweetness of getting back what was taken from you. Of all the triumphs I ever notched in my belt, none thrilled me more than the simple fact of having my life returned to me.

The reunion was held in Rapid City because that's where I wound up after my escape. Penny-pincher that he was, Slim had neglected the health of his car, and the heap ran out of gas before I'd driven twenty miles. If not for a traveling salesman who picked me up just before dark, I might still be wandering around those Badlands now, vainly searching for help. I asked him to drop me at the nearest police station, and once those cops found out who I was, they treated me like the crown prince of Ballyball. They fed me soup and

Coney Island hotdogs, they gave me new clothes and a warm bath, they taught me how to play pinochle. By the time the master arrived the next afternoon, I had already talked to two dozen reporters and posed for four hundred pictures. My kidnaping had been front-page news for more than a month, and when a stringer from the local press came snooping around the station house for some late-breaking crumbs, he recognized me from my photos and put out the word. The bloodhounds and ambulance chasers poured in after that. Flashbulbs popped like firecrackers all around me, and I bragged my head off into the wee hours of the morning, telling wild stories about how I'd outwitted my captors and stolen off before they could swap me for the loot. I suppose the bare facts would have done just as well, but I couldn't resist the urge to exaggerate. I reveled in my newfound celebrity, and after a while I grew giddy from the way those reporters looked at me, hanging on my every word. I was a showman, after all, and blessed with an audience like that one, I didn't have the heart to let them down.

The master put a stop to the nonsense the moment he walked in. For the next hour our hugs and tears occupied all my attention – but none of that was seen by the public. We sat alone in a back room of the constabulary, sobbing into each other's arms as two police officers guarded the door. After that, statements were made, papers were signed, and then he whisked me out of there, elbowing past a throng of gawkers and well-wishers in the street. Cheers went up, huzzahs rang out, but the master only paused long enough to smile and wave once to the rubberneckers before hustling me into a chauffeur-driven car parked at the curb. An hour and a half later, we were sitting in a private compartment on an eastbound train, headed for New England and the sandy shores of Cape Cod.

It wasn't until nightfall that I realized we weren't going to be stopping off in Kansas. With so much catching up to do with the master, so many things to describe and explain and recount, my head had been churning like a milkshake machine, and it was only after the lights were out and we were tucked into our berths that I thought to ask about Mrs Witherspoon. The master and I had been together for six hours by then, and her name hadn't come up once.

'What's the matter with Wichita?' I said. 'Ain't that just as good a place for us as Cape Cod?'

'It's a fine place,' the master said, 'but it's too hot this time of year. The ocean will be good for you, Walt. You'll recuperate faster.'

'And what about Mrs W.? When's she planning to join us?'

'She won't be along this time, kid.'

'Why not? You remember Florida, don't you? She loved it down there so much, we just about had to drag her out of the water. I never seen a body happier than she was sloshing around in them waves.'

'That might be so, but she won't be doing any swimming this summer. At least not with us.'

Master Yehudi sighed, filling the darkness with a soft, plaintive flutter of sound, and even though I was dead tired, just on the brink of dozing off, my heart began to speed up, pumping inside me like an alarm.

'Oh,' I said, trying not to betray my worry. 'And why's that?'

'I wasn't going to tell you tonight. But now that you've brought it up, I don't suppose there's any point in keeping it from you.'

'Tell me what?'

'Lady Marion is about to take the plunge.'

'Plunge? What plunge?'

'She's engaged to be married. If all goes according to plan, she'll be joined in holy wedlock before Thanksgiving.'

'You mean hitched? You mean coupled in matrimony for the rest of her natural life?'

'That's it. With a ring on her finger and a husband in her bed.'

'And that husband ain't you?'

'Perish the thought. I'm here with you, aren't I? How can I be back there with her if I'm here with you?'

'But you're her main squeeze. She don't have no right to ditch you like that. Not without your say-so.'

'She had to do it, and I didn't stand in her way. That woman's one in a million, Walt, and I don't want you breathing a word against her.'

'I'll breathe all the words I want. Somebody does you a bad turn, and I breathe fire.'

'She didn't do me a bad turn. Her hands were tied, and she made a promise that couldn't be broken. If I were you, boy, I'd thank her for making that promise every hour on the hour for the next fifty years.'

'Thank her? I spit on that trollop, master. I spit and curse on that two-faced bitch for doing you wrong.'

'Not when you find out why she did it, you won't. It's all because of you, little man. She put herself on the line for a pipsqueak named Walter Claireborne Rawley, and it was about the bravest, most selfless thing I've even seen a person do.'

'Bullroar. I don't have nothing to do with it. I wasn't even there.'

'Fifty thousand dollars, sport. You think that kind of money grows on bushes? When the ransom notes started coming in, we had to act fast.'

'It's a lot of dough, sure, but we must have earned twice that much by now.'

'Not even close. Marion and I couldn't even raise half that amount between us. We've done nicely for ourselves, Walt, but nowhere what you'd think. The overhead is enormous. Hotel bills, transportation, advertising – it all adds up, and we've just barely kept our heads above water.'

156

'Oh,' I said, doing some quick mental calculations on how much money we must have spent – and growing dizzy in the process.

'Oh is right. So what to do – that's the question. Whither goest us before it's too late? Old Judge Witherspoon turns us down. He hasn't talked to Marion since Charlie killed himself, and he's not about to interrupt his silence now. The banks laugh, the loan sharks won't touch us, and even if we sell the house, we're still going to fall short. So what to do – that's the question burning a hole in our stomachs. The clock's ticking, and every day we lose, the price is only going to go up.'

'Fifty thousand bucks to save my ass.'

'And a cheap price it was, too, considering your box-office potential in the years ahead. A cheap price, but we just didn't have it.'

'So where'd you go?'

'As I'm sure you understand by now, Mrs Witherspoon is a woman of manifold charms and allurements. I might have won a special place in her heart, but I wasn't the only man who carried the torch for her. Wichita teems with them, her suitors lurk behind every fencepost and fire hydrant. One of them, a young grain tycoon by the name of Orville Cox, has proposed to her five times in the past year. When you and I were out touring the sticks, young Orville was back in town, pressing his case pretty hard. Marion rebuffed him, of course, but not without a certain wistfulness and regret, and each time she said no, I think that wistfulness and regret grew a little stronger. Need I say more? She turned to Cox for the fifty thousand, a sum he was all too willing to part with, but only on the condition that she cast me aside and join him at the altar.'

'That's blackmail.'

'More or less. But this Orville really isn't such a bad

157

character. A little on the dull side, maybe, but Marion's going into it with her eyes open.'

'Well,' I sputtered, not knowing what to make of all this, 'I guess I owe her an apology. She came through for me like a real trooper.'

'That she did. Like an honest-to-goodness heroine.'

'But,' I continued, still not willing to give up, 'but that's all done with now. I mean, all bets is off. I got away from Slim on my own, and nobody had to fork out no fifty thousand. Orville's still got his rotten dough, and by rights that means old Mrs Witherspoon's still free.'

'Maybe so. But she's still planning to marry him. I talked to her just yesterday, and that was how things stood. She intends to go ahead with it.'

'We should break it up, master, that's what we should do. Storm right into the wedding and snatch her away.'

'Just like the movies, eh Walt?' For the first time since we'd started this dreadful conversation, Master Yehudi let out a laugh.

'You're damn straight. Just like a two-reeler punch-'em-up.'

'Let her go, Walt. Her mind's set on it, and there's nothing we can do to stop her.'

'But it's my fault. If it wasn't for that lousy kidnaping, none of this would have happened.'

'It's your uncle's fault, son, not yours, and you mustn't blame yourself – not now, not ever. Put it to rest. Mrs Witherspoon is doing what she wants to do, and we're not going to gripe about it. Understood? We're going to act like gentlemen, and not only are we not going to hold it against her, we're going to send her the prettiest wedding present any bride ever saw. Now get some sleep. We have a ton of work ahead of us, and I don't want you fretting about this business a second longer. It's done. The curtain is down, and the next act is about to begin.'

Master Yehudi talked a good game, but when we sat down

to breakfast in the dining car the next morning, his face looked wan and troubled – as if he'd been up all night, staring into the darkness and contemplating the end of the world. It occurred to me that he seemed thinner than he had in the past, and I wondered how this could have escaped my notice the day before. Had happiness made me that blind? I looked more closely, studying his face with as much detachment as I could. There was no question that something had changed in him. His skin was pinched and sallow, a certain haggardness had crept into the creases around his eyes, and all in all he looked somewhat diminished, less imposing than I'd remembered him. He'd been under duress, after all – first the ordeal of my kidnaping, then the blow of losing his woman – but I hoped that was all there was to it. Every now and then, I thought I detected a slight wince as he chewed his food, and once, toward the end of the meal, I unmistakably saw his hand dart under the table and clutch his belly. Was he unwell, or was it simply a passing attack of indigestion? And if he wasn't well, how bad was it?

He didn't say a word, of course, and since I was looking none too healthy myself, he managed to keep the spotlight on me throughout the breakfast.

'Eat up,' he said. 'You've dwindled down to a stick. Chomp down the waffles, son, and then I'll order you some more. We've got to put some meat on your bones, get you back to full strength.'

'I'm doing my best,' I said. 'It's not as though I got put up in some ritzy hotel. I lived on a steady diet of dog food with those bums, and my stomach's shrunken to the size of a pea.'

'And then there's the matter of your skin,' the master added, watching me struggle to get down another rasher of bacon. 'We'll have to do something about that, too. All those blotches. It looks like you've broken out with a case of the chicken pox.'

'No, sir, what I've got is the zits, and sometimes they're so sore, it hurts me just to smile.'

'Of course it does. Your poor body's gone haywire from all that captivity. Cooped up without any sunshine, sweating bullets day and night – it's no wonder you're a mess. The beach is going to do you a world of good, Walt, and if those pimples don't clear up, I'll show you how to take care of them and keep the new ones at bay. My grandmother had a secret remedy, and it hasn't failed yet.'

'You mean I don't have to grow another face?'

'This one will do. If you didn't have so many freckles, it wouldn't look so bad. Combine those with the acne, and it creates quite an effect. But don't brood, kid. Before long, the only thing you'll have to worry about is whiskers – and that's permanent, they stay with you until the bitter end.'

We spent more than a month in a little beach house on the Cape Cod shore, one day for every day I'd been locked up by Uncle Slim. The master rented it under a false name to protect me from the press, and for purposes of simplicity and convenience we posed as father and son. Buck was the alias he'd chosen: Timothy Buck for himself and Timothy Buck II for me, or Tim Buck One and Tim Buck Two. We got some good laughs out of that, and the funny thing was, it wasn't a whole lot different from Timbuktu where we were, at least as far as remoteness was concerned: high up on a promontory overlooking the ocean, with no neighbors for miles around. A woman named Mrs Hawthorne drove out from Truro every day to cook and clean for us, but other than kibbitzing with her, we pretty much kept to ourselves. We soaked up the sun, took long walks on the beach, ate clam chowder, slept ten or twelve hours every night. After a week of that loafer's regimen, I was feeling fit enough to try my hand at levitation again. The master started me off slowly with some routine ground exercises. Push-ups, jumping jacks, jogs on the beach, and when the time came to test the air again, we worked out behind the cliff, where Mrs Hawthorne couldn't spy on us. I was a little rusty at first, and I took some flops and spills, but after five or six days I was back in my old form, as limber and bouncy as I'd ever been. The fresh air was a great healer, and even if the master's remedy didn't do all he promised (a warm towel soaked in brine, vinegar, and drug-store astringents, applied to my face every four hours), half my zits began to fade on their own, no doubt from the sun-shine and the good food I was eating again.

My strength would have returned even more quickly, I think, if not for a nasty habit I developed during that holiday among the dunes and foghorns. Now that my hands were free to move again, they began to show a remarkable indepen-dence. They were filled with wanderlust, fidgety with urges to roam and explore, and no matter how many times I told them to stay put, they traveled wherever they damn pleased. I had only to crawl under the covers at night, and they would insist on flying to their favorite hot spot, a forest kingdom just south of the equator. There they would visit their friend, the great finger of fingers, the all-powerful one who ruled the universe by mental telepathy. When he called, no subject could resist. My hands were in his thrall, and short of tying them up in ropes again, I had no choice but to give them their freedom. So it was that Aesop's madness became my madness, and so it was that my pecker rose up to take control of my life. It no longer resembled the little squirt gun that Mrs Witherspoon had once cupped in her palm. It had gained in both size and stature since then, and its word was law. It begged to be touched, and I touched it. It cried out to be fondled, yanked, and squeezed, and I bowed to its whims with a willing heart. Who cared if I went blind? Who cared if my hair fell out? Nature was calling, and every night I ran to it as breathlessly and hungrily as Adam himself.

As for the master, I didn't know what to think. He seemed to be enjoying himself, and while his complexion and color undoubtedly improved, I witnessed three or four stomach-clutching episodes, and the facial twinges occurred almost regularly now, at every second or third meal. But his spirits couldn't have been brighter, and when he wasn't reading his Spinoza or working with me on the act, he kept himself busy on the telephone, haggling over arrangements for my upcoming tour. I was big stuff now. The kidnaping had seen to that, and Master Yehudi was more than ready to take full advantage of the situation. Hastily revising his plans for my career, he settled us into our Cape Cod retreat and went on the offensive. He was holding the chips now and could afford to play hard-to-get. He could dictate terms, press for new and unheard-of percentages from the booking agents, demand guarantees matched by only the biggest draws. I'd reached the top a lot sooner than either of us had expected, and before the master's wheelings and dealings were done, he'd booked me into scores of theaters up and down the East Coast, a string of one- and two-night stands that would keep us going until the end of the year. And not just in puny towns and villages – in real cities, the front-line places I'd always dreamed of going to. Providence and Newark; New Haven and Baltimore; Philadelphia, Boston, New York. The act had moved indoors, and from now on we'd be playing for high stakes. 'No more walking on water,' the master said, 'no more farm-boy costume, no more county fairs and chamber of commerce picnics. You're an aerial artist now, Walt, the one and only of your kind, and folks are going to pay top dollar for the privilege of seeing you perform. They'll dress up in their Sunday finery and sit in plush velvet seats, and once the theater goes dark and the spotlight turns on you, their eyes will fall out of their head. They'll die a thousand deaths, Walt. You'll prance and spin before them, and one by one they'll follow you up the stairs of heaven. By the time it's over, they'll be sitting in the presence of God.'

Such are the twists of fortune. The kidnaping was the worst

thing that had ever happened to me, and yet it turned out to be my big break, the fuel that finally launched me into orbit. I'd been given a month's worth of free publicity, and by the time I wriggled out of Slim's grasp, I was already a household name, the number-one cause célèbre in the land. The news of my escape created a stir, a second sensation on top of the first, and after that I could do no wrong. Not only was I a victim, I was a hero, a mighty-mite of spunk and derring-do, and beyond just being pitied, I was loved. How to figure such a business? I'd been thrown into hell. I'd been bound and gagged and given up for dead, and one month later I was everybody's darling. It was enough to fry your brain, to sizzle the boogers in your snout. America was at my feet, and with a man like Master Yehudi pulling the strings, the odds were it would stay there for a long time to come.

I'd outfoxed Uncle Slim, all right, but that didn't change the fact that he was still at large. The cops raided the shack in South Dakota, but other than a mess of fingerprints and a pile of dirty laundry, they found no trace of the culprits. I suppose I should have been scared, on the alert for more trouble, but curiously enough I didn't spend much time worrying. It was too peaceful on Cape Cod for any of that, and now that I'd bested my uncle once, I felt confident I could do it again – quickly forgetting how close a shave I'd just had. But Master Yehudi had promised to protect me, and I believed him. I wasn't going to stroll into any movie theaters on my own anymore, and as long as he was with me wherever I went, what could possibly happen? I thought about the kidnaping less and less as the days wore on. When I did think about it, it was mostly to relive my getaway and to wonder how badly I'd hurt Slim's leg with the car. I hoped it was real bad – that the fender had clipped him in the kneecap, maybe hard enough to shatter the bone. I wanted to have done some serious damage, to know that he'd be walking with a limp for the rest of his life.

But I was too busy with other things to feel much desire to look back. The days were full, crammed with preparations and rehearsals for my new show, and there weren't any blanks on my nighttime dance card either, considering how ready my dick was for dalliance and diversion. Between these nocturnal escapades and my afternoon exertions, I didn't have a spare moment to sulk or feel frightened. I wasn't haunted by Slim, I wasn't bogged down by Mrs Witherspoon's impending marriage. My thoughts were turned to a more immediate problem, and that was enough to keep my hands full: how to remake Walt the Wonder Boy into a theatrical performer, a creature fit for the confines of the indoor stage.

Master Yehudi and I had some mammoth conversations on this subject, but mostly we worked out the new routines by trial and error. Hour after hour, day after day, we'd stand on the windy beach making changes and corrections, struggling to get it right as flocks of seagulls honked and wheeled overhead. We wanted to make every minute count. That was our guiding principle, the object of all our efforts and furious calculations. Out in the boondocks I'd had every show to myself, a good hour's worth of performing time, even more if I'd felt in the mood. But vaudeville was a different brand of beer. I'd be sharing the bill with other acts, and the program had to be boiled down to twenty minutes. We'd lost the lake, we'd lost the impact of the natural sky, we'd lost the grandeur of my hundred-yard sallies and locomotion-struts. Everything had to be squeezed into a smaller space, but once we began to explore the ins and outs of it, we saw that smaller didn't necessarily mean worse. We had some new tools at our disposal, and the trick was to turn them to our advantage. For one thing, we had lights. The master and I both drooled at the thought of them, imagining all the effects they made possible. We could go from pitch black to brightness in the blink of an eye – and vice versa. We could dim the hall to squinty obscurity, throw spots from place to place, manipulate colors, make me appear and disappear at will. And then there was the music, which would sound far more ample and sonorous when played indoors. It wouldn't get lost in the background, it wouldn't be drowned out by traffic and merry-go-round noises. The instruments would become an integral part of the show, and they'd navigate the audience through a sea of shifting emotions, subtly cueing the crowd on how it should react. Strings, horns, woodwinds, drums: we'd have pros down in the pit with us every night, and when we told them what to play, they'd know how to put it across. But best of all, the crowd was going to be more comfortable. Undistracted by the buzzing of flies and the glare of the sun, people would be less prone to talk and lose their concentration. A hush would greet me the moment the curtain went up, and from beginning to end the performance would be controlled, advancing like clockwork from a few simple stunts to the wildest, most heart-stopping finale ever seen on a modern stage.

So we hashed out our ideas, batting it back and forth for a couple of weeks, and eventually we came up with a blueprint. 'Shape and coherence,' the master said. 'Structure, rhythm, and surprise.' We weren't going to give them a random collection of tricks. The act was going to unfold like a story, and little by little we'd build up the tension, leading the audience into bigger and better thrills as we went along, saving the best and most spectacular stunts for last.

The costume couldn't have been more basic: a white shirt open at the collar, loose black trousers, and a pair of white dance slippers on my feet. The white shoes were essential. They had to jump out at you, to create the greatest possible contrast with the brown floor of the stage. With only twenty minutes to work with, there was no time for costume changes or extra entrances and exits. We made the act continuous, to be performed without pause or interruption, but in our minds

165

we broke it down into four parts, and we worked on each part separately, as if each was an act in a play:

Part the First Solo clarinet, trilling a few bars of pastoral fluff. The melody suggests innocence, butterflies, dandelions bobbing in the breeze. The curtain goes up on a bare, brightly lit stage. I come on, and for the first two minutes I act like a know-nothing, a boob with a stick up my ass and pudding for brains. I bump into invisible objects strewn about me, encountering one obstacle after another as the clarinet is joined by a rumbling bassoon. I trip over a stone, I bang my nose against a wall, I catch my finger in a door. I'm the picture of human incompetence, a stumbling nincompoop who can barely stand on the ground – let alone rise above it. At last, after several near misses, I fall flat on my face. The trombone does a dipping glissando, I get some laughs. Reprise. But even clutzier than the first time. Again the sliding trombone, followed by a thumpity-thump on the snare drum, a boom on the kettle drum. This is slapstick heaven, and I'm on a collision course with thin ice. No sooner do I pick myself up and take a step than my foot snags on a roller skate and I fall again. Howls of laughter. I struggle to my feet, tottering about as I shake the cobwebs from my head, and then, just when the audience is beginning to get puzzled, just when it looks like I'm every bit as inept as I seem, I pull the first stunt.

Part the Second It has to look like an accident. I've just tripped again, and as I stagger forward, desperately trying to regain my balance, I reach out my hand and catch hold of something. It's the rung of an invisible ladder, and suddenly I'm hanging in midair – but only for a split second. It all happens so fast, it's hard to tell if I've left my feet or not. Before the audience can figure it out, I release my grip and tumble to the ground. The lights dim, then go off, plunging the hall into darkness. Music plays: mysterious strings, tremulous with wonder and expectation. A moment later, a spot-

166

light is turned on. It wanders left and right, then stops at the place occupied by the ladder. I stand up and begin to look for the invisible rung. When my hands make contact with the ladder again, I pat it gingerly, gaping in astonishment. A thing that isn't there is there. I pat it again, testing to make sure it's steady, and then begin to climb – very cautiously, one agonizing rung at a time. There's no doubt about it now. I'm off the ground, and the tips of my bright white shoes are dangling in the air to prove it. During my ascent, the spotlight expands, dissolving into a soft glow that eventually engulfs the entire stage. I reach the top, look down, and begin to grow frightened. I'm five feet off the ground now, and what the hell am I doing there? The strings vibrate again, underscoring my panic. I begin to climb down, but halfway to the floor I reach out with my hand and come against something solid – a plank jutting into the middle of the air. I'm flabbergasted. I run my fingers over this invisible object, and little by little curiosity gets the better of me. I slide my body around the ladder and crawl onto the plank. It's strong enough to hold my weight. I stand up and begin to walk, slowly crossing the stage at an altitude of three feet. After that, one prop leads to another. The plank becomes a staircase, the staircase becomes a rope, the rope becomes a swing, the swing becomes a slide. For seven minutes I explore these objects, creeping and tiptoeing upon them, gradually gaining confidence as the music swells. It looks as if I'll be able to cavort like this forever. Then, suddenly, I step off a ledge and begin to fall.

Part the Third I'm floating down to the ground with my arms spread, descending as slowly as someone in a dream. Just as I'm about to touch the stage, I stop. Gravity has ceased to count, and there I am, hovering six inches off the ground with no prop to support me. The theater darkens, and a second later I'm enclosed in the beam of a single spotlight. I look down, I look up, I look down again. I wiggle my toes. I turn my left foot this way and that. I turn my right foot this way and that. It's really happened. It's really true that I'm standing on air. A drumroll breaks the silence: loud, insistent, nerve-shattering. It seems to announce terrible risks, an assault on the impossible. I shut my eyes, extend my arms to their fullest, and take a deep breath. This is the exact midpoint of the performance, the moment of moments. With the spotlight still fixed on me, I begin to rise into the air, slowly and inexorably taking myself upward, climbing to a height of seven feet in one smooth heaven-bound soar. I pause at the top, count three long beats in my head, and then open my eyes. Everything turns to magic after that. With the music playing at full throttle, I go through an eight-minute routine of aerial acrobatics, darting in and out of the spotlight as I turn twists and somersaults and full gainers. One contortion flows into another, each stunt is more beautiful than the last. There is no sense of danger anymore. Everything has been turned into pleasure, euphoria, the ecstasy of seeing the laws of nature crumble before your eyes.

Part the Fourth After the final somersault, I glide back to my position at the center of the stage, seven feet off the ground. The music stops. A triple spotlight is thrown on me: one red, one white, one blue. The music starts up again: a stirring of cellos and French horns, loveliness beyond measure. The orchestra is playing 'America the Beautiful', the most cherished, most familiar song of all. When the fourth bar begins, I start to move forward, walking on the air above the heads of the musicians and out into the audience. I keep on walking as the music plays, traveling to the very back of the theater, eyes set before me as necks crane and people stand up from their seats. I reach the wall, turn, and begin to head back, walking in the same slow and stately manner as before. By the time I reach the stage again, the audience is one with me. I have touched them with my grace, let them share in the mystery of my godlike powers. I turn in midair, pause briefly once again, and then float down to the ground as the last notes of the song are played. I spread my arms and smile. And then I bow – just once – and the curtain comes down.

It wasn't too shabby. A trifle bloated at the end, perhaps, but the master wanted 'America the Beautiful' come hell or high water, and I couldn't talk him out of it. The opening pantomime sketch came straight from yours truly, and the master felt so keen about those pratfalls that he got a little carried away. A clown suit would make them even funnier, he said, but I told him no, it was just the opposite. If people expect a joke, you have to work a lot harder to make them laugh. You can't go whole hog from the start; you have to sneak up and goose them. It took me half a day of arguing to win that point, but on other matters I wasn't nearly so persuasive. The bit I worried about most was the end – the part where I had to leave the stage and go off on an aerial tour of the audience. I knew it was a good idea, but I still didn't have total confidence in my loft abilities. If I didn't maintain a height of eight and a half or nine feet, all sorts of problems could arise. People could jump up and swat at my legs, and even a weak, glancing blow would be enough to knock me off course. And what if someone actually grabbed hold of my ankle and wrestled me to the ground? A riot would break out in the theater, I'd wind up getting myself killed. This felt like a definite danger to me, but the master pooh-poohed my nervousness. 'You can do it,' he said. 'You got to twelve feet in Florida last winter, and I can't even remember the last time you dipped under ten. Alabama maybe, but you had a cold that day and your heart wasn't in it. You've gotten better, Walt. Little by little, you've shown improvement in every area. It's going to take some concentration, but nine feet isn't a stretch anymore. It's just another day at the office, a walk around the block and then home. No sweat. One time and you'll be over it. Believe me, son, it's going to go like gang-busters.'

The hardest trick was the ladder jump, and I must have spent as much time on that one as all the others put together. Most of the act was a recombination of turns I already felt comfortable with. The invisible props, the skyward rushes, the midair acrobatics – all those things were old hat to me by then. But the ladder jump was new, and the entire program hinged on my being able to pull it off. It might not sound like a big deal compared to those dramatic flourishes – just three inches off the ground for one tick of the clock – but the difficulty was in the transition, the lightning-fast two-step required to get me from one state to another. From flopping and careening madly about the stage, I had to go straight into liftoff, and it had to be done in one seamless movement, which meant tripping forward, grabbing the rung, and going up at the same time. Six months earlier, I never would have attempted such a thing, but I had made progress on reducing the length of my prelevitation trances. From six or seven seconds at the beginning of my career, I had brought them down to less than one, a nearly simultaneous fusion of thought and deed. But the fact remained that I still lifted off from a standing position. I had always done it that way; it was one of the fundamental tenets of my art, and just to conceive of such a radical change meant rethinking the whole process from top to bottom. But I did it. I did it, by gum, and of all the feats I accomplished as a levitator, this is the one I'm proudest of. Master Yehudi dubbed it the Scattershot Fling, and that's roughly what it felt like: a sensation of being in more than one place at the same time. Falling forward, I'd plant my feet on the ground for a fraction of a second, and then blink. The blink was crucial. It brought back the memory of the trance, and even the smallest vestige of that fibrillating blankness was enough to produce the necessary shift in me. I'd blink and raise my arm, latching my hand onto the unseen rung, and then I'd start going up. It wouldn't have been possible to sustain such a convoluted stunt for very long. Three quarters of a second was the limit, but that was all I needed, and once I perfected the move, it became the turning point of the show, the axis on which everything else revolved.

Three days before we left Cape Cod, the Pierce Arrow was delivered to our door by a man in a white suit. The driver had brought the thing all the way from Wichita, and when he stepped out and pumped the master's hand, grinning and gushing his hearty hellos, I assumed I was looking at the infamous Orville Cox. My first thought was to kick the four-flusher in the shins, but before I could deliver my scout's welcome, Master Yehudi saved me by addressing him as Mr Bigelow. It didn't take long to figure out that he was another one of Mrs Witherspoon's lunkhead admirers. He was a youngish guy of about twenty-four with a round face and a gee-whiz booster's laugh, and every other word that came from his mouth was 'Marion'. She must have done a hell of a snow job to conscript him into running such a long-distance errand for her, but he seemed pleased with himself and oh-so-proud to have done it. It made me want to puke. By the time the master suggested going into the house for a cool drink, I had already turned my back on him and was clomping up the wooden stairs.

I headed straight for the kitchen. Mrs Hawthorne was in there washing the dishes from lunch, her small bony figure perched on a stool beside the sink. 'Hi, Mrs H.,' I said, still churning inside, feeling as if the devil himself were doing handsprings in my head. 'What's for dinner tonight?'

'Flounder, mashed potatoes, and pickled beets,' she said, answering in her curt New England twang.

'Yum. I can't wait to sink my chompers into them beets. Make me a double portion, okay?'

That got a little smile from her. 'No problem, Master Buck,' she said, swiveling around on the stool to look at me. I took three or four steps in her direction, then went in for the kill.

'Good as your cooking is, ma'am,' I said, 'I'll bet you ain't never rustled up a dish half so tasty as this one.'

And then, before she could say another word, I flashed her a big smile, spread my arms, and lifted myself off the ground. I went up slowly, taking myself as high as I could without bumping my head against the ceiling. Once I'd reached the top, I hung there looking down at Mrs Hawthorne, and the shock and consternation that spread across her face were everything I'd hoped for. A choked howl died in her throat; her eyes rolled back into her head; and then she toppled off the stool, fainting onto the floor with a tiny thud.

As it happened, Bigelow and the master were just entering the house at that point, and the thud brought them running into the kitchen. Master Yehudi got there first, bursting through the door in the middle of my descent, but when Bigelow arrived a couple of seconds later, my feet were already touching the ground.

'What's this!' the master said, sizing up the situation in a single glance. He pushed me aside and bent down over Mrs Hawthorne's comatose body. 'What the hell is this!'

'Just a little accident,' I said.

'Accident my foot,' he said, sounding angrier than I'd heard him in months, perhaps years. I suddenly regretted the whole stupid prank. 'Go to your room, you idiot, and don't come out until I tell you. We have company now, and I'll deal with you later.'

I never did get to eat those beets, nor any other of Mrs Hawthorne's dishes for that matter. Once she recovered from her swoon, she promptly picked herself up and marched out the door, vowing never to set foot in our house again. I wasn't around to witness her departure, but that's what the master told me the next morning. At first I thought he was pulling my leg, but when she didn't show up by the middle of the day, I realized I'd scared the poor woman half to death. That's exactly what I'd wanted to do, but now that I'd done it, it didn't seem so funny to me anymore. She never even returned to collect her wages, and though we stayed on for another seventy-two hours ourselves, that was the last we ever saw of her.

Not only did the meals deteriorate, but I suffered a final indignity when Master Yehudi made me clean the house on the morning we packed up and left. I hated to be punished like that – sent off to bed without any supper, consigned to KP duty and household chores – but fume and bitch as I did about it, he was well within his rights. It didn't matter that I was the hottest child star since David loaded up his slingshot and let 'er rip. I had stepped out of line, and before my head swelled to the size of a medicine ball, the master had no choice but to crack down and let me have it.

As for Bigelow, the cause of my temperamental outburst, there isn't much to be said. He hung around for only a few hours, and by late afternoon a taxi came to fetch him – presumably to drive him to the nearest railroad station, where he would begin his long trip back to Kansas. I watched him leave from my second-floor window, despising him for his moronic cheerfulness and the fact that he was a buddy of Orville Cox, the man Mrs Witherspoon had chosen over me and the master. To make matters worse, Master Yehudi was on his best behavior, and it addled my spleen to see how politely he treated that twit of a bank clerk. Not only did he shake his hand, but he entrusted him with delivering his wedding present to the bride-to-be. Just as the cab door was about to close, he placed a large, beautifully wrapped package into the scoundrel's hands. I had no idea what was hidden in the box. The master hadn't told me, and though I fully intended to ask him about it at the first opportunity, so many hours passed before he released me from my prison, I clean forgot to when the moment arrived. As it turned out, seven years went by before I discovered what the gift was.

From Cape Cod we went to Worcester, half a day's drive to the west. It felt good to be traveling in the Pierce Arrow again, ensconced in our leather seats as of yore, and once we headed inland, whatever conflicts we'd been having were left behind like so many discarded candy wrappers, blowing out into the dune grass and the surf. Still, I didn't want to take anything for granted, and just to make sure there was no bad blood between us, I apologized to the master again. 'I done wrong,' I said, 'and I'm sorry,' and just like that the whole business was as stale as yesterday's news.

We holed up in the Cherry Valley Hotel, a dingy hooker's nest two doors down from the Luxor Theatre. That's where I'd been slotted for my first performance, and we rehearsed in that music hall every morning and afternoon for the next four days. The Luxor was a far cry from the grand entertainment palace I'd been hoping for, but it had a stage and curtains and a setup for lights, and the master assured me that the theaters would get better once we hit some of the larger stops on the tour. Worcester was a good quiet place to begin, he said, to familiarize myself with the feel of the stage. I caught on fast, learning my marks and cues without much trouble, but even so there were all sorts of kinks and glitches to be worked on: perfecting the spotlight sequences, coordinating the music with the stunts, choreographing the finale to avoid the balcony that jutted out over half the seats in the orchestra. The master was consumed by a thousand and one details. He tested the curtains with the curtain man, he adjusted the lights with the lighting men, he talked endlessly about music with the musicians. At no small expense, he hired seven of them to join us for the last two days of rehearsals, and he kept scribbling changes and corrections onto their scores until the last minute, desperate to get everything just right. I got a kick out of working with those guys myself. They were

174

a bunch of hacks and has-beens, old-timers who'd started out before I was born, and when you added it up, they must have spent twenty thousand nights in variety theaters and played for a hundred thousand different acts. Those geezers had seen everything, and yet the first time I came out and did my stuff for them, all hell broke loose. The drummer passed out, the bassoonist dropped his bassoon, the trombonist sputtered and went sour. It felt like a good sign to me. If I could impress those hard-boiled cynics, just think what I'd do when I got in front of a regular audience.

The hotel was conveniently located, but the nights in that fleabag almost did me in. With all the whores walking up and down the stairs and sauntering through the halls, my dick throbbed like a broken bone and gave me no rest. The master and I shared a double room, and I'd have to wait until I heard him snoring in the next bed before I dared to beat my meat. The buildup could be interminable. He liked to talk in the dark, discussing small points about that day's rehearsal, and rather than attend to the matter at hand (which was also in my hand), I'd have to think of polite answers to his questions. With every minute that passed, the agony became that much more crushing, that much more painful to bear. When he finally drifted off, I'd reach down and remove one of my dirty socks. That was my cum-catcher, and I'd hold it in my left hand while I got to work with my right, squirting jism into the bunched-up folds of cotton. After so much delay, it never took more than one or two tugs. I'd moan forth a quiet hymn of thanks and try to fall asleep, but once was rarely enough for me in those days. A hooker would burst out laughing in the hall, a bedspring would creak in an upstairs room, and my head would fill with every kind of fleshy obscenity. Before I knew it, my cock would stiffen, and I'd be at it again.

One night, I must have made too much noise. It was the eve of the Worcester performance, and I was winging my way

175

toward another sockful of bliss when the master suddenly woke up. Talk about a jolt to the nerves. When his voice broke through the darkness, it felt like the chandelier had landed on my head.

'What's the trouble, Walt?'

I dropped my unit as if it had sprouted thorns. 'Trouble?' I said. 'What do you mean trouble?'

'I mean that noise. That jostling and shaking and squeaking. That ruckus coming from your bed.'

'I got an itch. It's a doozy of an itch, master, and if I don't scratch hard, it'll never go away.'

'It's an itch, all right. An itch that starts in the loins and ends up all over the sheets. Give it a rest, kid. You'll tire yourself out, and a tuckered showman is a sloppy showman.'

'I ain't tuckered. I'm fit as a fiddle and raring to go.'

'For the time being maybe. But wanking takes its toll, and before long you'll start to feel the strain. I don't need to tell you what a precious thing a pecker is. You get too fond of it, though, and it's liable to turn into a stick of dynamite. Preserve the bindu, Walt. Save it for when it really counts.'

'Preserve the what?'

'The bindu. An Indian term for the stuff of life.'

'You mean the stickum?'

'That's right, the stickum. Or whatever else you want to call it. There must be a hundred names, but they all mean the same thing.'

'I like bindu. It beats them others hands down.'

'Just so long as you don't beat yourself down, little man. We have some big days and nights ahead of us, and you're going to need every ounce of strength you've got.'

None of it mattered. Tired or not tired, preserving the bindu or producing it in buckets, I broke from the gate like a bat out of hell. We stunned them in Worcester. We wowed them in Springfield. They dropped their drawers in Bridgeport. Even the mishap in New Haven proved to be a blessing in disguise, since it buttoned the lips of the doubters once and for all. With so much talk about me circulating in the air, I suppose it was natural that some people should begin to suspect fraud. They believed the world was set up in a certain way, and there was no place in it for a person of my talents. To do what I could do upset all the rules. It contradicted science, overturned logic and common sense, made mince-meat of a hundred theories, and rather than change the rules to accommodate my act, the big shots and professors decided I was cheating. The newspapers were full of that stuff in every town we went to: debates and arguments, charges and countercharges, all the pros and cons you could count. The master took no part in it. He stood outside the fray, grinning happily as the box-office receipts rolled in, and when reporters pressed him to give a comment, his answer was always the same: 'Come to the theater and judge for yourself.'

After two or three weeks of mounting controversy, things finally came to a head in New Haven. I hadn't forgotten that this was the home of Yale College – and that if not for the villainies and outrages committed in Kansas two years before, it also would have been my brother Aesop's home. It sad-dened me to be there, and all day prior to the performance I sat in the hotel room with a heavy heart, remembering the crazy times we'd lived through together and thinking about what a great man he would have become. When we finally left for the theater at six o'clock, I was an emotional wreck, and try as I did to get my bearings, I turned in the flattest performance of my career. My timing was off, I wobbled during my spins, and my loft was a disgrace. When the moment came to crank it up and fly out over the heads of the audience, the dreaded bomb finally went off. I couldn't maintain altitude. By sheer will-power I'd managed to lift myself to seven and a half feet, but that was the best I could do, and I started the finale with grave misgivings, knowing that a tall person with only moderate reach could nab me without bothering to jump. After that, things went from bad to worse. Halfway out over the orchestra seats, I decided to make a last gallant effort to see if I couldn't get myself a little higher. I wasn't hoping for miracles – just a little breathing room, maybe six or eight more inches. I paused for a moment to regroup, hovering in place as I shut my eyes and concentrated on my task, but once I started moving again, my altitude was just as dismal as before. Not only was I not going up, but after a few seconds I realized that I was actually beginning to sink. It happened slowly, ever so slowly, an inch or two for every yard I went forward, and yet the decline was irreversible – like air leaking out of a balloon. By the time I reached the back rows, I was down to six feet, a sitting duck for even the shortest dwarf. And then the fun began. A bald-headed goon in a red blazer shot out of his seat and whacked me on the heel of my left foot. I spun out from the blow, tilting like a lopsided parade float, and before I could right my balance, someone else batted my other foot. That second bump clinched it. I tumbled out of the air like a dead sparrow and landed forehead-first on the rim of a metal chair back. The impact was so sudden and so fierce, it knocked me out cold.

I missed the bedlam that followed, but by all accounts it was a honey of a rumble: nine hundred people shouting and jumping every which way, an outbreak of mass hysterics that spread through the hall like a brushfire. Unconscious though I might have been, my fall had proved one thing, and it had proved it beyond a shadow of a doubt for all time. The act was real. There were no invisible wires attached to my limbs, no helium bubbles hidden under my clothes, no silent engines strapped around my waist. One by one, members of the audience passed my dormant body around the theater, groping and pinching me with their curious fingers as if were some kind of medical specimen. They stripped off my costume, they looked inside my mouth, they spread my cheeks and peered into my bunghole, and not one of them found a damned thing that God himself hadn't put there. Meanwhile, the master had sprung from his position backstage and was fighting his way toward me. By the time he'd leapfrogged over nineteen rows of customers and wrested me from the last pair of arms, the verdict was unanimous. Walt the Wonder Boy was the real goods. The act was on the up-and-up, and what you saw was what you got, amen.

The first of the headaches came that night. Considering how I'd crash-landed on the chair back, it was no surprise that I should have felt some twinges and aftereffects. But this pain was monstrous – a horrific jackhammer assault, an endless volley of hailstones pounding against the inner walls of my skull – and it woke me from a deep sleep in the middle of the night. The master and I had connecting rooms with a bathroom in between, and once I'd found the courage to pry myself out of bed, I staggered toward the bathroom, praying I'd find some aspirins in the medicine cabinet. I was so woozy and distracted by the pain, I didn't notice that the bathroom light was already on. Or, if I did notice, I didn't pause to think about why that light should be burning at three o'clock in the morning. As I soon found out, I wasn't the only person who had left his bed at that ungodly hour. When I opened the door and stepped into the dazzling white-tiled room, I nearly stumbled into Master Yehudi. Dressed in his lavender silk pajamas, he was clutching the sink with his two hands and doubled over in pain, gasping and retching as if his insides had caught fire. The siege lasted for another twenty or thirty seconds, and it was such a terrible thing to witness, I almost forgot I was in pain myself.

Once he saw that I was there, he did everything he could to cover up what had just happened. He turned his grimaces into forced, histrionic smiles; he straightened up and threw back his shoulders; he slicked down his hair with his palms. I wanted to tell him that he should stop pretending, that I was on to his secret now, but my own pain was so bad that I couldn't summon the words to do it. He asked me why I wasn't asleep, and when he learned about my headache, he took charge of the situation by rushing about and playing doctor: shaking aspirins out of the bottle, filling up a glass with water, examining the bump on my forehead. He talked so much during these ministrations, I couldn't get a word in edgewise.

'We're quite a pair, aren't we?' he said, as he carried me to my room and tucked me into bed. 'First you take a nosedive and clunk your bean, and then I gorge myself on rancid cherrystones. I should learn to lay off those buggers. Every time I eat them, I come down with the goddamn bends.'

It wasn't a bad story, especially for one he'd made up on the spur of the moment, but it didn't fool me. No matter how much I wanted to believe him, I wasn't fooled for a second.

By the middle of the next afternoon, the worst of the headache was gone. A dull throbbing persisted near my left temple, but it wasn't enough to keep me off my feet. Since the bump was on the right side of my forehead, it would have made more sense for the tender spot to be there, but I was no expert on these matters and didn't dwell on the discrepancy. All I cared about was that I was feeling better, that the pain was subsiding, and that I would be ready for the next performance.

What worries I did have were centered around the master's condition – or whatever it was that had caused the gruesome attack I'd seen in the bathroom. The truth couldn't be hidden anymore. His sham had been exposed, and yet because he seemed so much better the next morning, I didn't dare to mention it. My nerve simply failed me, and I couldn't bring myself to open my mouth. I'm not proud of how I acted, but the thought that the master had been struck by some terrible disease was too frightening even to consider. Rather than jump to morbid conclusions, I let him cow me into accepting his version of the incident. Cherrystone clams my eye. He'd clammed up on me all right, and now that I'd seen what I shouldn't have seen, he'd make sure I'd never see it again. I could count on him for that kind of performance. He'd gut it out, he'd put up a tough front, and little by little I'd begin to think I hadn't seen it after all. Not because I would believe such a lie – but because I'd be too afraid not to.

From New Haven we went to Providence; from Providence to Boston; from Boston to Albany; from Albany to Syracuse; from Syracuse to Buffalo. I remember all those stops, all those theaters and hotels, all the performances I gave, everything about everything. It was late summer, early fall. Little by little, the trees lost their greenness. The world turned red and yellow and orange and brown, and everywhere we went the roads were lined with the strange spectacle of mutating color. The master and I were on a roll now, and it seemed that nothing could stop us anymore. I played to packed houses in every city. Not only did the shows sell out, but hundreds more were turned away at the box office every night. Scalpers did a bang-up business, peddling tickets for three, four, even five times their face value, and every time we pulled up in front of a new hotel, there would be a crowd of people waiting at the entrance, desperate fans who'd stood for hours in the rain and frost just to get a glimpse of me.

My fellow performers were a little envious, I think, but the truth was they'd never had it so good. When the mobs poured in to see my act, they saw the other acts, too, and that meant money in all our pockets. Over the course of those weeks and months, I topped bills that included every kind of wigged-out entertainment. Comics, jugglers, falsetto singers, birdcallers, midget jazz bands, dancing monkeys – they all took their spills and did their turns before I came on. I liked watching that loopy stuff, and I did my best to make pals backstage with anyone who seemed friendly, but the master wasn't too keen on having me mix with my cohorts. He was standoffish with most of them and urged me to follow his example. 'You're the star,' he'd whisper. 'Act like it. You don't have to give those chumps the time of day.' It was a small bone of contention between us, but I figured I'd be on the vaudeville circuit for years to come, and I saw no point in making enemies when I didn't have to. Unbeknownst to me, however, the master had been hatching his own plans for our future, and by the end of September he was already talking out loud about a one-man spring tour. That was how it was with Master Yehudi: the better things went for us, the higher he set his sights. The current tour wouldn't be over until Christmas, and yet he couldn't resist looking beyond it to something even more spectacular. The first time he mentioned it to me, I gulped at the pure ballsiness of the proposition. The idea was to work our way east from San Francisco to New York, playing the ten or twelve biggest cities for special command performances. We'd book the shows in indoor arenas and football stadiums like Madison Square Garden and Soldier's Field, and no crowd would ever be smaller than fifteen thousand. 'A triumphal march across America' was how he described it, and by the time he finished his sales pitch, my heart was pounding four times faster than normal. Christ, could that man talk. His mouth was one of the great huckster machines of all time, and once he got it going full tilt, the dreams poured out of it like smoke rushing through a chimney.

'Shit, boss,' I said. 'If you can swing a tour like that, we'll rake in millions.'

'I'll swing it all right,' he said. 'Just keep up the good work, and it's in the bag. That's all it takes, Walt. You keep on doing what you've been doing, and Rawley's March is a sure thing.'

Meanwhile, we were gearing up for my first theatrical performance in New York. We wouldn't be there until Thanksgiving weekend, still a long way down the road, but we both knew it was going to be the highlight of the season, the pinnacle of my career so far. Just thinking about it was enough to make me dizzy. Add ten Bostons to ten Philadelphias, and they wouldn't equal one New York. Put eighty-six performances in Buffalo together with ninety-three in Trenton, and the sum wouldn't amount to a minute's worth of stage time in the Big Apple. New York was top banana, ground zero on the show business map, and no matter how many raves I got in other cities, I wouldn't be anything until I took my act to Broadway and let them see what I could do. That's why the master had booked New York for so late in the tour. He wanted me to be an old hand by the time we got there, a seasoned, battle-tested soldier who knew what bullets tasted

183

like and could roll with any punch. I became that vet with time to spare. By October twelfth, I'd done forty-four variety theater gigs, and I felt ready, as lean and mean as I'd ever be, and yet we still had more than a month to go. I had never endured such suspense. New York ate at me day and night, and after a while I didn't think I could stand it anymore.

We played Richmond on the thirteenth and fourteenth, Baltimore on the fifteenth and sixteenth, and then headed for Scranton, Pennsylvania. I turned in a good performance there, certainly up to snuff and no worse than any of the others, but immediately upon finishing the show, just as I took my bow and the curtain came down, I passed out and fell to the floor. I had felt perfectly fine until that moment, going through my aerial turns with all the ease and aplomb I was accustomed to, but as soon as my feet touched the stage for the last time, I felt as if I weighed ten thousand pounds. I held my position just long enough for the smile, the bow, and the closing of the curtain, and then my knees buckled, my back gave way, and my body was thrust to the ground. When I opened my eyes in the dressing room five minutes later, I felt a little light-headed, but it seemed that the crisis had passed. But then I stood up, and it was precisely then that the headache returned, ripping through me with a blast of savage, blinding pain. I tried to take a step, but the world was swimming, undulating like a belly dancer in a funhouse mirror, and I couldn't see where I was going. By the time I took a second step, I had already lost my balance. If the master hadn't been there to catch me, I would have fallen flat on my face again.

Neither one of us was ready to panic at that point. The headache and dizziness could have been caused by any number of things – fatigue, a touch of the flu, an ear infection – but just to play it safe, the master called Wilkes-Barre and canceled my performance for the following night. I slept soundly in the Scranton hotel, and by the next morning I was well again, utterly free of pain and discomfort. My recovery defied all logic, but we both accepted it as one of those things, a fluke that didn't deserve to be second-guessed. We set off for Pittsburgh in good spirits, glad of the day off, and once we got there and checked into the hotel, we actually took in a movie together to celebrate my return to form. The next night, however, when I did my show at the Fosberg Theatre, it was Scranton all over again. I turned in a jewel of a perform-ance, and just as the curtain came down and the act was done, I collapsed. The headache started up again immediately after I opened my eyes, and this time it didn't go away in one night. When I woke up the next morning, the daggers were still lodged in my skull, and they didn't leave until four o'clock in the afternoon – several hours after Master Yehudi had been forced to cancel that night's performance.

Everything pointed to the knock on the head I'd received in New Haven. That was the most likely cause of my problem, and yet if I'd been walking around with a concussion for the past few weeks, it must have been the mildest concussion in medical history. How else to account for the odd and unset-tling fact that as long as I kept my feet on the ground, I remained in good health? The headaches and dizzy spells came only after I performed, and if the link between levitating and my new condition was as definite as it seemed, then the master wondered if my brain hadn't been jarred in such a way as to put undue pressure on my cranial arteries every time I went up into the air, which in turn caused the excruciat-ing attacks when I came down. He wanted to put me in the hospital and have some X-rays taken of my skull. 'Why chance it?' he said. 'We've hit the flat part of the tour, and a week or ten days off might be just what you need. They'll do some tests, probe around in your neurological gearbox, and maybe they'll figure out what this cursed thing is.'

'No way,' I said. 'I ain't going into no hospital.'

'The only cure for a concussion is rest. If that's what it is, then you don't have any choice.'

'Forget it. I'd sooner work on a chain gang than park my butt in one of them joints.'

'Think of the nurses, Walt. All those sweet little gals in white uniforms. You'll have a dozen honeybuns doting on you night and day. If you play it smart, you might even see some action.'

'You can't tempt me. Nobody's going to turn me into a sucker. We're signed up to do some shows, and I aim to do them – even if it kills me.'

'Reading and Altoona aren't where the action is, son. We can skip Elmira and Binghampton, and it won't make a pea-shooter's worth of difference. I'm thinking about New York, and I know you are, too. That's the one you've got to be in shape for.'

'My head don't hurt when I do the act. That's the bottom line, chief. As long as I can go on, I gotta go on. Who cares if I smart some afterwards? I can live with pain. Life's a pain anyway, and the only good thing about it is when I'm up on stage doing my act.'

'Problem is, the act is wiping you out. You keep coming down with those headaches, and you won't be Walt the Wonder Boy much longer. I'll have to change your name to Mr Vertigo.'

'Mr Who?'

'Mr Dizzy-in-the-Head. Mr Fear-of-Heights.'

'I ain't afraid of nothing. You know that.'

'You're all guts, kid, and I love you for it. But there comes a time in every levitator's career when the air is fraught with peril, and I'm afraid we've come to that time now.'

We kept on jawing about these things for the next hour, and in the end I wore him down enough to give me one last chance. That was the bargain. I'd play Reading the next night, and headache or no headache, if I was well enough to go on in Altoona the night after that, I would perform as scheduled. It was a crazy thing to push for, but that second attack had scared me stiff, and I was afraid it meant I was losing my touch. What if the headaches were only the first step? I figured my only hope was to fight my way through it, to go on performing until I got better or couldn't take it anymore – and then see what happened. I was so unhinged, I really didn't care if my brain burst into a thousand pieces. Better to be dead than to lose my powers, I told myself. If I couldn't be Walt the Wonder Boy, I didn't want to be anyone.

Reading turned out badly, much worse than I had feared. Not only did my gamble not pay off, but the results were even more catastrophic than before. I did the show and collapsed, just as I'd known I would, but this time I didn't wake up in the dressing room. Two stagehands had to carry me across the street to the hotel, and when I opened my eyes fifteen or twenty minutes later, I didn't even have to stand up to feel the pain. The instant the light hit my pupils, the agony began. A hundred trolley cars jumped the rails and converged on a spot behind my left temple; airplanes crashed there; trucks collided there; and then two little green gremlins picked up hammers and started driving stakes through my eyeballs. I writhed about on the bed, howling for someone to put me out of my misery, and by the time the master summoned the hotel quack to come upstairs and administer a hypo, I was fit to be tied, a toboggan of flames twisting and plunging through the valley of the shadow of death.

I woke up in a Philadelphia hospital ten hours later, and for the next twelve days I didn't budge. The headache continued for another forty-eight hours, and they kept me under such heavy sedation that I can't remember anything until the third day, when I finally woke up again and discovered that the pain was gone. After that, they subjected me to all kinds of examinations and procedures. Their curiosity was inexhaustible, and once they got started they didn't leave me alone. Every hour on the hour a different doctor would walk into the room and put me through my paces. My knees were tapped with hammers, cookie-cutters were rolled over my skin, flashlights were shone in my eyes; I gave them piss and blood and shit; they listened to my heart and looked into my ears; they X-rayed me from conk to toe. There was nothing to live for anymore except science, and those boys in the white coats did a thorough job of it. Within a day or two they turned me into a quivering naked germ, a microbe trapped in a maze of needles, stethoscopes and tongue depressors. If the nurses had been good to look at, there might have been some relief, but the ones I got were all old and ugly, with fat behinds and hair on their chins. I'd never come across such a crew of dog-show contestants, and whenever one of them came in to take my temperature or read my chart, I'd shut my eyes and pretend I was asleep.

Master Yehudi sat by my side throughout this ordeal. The press had got wind of my whereabouts, and for the first week or so the papers were full of updates about my condition. The master read these articles out loud to me every day. I found some comfort in the hullaballoo while I was listening, but the moment he stopped reading, boredom and cussedness would close in on me again. Then the New York stock market crashed, and I got pushed off the front pages. I wasn't paying much attention, but I figured the crisis was only temporary, and once that Black Tuesday business was over I'd be back in the headlines where I belonged. All those stories about people jumping out of windows and shooting themselves in the head struck me as tabloid flimflam, and I shrugged them off like so many fairy tales. The only thing I cared about was getting the show back on the road. My headache was gone and I felt terrific, one-hundred-percent normal. When I opened my eyes in the morning and saw Master Yehudi sitting by my bed, I would begin the day by asking the same question I'd asked the day before: When do I get out of here?

188

And every day he would give me the same answer: As soon as the test results are in.

When they did come in, I couldn't have been more pleased. After all that rigmarole of pricking and poking, all those tubes and suction cups and rubber gloves, the doctors couldn't find a thing wrong with me. No concussion, no brain tumor, no blood disease, no inner-ear imbalance, no lumps, no mumps, no bumps. They gave me a clean bill of health and declared me the fittest specimen of fourteen-year-old manhood they'd ever seen. As far as the headaches and dizziness went, they couldn't determine the precise cause. It might have been a bug that had already passed through my system. It might have been something I'd eaten. Whatever it was, it wasn't there anymore, and if by chance it *was* there, it was too small to be detected – not even by the strongest microscope on the planet.

'Hot diggity,' I said, when the master broke the news to me. 'Hot diggity dog.'

We were alone in my room on the fourth floor, sitting side by side on the edge of the bed. It was early morning, and the light was pouring in on us through the slats of the venetian blinds. For three or four seconds, I felt as happy as I've ever been in my life. I felt so happy I wanted to scream.

'Not so fast, son,' the master said. 'I haven't finished yet.'

'Fast? Fast's the name of the game, boss. The faster the better. We've already missed eight shows, and the sooner we pack up and get me out of here, the sooner we get to where we're going. Which city we booked in next? If it ain't too far, we might even make it by curtain time.'

The master took hold of one of my hands and squeezed. 'Calm down, Walt. Take a deep breath, close your eyes, and listen to what I have to say.'

It didn't sound like a joke, so I did what he asked and tried to sit still.

'Good.' He spoke that one word and stopped. There was a

long pause before he spoke again, and in that interval of darkness and silence, I knew that something awful was about to happen. 'There aren't going to be any more shows,' he said at last. 'We're all washed up, kid. Walt the Wonder Boy is kaput.'

'Don't josh me, master,' I said, opening my eyes and looking at his glum, determined face. I kept waiting for him to throw me a wink and burst out laughing, but he just sat there gazing at me with those dark eyes of his. If anything, his expression grew even sadder.

'I wouldn't tease at a moment like this,' he said. 'We've come to the end of the line, and there's not a fucking thing we can do about it.'

'But the docs just gave me the thumbs up. I'm healthy as a horse.'

'That's the trouble. There's nothing wrong with you – which means there's nothing to be cured. Not with rest, not with medicine, not with exercise. You're perfectly well, and because you're well, your career is over.'

'That's crazy talk, master. It don't make a bit of sense.'

'I've heard about cases like yours before. They're very rare. The literature speaks of only two of them, and they're separated in time by hundreds of years. A Czech levitator in the early nineteenth century had what you have, and before that there was Antoine Dubois, a Frenchman who was active during the reign of Louis the Fourteenth. As far as I know, those are the only two recorded cases. You're the third, Walt. In all the annals of levitation, you're just the third one to confront this problem.'

'I still don't know what you're talking about.'

'Puberty, Walt, that's what. Adolescence. The bodily changes that turn a boy into a man.'

'You mean my boners and such? My curly hairs and the crack in my voice?'

'Just so. All the natural transformations.'

'Maybe I've been whacking off too much. What if I stopped that tomfoolery? You know, preserved the bindu a little more. Do you think that would help?'

'I doubt it. There's only one cure for your condition, but I wouldn't dream of inflicting it on you. I've already put you through enough.'

'I don't care. If there's a way to fix it, then that's what we've got to do.'

'I'm talking about castration, Walt. You cut off your balls, and then maybe there's a chance.'

'Did you say *maybe*?'

'Nothing's guaranteed. The Frenchman did it, and he went on levitating until he was sixty-four. The Czech did it, and it didn't do an ounce of good. The mutilation went for naught, and two months later he jumped off the Charles Bridge and killed himself.'

'I don't know what to say,'

'Of course you don't. If I were in your shoes, I wouldn't know what to say either. That's why I'm suggesting we pack it in. I don't expect you to do a thing like that. No man could ask that of another man. It wouldn't be human.'

'Well, seeing that the verdict is sort of fuzzy, it wouldn't be too smart to risk it, would it? I mean, if I give up being Walt the Wonder Boy, at least I've got my balls to keep me company. I wouldn't want to be in a position where I wound up losing both.'

'Exactly. Which is why the subject is closed. There's no point in talking about it anymore. We've had a good run, and now it's over. At least you get to quit while you're still on top.'

'But what if the headaches go away?'

'They won't. Believe me they won't.'

'How can you know? Maybe those other guys still got them, but what if I'm different?'

'You're not. It's a permanent condition, and there's no cure for it. Short of taking the risk we've already rejected, the headaches will be with you for the rest of your life. For every minute you spend in the air, you'll be racked with pain for three hours on the ground. And the older you are, the worse that pain will be. It's gravity's revenge, son. We thought we had it licked, but it turns out to be stronger than we are. That's the way it goes. We won for a while, and now we've lost. So be it. If that's what God wants, then we have to bow to his will.'

It was all so sad, so depressing, so futile. I'd struggled to make a success of myself for so long, and now, just when I was about to become one of the immortals of history, I had to turn my back on it and walk away. Master Yehudi swallowed this poison without flinching a muscle. He accepted our fate like a stoic and refused to make a fuss. It was a noble stance, I suppose, but it wasn't in my repertoire to take bad news lying down. Once we'd run out of things to say, I stood up and started kicking the furniture and punching the walls, storming about the room like some nutso shadowboxer. I knocked over a chair, sent the night table clattering to the floor, and cursed my bad luck with vocal chords going at full blast. Wise old man that he was, Master Yehudi did nothing to stop me. Even when a couple of nurses rushed into the room to see what the trouble was, he calmly shooed them out, explaining he would cover any damages in full. He knew how I was built, and he knew that my fury needed a chance to express itself. No bottling up for me; no turning the other cheek for Walt. If the world hit me, I had to hit back.

Fair enough. Master Yehudi was smart to let me carry on like that, and I'm not going to blame him if I acted like a dumbbell and carried it too far. Right in the middle of my outburst, I came up with what had to be my all-time stupidest idea, the howler to end all howlers. Oh, it seemed pretty clever at the time, but that was only because I still couldn't face up to what had happened – and once you deny the facts, you're only asking for trouble. But I was desperate to prove the master wrong, to show him that his theories about my condition were so much flat fizzy water. So, right there in that Philadelphia hospital room, on the third day of November 1929, I made a sudden, last-ditch attempt to resurrect my career. I stopped punching the wall, turned around and faced the master, and then spread my arms and lifted myself off the ground.

'Look!' I shouted at him. 'Take a good look and tell me what you see!'

The master studied me with a dark, mournful expression. 'I see the past,' he said. 'I see Walt the Wonder Boy for the last time. I see someone who's about to be sorry for what he just did.'

'I'm as good as I ever was!' I yelled back at him. 'And that's the goddamned best in the world!'

The master glanced down at his watch. 'Ten seconds,' he said. 'For every second you stay up there, you'll have three minutes of pain. I guarantee it.'

I figured I'd put my point across, so rather than risk another long bout of agony, I decided to come down. And then it happened – just as the master had promised it would. The instant my toes touched the ground, my head cracked open again, exploding with a violence that sucked the daylights out of me and made me see stars. Vomit burst through my windpipe and landed on the wall six feet away. Switchblades opened in my skull, tunneling deep into the center of my brain. I shook, I howled, I fell to the floor, and this time I didn't have the luxury of fainting. I thrashed about like a flounder with a hook in his eye, and when I pleaded for help, imploring the master to call in a doctor to give me a shot, he just shook his head and walked away. 'You'll get over it,' he said. 'In less than an hour, you'll be as good as new.' Then, without offering me a single word of comfort, he quietly straightened up the mess in the room and started packing my bag.

That was the only treatment I deserved. His words had fallen on deaf ears, and that left him with no choice but to back off and let my actions speak for themselves. So the pain spoke to me, and this time I listened. I listened for forty-seven minutes, and by the time class was out, I'd learned everything I needed to know. Talk about a crash course in the ways of the world. Talk about boning up on sorrow. The pain fixed me but good, and when I walked out of the hospital later that morning, my head was more or less screwed on straight again. I knew the facts of life. I knew them in every crevice of my soul and every pore of my skin, and I wasn't about to forget them. The glory days were over. Walt the Wonder Boy was dead, and there wasn't a chance in hell he'd ever show his face again.

We walked back to the master's hotel in silence, wending our way through the city streets like a pair of ghosts. It took ten or fifteen minutes to get there, and when we reached the entrance I couldn't think of anything better to do than stick out my hand and try to say good-bye.

'Well,' I said. 'I guess this is where we part company.'

'Oh?' the master said. 'And why is that?'

'You'll be looking for a new boy now, and there ain't much point in hanging around if I'm just going to be in the way.'

'And why would I look for a new boy?' He seemed genuinely astonished by the suggestion.

'Because I'm a dud, that's why. Because the act is finished, and I ain't no good to you no more.'

'You think I'd drop you like that?'

'Why not? Fair is fair, and if I can't deliver the goods, it's only right for you to start making other plans.'

'I have made plans. I've made a hundred of them, a thousand of them. I've got plans up my sleeves and plans in my socks. My whole body's crawling with plans, and before the

194

itch works me into a frenzy, I want to pluck them out and put them on the table for you.'

'For me?'

'Who else, squirt? But we can't have a serious discussion standing in the doorway, can we? Come on up to the room. We'll order some lunch and get down to brass tacks.'

'I still don't get it.'

'What's to get? We might be out of the levitation business, but that doesn't mean we've closed up shop.'

'You mean we're still partners?'

'Five years is a long time, son. After all we've been through together, I've sort of grown attached. I'm not getting any younger, you know. It wouldn't make sense to start looking for someone else. Not now, not at my age. It took me half a life to find you, and I'm not going to kiss you off because we've had a few setbacks. Like I said, I've got some plans to discuss with you. If you like those plans and want in, you're in. If not, we divide up the money and part ways.'

'The money. Jesus God, I clean forgot about the money.'

'You've had other things on your mind.'

'I've been so low in the dumps, my noodle's been on holiday. So how much we got? What's it tote up to in round figures, boss?'

'Twenty-seven thousand dollars. It's sitting in the hotel safe, and it's all ours free and clear.'

'And here I thought I was down-and-out broke again. It kind of puts things in a different light, don't it? I mean, twenty-seven grand's a nice little booty.'

'Not bad. We could have done worse.'

'So the ship ain't sunk after all.'

'Not by a long shot. We did okay for ourselves. And with hard times coming, we'll be pretty snug. Dry and warm in our little boat, we'll sail the seas of adversity a lot better than most.'

'Aye aye, sir.'

'That's it, mate. All aboard. As soon as the wind is up, we'll lift anchor – and with a heave and a ho we'll be off!'

I would have traveled to the ends of the earth with him. By boat, by bicycle, by crawling on my belly – it didn't matter what means of transportation we used. I just wanted to be where he was and to go where he went. Until that conversation in front of the hotel, I thought I'd lost everything. Not only my career, not only my life, but my master as well. I assumed he was finished with me, that he'd kick me out and never give it a second thought, but now I knew different. I wasn't just a paycheck to him. I wasn't just a flying machine with a rusty engine and damaged wings. For better or worse, we were booked for the duration, and that counted more to me than all the seats in all the theaters and football stadiums put together. I'm not saying that things weren't black, but they weren't half as black as they could have been. Master Yehudi was still with me, and not only was he with me, he was carrying a pocketful of matches to light the way.

So we went upstairs and ate our lunch. I don't know about a thousand plans, but he certainly had three or four of them, and he'd thought each one through pretty carefully. The guy just wouldn't quit. Five years of hard work had flown out of the window, decades of scheming and preparation had turned to dust overnight, and there he was bubbling over with new ideas, plotting our next move as if everything still lay before us. They don't make them like that anymore. Master Yehudi was the last of a breed, and I've never run across the likes of him since: a man who felt perfectly at home in the jungle. He might not have been the king, but he understood its laws better than anyone else. Bash him in the gut, spit in his face, break his heart, and he'd bounce right back, ready to take on all comers. Never say die. He didn't just live by that motto, he was the man who invented it.

The first plan was the simplest. We'd move to New York and live like regular people. I'd go to school and get a good

196

education, he'd start up a business and make money, and we'd both live happily ever after. I didn't say a word when he finished, so he passed on to the next one. We'd go out on tour, he said, giving lectures at colleges, churches, and ladies' garden clubs on the art of levitation. There'd be a big demand for us, at least for the next six months or so, and why not continue to cash in on Walt the Wonder Boy until the last lingering bits of my fame had dried up? I didn't like that one either, so he shrugged and moved on to the next. We'd pack up our belongings, he said, get into the car, and drive out to Hollywood. I'd start a new career as a movie actor, and he'd be my agent and manager. What with all the notices I'd had from the act, it wouldn't be hard to swing me a tryout. I was already a big name, and given my flair for slapstick, I'd probably land on my feet in no time.

'Ah,' I said. 'Now you're talking.'

'I figured you'd go for it,' the master said, leaning back in his chair and lighting up a fat Cuban cigar. 'That's why I saved it for last.'

And just like that, we were off to the races again.

We checked out of the hotel early the next morning, and by eight o'clock we were on the road, heading west to a new life in the sunny hills of Tinseltown. It was a long, grueling drive back in those days. There were no superhighways or Howard Johnsons, no six-lane bowling alleys stretching back and forth between coasts, and you had to twist your way through every little town and hamlet, following whatever road would take you in the right direction. If you got stuck behind a farmer hauling a load of hay with a Model-T tractor, that was your tough luck. If they were digging up a road somewhere, you'd have to turn around and find another road, and more often than not that meant going hours out of your way. Those were the rules of the game back then, but I can't say I was perturbed by the slow going. I was just a passenger, and if I felt like dozing off for an hour or two in the back seat, there was nothing to stop me. A few times, when we hit a particularly deserted stretch of road, the master let me take over at the wheel, but that didn't happen often, and he wound up doing ninety-eight percent of the driving. It was a hypnotic sort of experience for him, and after five or six days he fell into a wistful, ruminating state of mind, more and more lost in his own thoughts as we pushed toward the middle of the country. We were back in the land of big skies and flat, dreary expanses, and the all-enveloping air seemed to drain some of the enthusiasm out of him. Maybe he was thinking about Mrs Witherspoon, or maybe some other person from his past had come back to haunt him, but more than likely he was pondering questions about life and death, the big scary stuff that worms its way into your head when there's nothing to distract you. Why am I here? Where am I going? What happens to me after I've drawn my last breath? These are weighty subjects, I know, but after mulling over the master's actions on that trip for more than half a century, I believe I know whereof I speak. One conversation stands out in memory, and if I'm not wrong in how I interpreted what he said, it shows the sorts of things that were beginning to prey on his spirit. We were somewhere in Texas, a little past Fort Worth, I think, and I was jabbering on to him in that breezy, boastful way of mine, talking for no other reason than to hear myself talk.

'California,' I said. 'It never snows there, and you can swim in the ocean all year round. From what folks say, it's the next best thing to paradise. Makes Florida look like a muggy swamp by comparison.'

'No place is perfect, kid,' the master said. 'Don't forget the earthquakes and the mudslides and the droughts. They can go for years without rain there, and when that happens, the whole state turns into a tinderbox. Your house can burn down in less time than it takes to flip an egg.'

'Don't worry about that. Six months from now, we'll be living in a stone castle. That stuff can't burn – but just to play it safe, we'll have our own fire department on the premises. I'm telling you, boss, the flicks and me was made for each other. I'm going to rake in so much dough, we'll have to open a new bank. The Rawley Savings and Loan, with national headquarters on Sunset Boulevard. You watch and see. In no time at all, I'm going to be a star.'

'If everything goes well, you'll be able to earn your crust of bread. That's the important thing. It's not as if I'm going to be around forever, and I want to make sure you can fend for yourself. It doesn't matter how you do it. Actor, cameraman, messenger boy – one trade's as good as another. I just need to know there'll be a future for you after I'm gone.'

'That's old man talk, master. You ain't even fifty yet.'

'Forty-six. Where I come from, that's pretty long in the tooth.'

'Swizzle sticks. You get out in that California sun, it'll add ten years to your life the first day.'

'Maybe so. But even if it does, I still have more years behind me than in front of me. It's simple mathematics, Walt, and it can't do us any harm to prepare for what's ahead.'

We switched onto another subject after that, or maybe we just stopped talking altogether, but those dark little comments of his loomed larger and larger to me as the days dragged on. For a man who worked so hard at hiding his feelings, the master's words were tantamount to a confession. I'd never heard him open up like that before, and even though he couched it in a language of *what ifs* and *what thens*, I wasn't so stupid as to ignore the message buried between the lines. My thoughts went back to the stomach-clutching scene in the New Haven hotel. If I hadn't been so bogged down with my own troubles since then, I would have been more vigilant. Now, with nothing better to do than stare out the window and count the days until we got to California, I resolved to watch his every move. I wasn't going to be a coward this time. If I caught him grimacing or grabbing his stomach again, I was going to speak up and call his bluff – and hustle him to the first doctor I could find.

He must have noticed my worry, for not long after that conversation, he clamped down on the gloom-and-doom talk and started whistling a different song. By the time we left Texas and crossed into New Mexico, he seemed to perk up considerably, and alert as I was for signs of trouble, I couldn't detect a single one – not even the smallest hint. Little by little, he managed to pull the wool over my eyes again, and if not for what happened seven or eight hundred miles down the road, it would have been months before I suspected the truth, perhaps even years. Such was the master's power. No one could match him in a battle of wits, and every time I tried, I wound up feeling like a horse's ass. He was so much quicker than I was, so much defter and more experienced, he could fake me out of my pants before I even put them on. There was never any contest. Master Yehudi always won, and he went on winning to the bitter end.

The most tedious part of the trip began. We spent days riding through New Mexico and Arizona, and after a while it felt like we were the only people left in the world. The master was fond of the desert, however, and once we entered that barren landscape of rocks and cacti, he kept pointing out curious geological formations and delivering little lectures on the incalculable age of the earth. To be perfectly honest, it left me pretty cold. I didn't want to spoil the master's fun, so I kept my mouth shut and pretended to listen, but after four thousand buttes and six hundred canyons, I'd had enough of the scenic tour to last me a lifetime.

'If this is God's country,' I finally said, 'then God can have it.'

'Don't let it get you down,' the master said. 'It goes on forever out here, and counting the miles won't shorten the trip. If you want to get to California, this is the road we have to take.'

'I know that. But just because I put up with it don't mean I have to like it.'

'You might as well try. The time will go faster that way.'

'I hate to be a party pooper, sir, but this beauty stuff's a great big ho-hum. I mean, who cares if a place looks crummy or not? As long as it's got some people in it, it's bound to be interesting. Subtract the people, and what's left? Emptiness, that's what. And emptiness don't do a thing for me but lower my blood pressure and make my eyelids droop.'

'Then close your eyes and get some sleep, and I'll commune with nature myself. Don't fret, little man. It won't be long now. Before you know it, you'll have all the people you want.'

The darkest day of my life dawned in western Arizona on November sixteenth. It was a bone-dry morning like all the others, and by ten o'clock we were crossing the California border to begin our glide through the Mojave toward the coast. I let out a little whoop of celebration when we passed that milestone and then settled in for the last leg of the journey. The master was clipping along at a nice speed, and we figured we'd make it to Los Angeles in time for dinner. I remember arguing in favor of a swank restaurant for our first night in town. Maybe we'd run into Buster Keaton or Harold Lloyd, I said, and wouldn't that be a thrill, huh? Imagine shaking hands with those guys over a mound of baked Alaska in some posh supper club. If they were in the mood for it, maybe we could get into a pie fight and tear the joint apart. The master was just beginning to laugh at my description of this screwy scene when I looked up and saw something on the road in front of us. 'What's that?' I said. 'What's what?' the master said. And a couple of moments later, we were running for our lives.

The *what* was a gang of four men spread out across the narrow turnpike. They were standing in a row – two, three hundred yards up ahead – and at first it was tough to make them out. What with the glare from the sun and the heat rising off the ground, they looked like spectres from another planet, shimmering bodies made of light and thin air. Fifty yards closer, and I could see that their hands were raised over their heads, as if they were signaling us to stop. At that point I took them for a crew of road workers, and even when we got still closer and I saw that they had handkerchiefs over their faces, I didn't think twice about it. It's dusty out here, I said to myself, and when the wind blows a man needs some protection. But then we were sixty or seventy yards away, and suddenly I could see that all four of them were holding shiny metal objects in their upraised hands. Just when I realized they were guns, the master slammed on the brakes, skidded to a stop, and threw the car into reverse. Neither one of us said a word. Gas pedal to the floor, we backed up with the engine whining and the chassis shaking. The four desperadoes took off after us, running up the road as their gun barrels glinted in the light. Master Yehudi had turned his head in the other direction to look through the rear window, and he couldn't see what I saw, but as I watched the men gaining ground on us, I noticed that one of them ran with a limp. He was a scrawny, chicken-necked sack of bones, but in spite of his handicap he moved faster than the others. Before long, he was out in the lead by himself, and that was when the handkerchief slipped off his face and I got my first real look at him. Dust was flying in all directions, but I would have known that mug anywhere. Edward J. Sparks. The one and only was back, and the moment I laid eyes on Uncle Slim, I knew my life was ruined forever.

I shouted through the noise of the straining engine: 'They're catching up to us! Turn around and go forward! They're close enough to shoot!'

It was a rough call. We couldn't go fast enough in reverse to get away, and yet the time it took to turn around would slow us down even more. But we had to risk it. If we didn't increase our speed in about four seconds, we wouldn't have a chance.

Master Yehudi swung out sharply to the right, angling into a frantic, backwards U-turn as he shifted into first. The gears made a hideous, grinding noise, the back wheels jumped off the edge of the road and hit some stray rocks, and then we were spinning, flailing without traction as the car groaned and shook. It took a second or two before the tires caught hold again, and by the time we shot out of there with our nose pointed in the right direction, the guns were coughing behind us. One shell snagged a back tire, and the instant the rubber blew out, the Pierce Arrow lurched wildly to the left. The master rolled with it and never lifted his foot from the floor. Steering like a madman to keep us on the road, he was already shifting into third when another bullet came blasting through the back window. He let out a howl, and his hands flew off the steering wheel. The car bucked off the road, bounced onto the rock-strewn desert floor, and a moment later blood started gushing out of his right shoulder. God knows where he found the strength, but he managed to grab hold of the wheel again and give it another try. It wasn't his fault that it didn't work. The car was careening out of control by then, and before he could get us turned back toward the road, the left front tire skidded up the ramp of a large protruding stone and the whole machine tipped over.

The next hour was a blank. The jolt flung me out of my seat, and the last thing I remember is flying through the air in the master's direction. Somewhere between takeoff and landing, I must have clunked my head against the dashboard or steering wheel, for by the time the car stopped moving, I was already out cold. Dozens of things happened after that, but I missed them all. I missed seeing Slim and his men swoop down on the car and rob us of the strongbox in the trunk. I missed seeing them slash the other three tires. I missed seeing them open our suitcases and scatter our clothes on the ground. Why they didn't shoot us after that is still something of a mystery to me. They must have talked about whether to kill us or not, but I heard nothing of what they said and can't begin to speculate on why we were spared. Maybe we looked dead already, or maybe they just didn't give a damn. They had the strongbox with all our money in it, and even if we were still breathing when they left, they probably figured we'd die from our injuries anyway. If there was any comfort in being robbed of every cent we had, it came from the smallness of the sum they walked off with. Slim must have thought we had millions. He must have been counting on a once-in-a-lifetime jackpot, but all he got from his efforts was a paltry twenty-seven thousand dollars. Split that into four, and the shares didn't add up to much. No more than a pittance, really, and it made me glad to think about his disappointment. For years and years, it warmed my soul to imagine how crushed he must have been.

I think I was out for an hour – but it could have been more than that, it could have been less. However long it was, when I woke up I found myself lying on top of the master. He was still unconscious, and the two of us were wedged against the door on the driver's side, limbs tangled together and our clothes soaked in blood. The first thing I saw when my eyes blinked into focus was an ant marching over a small stone. My mouth was filled with crumbled bits of dirt, and my face was jammed flat against the ground. That was because the window had been open at the time of the crash, and I suppose that was a piece of luck, if *luck* is a word that can be used in describing such things. At least my head hadn't gone through the glass. There was that to be thankful for, I suppose. At least my face hadn't been cut to shreds.

My forehead hurt like hell and my body was bruised all over, but no bones were broken. I found that out when I stood up and tried to open the door above me. If any real damage had been done, I wouldn't have been able to move. Still, it wasn't easy to push that thing out on its hinges. It weighed half a ton, and what with the strange tilt of the car and the difficulty of getting any leverage on it, I must have struggled for five minutes before clambering through the hatch. Warm air hit my face, but it felt cool after the sweatbox confines of the Pierce Arrow. I sat on my perch for a couple of seconds, spitting out dirt and sucking in the languid breeze, but then my hands slipped, and the moment I touched the red-hot surface of the car, I had to jump off. I crashed to the ground, picked myself up, and began staggering around the car to the other side. On the way, I caught sight of the open trunk and noticed that the money box was missing, but since that was already a foregone conclusion, I didn't pause to think about it. The left side of the car had landed on a stone outcrop, and there was a small space between the ground and the door –

about six or eight inches. It wasn't wide enough to stick my head through, but by lying flat on the ground I could see far enough inside to get a glimpse of the master's head dangling out the window. I can't explain how it happened, but the moment I spotted him through that narrow crack, his eyes opened. He saw me looking at him, and a moment later he twisted his face into something that resembled a smile. 'Get me out of here, Walt,' he said. 'My arm's all busted up, and I can't move on my own.'

I ran around to the other side of the car again, took off my shirt, and bunched it up in my hands, improvising a pair of makeshift mittens to protect my palms against the burning metal. Then I scrambled to the top, braced myself along the edge of the open door, and reached in to pull the master out. Unfortunately, his right shoulder was the bad one, and he couldn't extend that arm. He made an effort to turn his body around and give me his other arm, but that took work, real work, and I could see how excruciating the pain was for him. I told him to stay still, removed the belt from my pants, and then tried again by lowering the leather strap into the car. That seemed to do the trick. Master Yehudi grabbed hold of it with his left hand, and I began to pull. I don't want to remember how many times he bumped himself, how many times he slipped, but we both fought on, and after twenty or thirty minutes we finally got him out.

And there we were, marooned in the Mojave Desert. The car was wrecked, we had no water, and the closest town was forty miles away. That was bad enough, but the worst part of our predicament was the master's wound. He'd lost an awful lot of blood in the past two hours. Bones were shattered inside him, muscles were torn, and the last bits of his strength had been spent on crawling out of the car. I sat him down in the shade of the Pierce Arrow and then ran off to collect some of the clothing scattered about on the ground. One by one, I picked up his fine white shirts and custom-made silk ties, and when my arms were too full to hold anymore, I carried them back to use as bandages. It was the best idea I could think of, but it didn't do much good. I linked the ties together, tore the shirts into long strips, and wrapped him as tightly as I could – but the blood came seeping through before I was finished.

'We'll rest here for a while,' I said. 'Once the sun starts going down, we'll see if we can't stand you on your feet and get moving.'

'It's no good, Walt,' he said. 'I'm never going to make it.'

'Sure you will. We'll start walking down the road, and before you know it, a car will come along and pick us up.'

'There hasn't been a car by here all day.'

'That don't matter. Someone's bound to turn up. It's the law of averages.'

'And what if no one comes?'

'Then I'll carry you on my back. One way or another, we're going to get you to a sawbones and see that he patches you up.'

Master Yehudi closed his eyes and whispered through the pain. 'They took the money, didn't they?'

'You got that one right. It's all gone, every last penny of it.'

'Oh well,' he said, doing his best to crack a smile. 'Easy come, easy go, eh Walt?'

'That's about the size of it.'

Master Yehudi started to laugh, but the jostling hurt too much for him to continue. He paused to get a grip on himself, and then, apropos of nothing, he looked into my eyes and announced: 'Three days from now, we would have been in New York.'

'That's ancient history, boss. One day from now, we're going to be in Hollywood.'

The master looked at me for a long time without saying anything. Then, unexpectedly, he reached out and took hold of my arm with his left hand. 'Whatever you are,' he finally said, 'it's because of me. Isn't that so, Walt?'

'Of course it is. I was a no-good bum before you found me.'

'I just want you to know that it works both ways. Whatever I am, it's because of you.'

I didn't know how to answer that one, so I didn't try. Something strange was in the air, and all of a sudden I couldn't tell where we were going anymore. I wouldn't say that I was scared – at least not yet – but my stomach was beginning to twitch and flutter, and that was always a sure sign of atmospheric disturbance. Whenever one of those fandangos started up inside me, I knew the weather was about to change.

'Don't worry, Walt,' the master continued. 'Everything's going to be all right.'

'I hope so. The way you're looking at me now, it's enough to give a guy the heebie-jeebies.'

'I'm thinking, that's all. Thinking things through as carefully as I can. You shouldn't let that upset you.'

'I ain't upset. As long as you don't pull a fast one on me, I won't be upset at all.'

'You trust me, don't you, Walt?'

'Sure I trust you.'

'You'd do anything for me, wouldn't you?'

'Sure, you know that.'

'Well, what I want you to do for me now is climb back into the car and fetch the pistol from the glove compartment.'

'The gun? What do you want that for? There's no robbers to shoot now. It's just us and the wind out here – and whatever wind there is, it ain't much to speak of.'

'Don't ask questions. Just do as I say and bring me the gun.'

Did I have any choice? Yes, I probably did. I probably could have refused, and that would have ended the matter right then and there. But the master had given me an order, and I wasn't about to give him any lip – not then, not at a time like that. He wanted the gun, and as far as I was concerned, it was my job to get it for him. So, without another word, I scrambled into the car and got it.

'Bless you, Walt,' he said when I handed it to him a minute later. 'You're a boy after my own heart.'

'Just be careful,' I said. 'That weapon's loaded, and the last thing we need is another accident.'

'Come here, son,' he said, patting the ground next to him. 'Sit down beside me and listen to what I have to say.'

I'd already begun to regret everything. The sweet tone in his voice was the giveaway, and by the time I sat down, my stomach was turning cartwheels, pole-vaulting straight into my esophagus. The master's skin was chalk-white. Little dots of sweat clung to his mustache, and his limbs were trembling with fever. But his gaze was steady. Whatever force he still had was locked inside his eyes, and he kept those eyes fixed on me the whole time he talked.

'Here's how it is, Walt. We're in a nasty spot, and we have to get ourselves out of it. If we don't do it pretty soon, we're both going to croak.'

'That could be. But it don't make sense to leave until the temperature cools off a bit.'

'Don't interrupt. Hear me out first, and then you'll have your say.' He stopped for a moment to wet his lips with his tongue, but he was too low on saliva for the gesture to do him any good. 'We have to stand up and walk away from here. That's definite, and the longer we wait, the worse it's going to be. Problem is, I can't stand up and I can't walk. Nothing's going to change that. By the time the sun goes down, I'll only be weaker than I am now.'

'Maybe yes, maybe no.'

'No maybes about it, sport. So instead of sitting around and losing precious time, I have a proposition for you.'

'Yeah, and what's that?'

'I stay here, and you go off on your own.'

'Forget it. I ain't budging from your side, master. I made that promise a long time ago, and I intend to stick by it.'

'Those are fine sentiments, boy, but they're only going to cause you trouble. You've got to get out of here, and you can't do that with me dragging you down. Face the facts. This is the last day we're ever going to spend together. You know that, and I know that, and the faster we get it into the open, the better off we're going to be.'

'Nothing doing. I don't buy that for a second.'

'You don't want to leave me. It's not that you think you shouldn't go, but it pains you to think of me lying here in this condition. You don't want me to suffer, and I'm grateful to you for that. It shows you've learned your lessons well. But I'm offering you a way out, and once you think about it a little bit, you'll realize it's the best solution for both of us.'

'What's the way out?'

'It's very simple. You take this gun and shoot me through the head.'

'Come on, master. This is no time for jokes.'

'It's no joke, Walt. First you kill me, and then you go on your way.'

'The sun's got to your head, and it's turned you bonkers. You caught a bullet in the shoulder, that's all. Sure it hurts, but it's not as though it's going to kill you. The docs can mend those things one, two, three.'

'I'm not talking about the bullet. I'm talking about the cancer in my belly. We don't have to fool each other about that anymore. My gut's all mangled and destroyed, and I don't have more than six months to live. Even if I could get out of here, I'm done for anyway. So why not take matters into our own hands? Six months of pain and agony – that's what I've got to look forward to. I was hoping to get you started on something new before I kicked the bucket, but that wasn't meant to be. Too bad. Too bad about a lot of things, but you'll be doing me a big favor if you pull the trigger now, Walt. I'm depending on you, and I know you won't let me down.'

'Cut it out. Stop this talk, master. You don't know what you're saying.'

'Death isn't so terrible, Walt. When a man comes to the end of the line, it's the only thing he really wants.'

'I won't do it. Not in a thousand years I won't. You can ask me till kingdom come, but I'll never raise a hand against you.'

'If you won't do it, I'll have to do it myself. It's a lot harder that way, and I was hoping you'd spare me the trouble.'

'Jesus God, master, put the gun down.'

'Sorry, Walt. If you don't want to see it, then say your goodbyes now.'

'I ain't saying nothing. You won't get a word out of me until you put that gun down.'

But he wasn't listening anymore. Still looking into my eyes, he raised the pistol against his head and cocked the hammer. It was as if he was daring me to stop him, daring me to reach out and grab the gun, but I couldn't move. I just sat there and watched, and I didn't do a thing.

His hand was shaking and sweat was pouring off his forehead, but his eyes were still steady and clear. 'Remember the good times,' he said. 'Remember the things I taught you.' Then, swallowing once, he shut his eyes and squeezed the trigger.

III

It took me three years to track down Uncle Slim. For more than a thousand days I roamed the country, hunting the bastard in every city from San Francisco to New York. I lived from hand to mouth, scrounging and hustling as best I could, and little by little I turned back into the beggar I was born to be. I hitchhiked, I traveled on foot, I rode the rails. I slept in doorways, in hobo jungles, in flophouses, in open pastures. In some cities, I threw my hat on the sidewalk and juggled oranges for the passersby. In other cities, I swept floors and emptied garbage cans. In still other cities, I stole. I pilfered food from restaurant kitchens, money from cash registers, socks and underwear from the bins at Woolworth's – whatever I could lay my hands on. I stood in breadlines and snored through sermons at the Salvation Army. I tap-danced on street corners. I sang for my supper. Once, in a movie theater in Seattle, I earned ten dollars from an old man who wanted to suck my cock. Another time, on Hennepin Avenue in Minneapolis, I found a hundred-dollar bill lying in the gutter. In the course of those three years, a dozen people walked up to me in a dozen different places and asked if I was Walt the Wonder Boy. The first one took me by surprise, but after that I had my answer ready. 'Sorry, pal,' I'd say. 'Never heard of him. You must be confusing me with someone else.' And before they could insist, I'd tip my cap and vanish into the crowd.

I was pushing eighteen by the time I caught up with him. I'd grown to my full height of five feet five and a half inches, and Roosevelt's inauguration was just two months away. Bootleggers were still in business, but with Prohibition about to give up the ghost, they were selling off their last bits of stock and exploring new lines of crooked investment. That's how I found my uncle. Once I realized that Hoover was going to be thrown out, I started knocking on the door of every rum-runner I could find. Slim was just the sort to latch onto a dead-end operation like illegal booze, and the odds were that if he'd begged someone for a job, he would have done it close to home. That eliminated the east and west coasts. I'd already lost enough time in those places, so I began zeroing in on all his old haunts. When nothing happened in Saint Louis, Kansas City, or Omaha, I fanned out through wider and wider swatches of the Midwest. Milwaukee, Cincinnati, Minneapolis, Chicago, Detroit. From Detroit I went back to Chicago, and even though I hadn't turned up any leads on three previous visits there, the fourth one changed my luck. Forget about lucky three. Three strikes and you're out, but four balls and you walk, and when I returned to Chicago in January of 1933, I finally got to first base. The trail led to Rockford, Illinois – just eighty miles down the road – and that's where I found him: sitting in a warehouse at three o'clock in the morning, guarding two hundred smuggled cases of bonded Canadian rye.

It would have been easy to shoot him right then and there. I had a loaded gun in my pocket, and seeing that it was the same gun the master had used on himself three years before, there would have been a certain justice in turning that gun on Slim now. But I had different plans, and I'd been nurturing them for so long, I wasn't about to let myself get carried away. It wasn't enough just to kill Slim. He had to know who his executioner was, and before I allowed him to die, I wanted him to live with his death for a good little moment. Fair was fair, after all, and if revenge couldn't be sweet, why bother with it in the first place? Now that I'd entered the pastry shop, I aimed to gorge myself on a whole platterful of goodies.

The plan was nothing if not complicated. It was all mixed up with memories from the past, and I never would have thought of it without the books that Aesop read to me back on the farm in Cibola. One of them, a large tome with a ragged blue cover, was about King Arthur and the knights of the Round Table. Except for my namesake Sir Walter, these boys in the metal suits were my top heroes, and I asked for that collection more than any other. Whenever I was most in need of company (nursing my wounds, say, or just feeling low from my struggles with the master), Aesop would break off from his studies and come upstairs to sit with me, and I never forgot how comforting it was to listen to those tales of black magic and adventure. Now that I was alone in the world, they came back to me often. I was on a quest of my own, after all. I was looking for my own Holy Grail, and a year or so into my search, a curious thing started to happen: the cup in the story started turning into a real cup. Drink from the cup and it will give you life. But the life I was looking for could only begin with my uncle's death. That was my Holy Grail, and there could be no real life for me until I found it. Drink from the cup and it will give you death. Little by little, the one cup turned into the other cup, and as I went on moving from place to place, it gradually dawned on me how I was going to kill him. I was in Lincoln, Nebraska, when the plan finally crystallized – hunched over a bowl of soup at the Saint Olaf Lutheran Mission – and after that there were no more doubts. I was going to fill a cup with strychnine and make the bastard drink it. That was the picture I saw, and from that day on it never left me. I'd hold a gun to his head and make him drink down his own death.

So there I was, sneaking up behind him in that cold, empty warehouse in Rockford, Illinois. I'd spent the past three hours crouched behind a stack of wooden boxes, waiting for Slim to get drowsy enough to nod off, and now the moment was upon me. Considering how many years had gone into planning for this moment, it was remarkable how calm I felt.

'Howdy there, unc,' I said, whispering into his ear. 'Long time no see.'

The gun was pressed into the back of his head, but just to

make sure he got the point, I cocked the hammer with my thumb. A bare, forty-watt bulb hung above the table where Slim was sitting, and all the tools of his night watchman's trade were spread out before him: a thermos of coffee, a bottle of rye, a shot glass, the Sunday funnies, and a thirty-eight revolver.

'Walt?' he said. 'Is that you, Walt?'

'In the flesh, buddy. Your number-one favorite nephew.'

'I didn't hear a thing. How the hell'd you sneak up on me like that?'

'Put your hands on the table and don't turn around. If you try to reach for the gun, you're a dead man. Got it?'

He let out a nervous little laugh. 'Yeah, I got it.'

'Sort of like old times, huh? One of us sits in a chair, and the other one holds a gun on him. I thought you'd appreciate my sticking to family tradition.'

'You got no call to be doing this, Walt.'

'Shut up. You start to plead with me, and I plug you on the spot.'

'Jesus, kid. Give a guy a break.'

I sniffed the air behind his head. 'What's that smell, unc? You haven't shit your pants already, have you? I thought you were supposed to be tough. All these years, I've been walking around remembering what a tough guy you were.'

'You're nuts. I ain't done nothing.'

'Sure smells like a turd to me. Or is that just fear? Is that what fear smells like on you, Eddie boy?'

The gun was in my left hand, and in my right I was holding a satchel. Before he could continue the conversation – which was already grating on my nerves – I swung the bag around past his head and plunked it on the table before him. 'Open it,' I said. As he was unzipping the satchel, I moved around to the side of the table and pocketed his gun. Then, slowly pulling my own gun away from his head, I continued walking until I was directly opposite him. I kept the gun pointed at his face as he reached in and dug out the contents of the bag: first the screw-top jar filled with the poisoned milk, then the silver chalice. I'd pinched that thing from a Cleveland pawnshop two years before and had been carrying it with me ever since. The metal wasn't pure – just silver plate – but it was embossed with little figures on horseback, and I'd polished it up that evening until it glowed. Once it was sitting on the table with the jar, I backed up a couple of feet to give myself a broader view. The show was about to start, and I didn't want to miss a thing.

Slim looked old to me, as old as the hills. He'd aged twenty years since I'd last seen him, and the expression in his eyes was so hurt, so filled with pain and confusion, a lesser man than myself might have felt some pity for him. But I felt nothing. I wanted him to be dead, and even as I looked into his face, searching it for the smallest sign of humanity or goodness, I thrilled at the idea of killing him.

'What's all this?' he said.

'Cocktail hour. You're going to pour yourself a good stiff drink, amigo, and then you're going to drink to my health.'

'It looks like milk.'

'One hundred percent – and then some. Straight from Bessie the cow.'

'Milk's for kids. I can't stand the taste of that shit.'

'It's good for you. Makes for strong bones and a sunny disposition. Old as you look now, unc, it might not be such a bad idea to sip from the fountain of youth. It'll work wonders, believe me. A few sips of that liquid there, and you'll never look a day older than you do now.'

'You want me to pour the milk into the cup. Is that what you're saying?'

'Pour the milk into the cup, lift it in the air and say "Long life to you, Walt," and then start drinking. Drink the whole thing down. Drink it to the last drop.'

'And then what?'

'Then nothing. You'll be doing the world a great service, Slim, and God will reward you.'

'There's poison in this milk, ain't there?'

'Maybe there is, maybe there isn't. There's only one way to find out.'

'Shit. You gotta be crazy if you think I'm going to drink that stuff.'

'You don't drink it, a bullet goes into your head. You drink it, and maybe you've got a chance.'

'Sure. Just like that Chinaman in hell.'

'You never know. Maybe I'm doing this just to scare you. Maybe I want to drink a little toast with you before we get down to business.'

'Business? What kind of business?'

'Past business, present business. Maybe even future business. I'm broke, Slim, and I need a job. Maybe I'm here to ask your help.'

'Sure, I'll help you get a job. But I don't have to drink no milk to do that. If you want me to, I'll talk to Bingo first thing tomorrow morning.'

'Good. I'll hold you to that. But first we're going to drink our vitamin D.' I stepped forward to the edge of the table, reached out with the gun, and jabbed it under his chin – hard enough to make his head snap back. 'And we're going to drink it now.'

Slim's hands were trembling by then, but he went ahead and unscrewed the top of the jar. 'Don't spill it,' I said, as he started pouring the milk into the chalice. 'You spill one drop and I squeeze the trigger.' The white liquid flowed from one container into the other, and none of it landed on the table. 'Good,' I said, 'very good. Now lift the cup and say the toast.'

'Long life to you, Walt.'

The skunk was sweating bullets. I breathed in the whole foul stench of him as he brought the goblet to his lips, and I was glad, glad that he knew what was coming. I watched the terror mount in his eyes, and suddenly I was trembling along with him. Not from shame or regret – but from joy.

'Snark it down, you old fuck,' I said. 'Open your gullet and make with the glug-glug-glug.'

He shut his eyes, held his nose like a kid about to take his medicine, and started to drink. He was damned if he did and damned if he didn't, but at least I'd held out a little scrap of hope to him. Better that than the gun. Guns killed you for sure, but maybe I was only teasing him about the milk. And even if I wasn't, maybe he'd get lucky and survive the poison. When a man has only one chance, he's going to take it, even if it's the longest long shot on the board. So he plugged up his nose and went for it, and in spite of how I felt about him, I'll say this for the creep: he took his medicine like a good boy. He downed his death as if it were a dose of castor oil, and even though he shed some tears along the way, gasping and whimpering after each swallow, he gulped on bravely until it was gone.

I waited for the poison to kick in, standing there like a dummy as I watched Slim's face for signs of distress. The seconds ticked by, and still the bastard didn't keel over. I'd been expecting immediate results – death after one or two swallows – but the milk must have buffered the sting, and by the time my uncle slammed the empty cup down on the table, I was already wondering what had gone wrong.

'Fuck you,' he said. 'Fuck you, you bluffing son of a bitch.'

He must have seen the astonishment in my face. He'd drunk enough strychnine to kill an elephant, and yet there he was standing up and shoving his chair to the floor, grinning like a leprechaun who'd just won at Russian roulette. 'Stay where you are,' I said, gesturing at him with the gun. 'You'll be sorry if you don't.'

For all response, Slim burst out laughing. 'You don't have the guts, asshole.'

And he was right. He turned around and started walking

away, and I couldn't bring myself to fire the gun. He was giving me his back as a target, and I just stood there watching him, too shaken to pull the trigger. He took one step, then another step, and began disappearing into the shadows of the warehouse. I listened to his mocking, lunatic laughter bounce off the walls, and just when I couldn't stand it anymore, just when I thought he'd licked me for good, the poison caught up with him. He'd managed to take twenty or thirty steps by then, but that was as far as he got, which meant that I had the last laugh after all. I heard the sudden, choked-off gurgling in his throat, I heard the thud of his body hitting the floor, and when I finally stumbled my way through the dark and found him, he was flat-out stone dead.

Still, I didn't want to take anything for granted, so I dragged his corpse back toward the light to have a better look, pulling him face-down by the collar across the cement floor. I stopped a few feet from the table, but just when I was about to crouch down and put a bullet through Slim's head, a voice interrupted me from behind.

'Okay, buster,' the voice said. 'Drop the gat and put your hands in the air.'

I let go of the gun, I raised my hands, and then, very slowly, I turned around to face the stranger. He didn't strike me as anything special: a nondescript sort of guy in his late thirties or early forties. He was dressed in spiffy blue pinstripes and expensive black shoes and sported a peach-colored hanky in his front pocket. At first I thought he was older, but that was only because his hair had turned white on him. Once you looked into his face, you realized he wasn't old at all.

'You just knocked off one of my men,' he said. 'That's a no-no, kid. I don't care how young you are. You do something like that, you gotta pay the penalty.'

'Yeah, that's right,' I said, 'I killed the son-of-a-bitch. He had it coming, and I did him in. That's the way you treat vermin, mister. They crawl into your house, you get rid of

222

them. You can shoot me if you want, I don't care. I done what I came to do, and that's all that matters. If I die now, at least I'm going to die happy.'

The man's eyebrows went up about a sixteenth of an inch, then fluttered there for a moment in surprise. My little speech had thrown him, and he wasn't sure how to react. After thinking it over for a couple of seconds, it looked as if he decided to be amused. 'So you want to die now,' he said. 'Is that it?'

'I didn't say that. You're the one holding the gun, not me. If you want to pull the trigger, there's not a hell of a lot I can do about it.'

'And what if I don't shoot? What am I supposed to do with you then?'

'Well, seeing as how you just lost one of your men, you might think about hiring someone to replace him. I don't know how long Slim was on the payroll, but it must have been long enough for you to figure out what a crud-brained bucket of slime he was. If you didn't know that, I wouldn't be standing here now, would I? I'd be stretched out on the floor with a bullet in my heart.'

'Slim had his faults. I'm not going to argue with you about that.'

'You didn't lose much of anything, mister. You look at the plus and minus, and you'll see you're better off without him. Why pretend to feel sorry for a no-good nobody like Slim? Whatever he did for you, I'll do better. That's a promise.'

'You got some mouth on you, shorty.'

'After what I've been through these past three years, it's about the only thing I got left.'

'And what about a name? You still got one of those?'

'Walt.'

'Walt what?'

'Walt Rawley, sir.'

'Do you know who I am, Walt?'

223

'No, sir. I don't have a clue.'

'The name's Bingo Walsh. You ever hear of me?'

'Sure, I've heard of you. You're Mr Chicago. Right-hand man to Boss O'Malley. You're King of the Loop, Bingo, the shaker and mover who cranks the wheel and makes things spin.'

He couldn't help smiling at the buildup. You tell a number-two guy he's number one, and he's bound to appreciate the compliment. Considering that he still hadn't lowered the gun, I was in no mood to spread unkind words about him. As long as it kept me alive, I'd stand there scratching his back until the cows came home.

'Okay, Walt,' he said. 'We'll give it a shot. Two, three months, and then we'll see where we stand. Sort of a trial period to get acquainted. But if you don't pan out by then, I dump you. I send you off on a long trip.'

'To the same place where Slim just went, I suppose.'

'That's the deal I'm offering. Take it or leave it, kid.'

'It sounds fair to me. If I can't do the job, you cut off my head with an axe. Yeah, I can live with that. Why the hell not? If I can't catch on with you, Bingo, what's the use of living anyway?'

That was how my new career began. Bingo broke me in and taught me the ropes, and little by little I became his boy. The two-month trial period was hard on my nerves, but my head was still attached to my body by the time it ended, and after that I found myself warming to the business. O'Malley had one of the largest setups in Cook County, and Bingo was responsible for running the show. Gambling parlors, numbers operations, whorehouses, protection squads, slot machines – he managed all these enterprises with a firm hand, accountable to no one but the boss himself. I met up with him at a tumultuous moment, a period of transition and new opportunities, and by the time the year was out he'd solidified his position as one of the cleverest talents in the Midwest. I was lucky to have him as my mentor. Bingo took me under his wing, I kept my eyes open and listened to what he said, and my whole life turned around. After three years of desperation and hunger, I now had food in my stomach, money in my pocket, and decent clothes on my back. I was suddenly on my way again, and because I was Bingo's boy, doors opened whenever I knocked.

I started out as a gofer, running errands for him and doing odd little jobs. I lit his cigarettes and took his suits to the cleaners; I bought flowers for his girlfriends and polished the hubcaps on his car; I hopped to his commands like an eager pup. It sounds humiliating, but the fact was I didn't mind being a lackey. I knew my chance would come, and in the meantime I was just thankful he'd taken me on. It was the Depression, after all, and where else was someone like me going to get a better deal? I had no education, no skills, no training for anything except a career that was already finished, so I swallowed my pride and did what I was told. If I had to lick boots to earn my living, then so be it, I'd turn myself into the best bootlicker around. Who cared if I had to listen to Bingo's stories and laugh at his jokes? The guy wasn't a bad storyteller, and the truth was, he could be pretty funny when he wanted to be.

Once I proved my loyalty to him, he didn't hold me back. By early spring I was already climbing the ladder, and from then on the only question was how fast it would take me to get to the next rung. Bingo paired me with an ex-pug named Stutters Grogan, and Stutters and I began going the rounds of bars, restaurants, and candy stores to collect O'Malley's weekly protection money. As his name suggests, Stutters wasn't much on speechmaking, but I had a vivid way with words, and whenever we came across a slacker or deadbeat, I would paint such colorful pictures of what happened to clients who reneged on their payments that my partner rarely had to employ his fists. He was a useful prop, and it was good to have him for purposes of either-or demonstrations, but I prided myself on being able to settle conflicts without having to call on his services. Eventually, word got back to Bingo about my good track record, and he moved me up to a position on the South Side running numbers. Stutters and I had worked well together, but I preferred being on my own, and for the next six months I pounded the sidewalks in a dozen different colored neighborhoods, chatting up my regulars as they parted with their nickels and dimes for a shot at winning a few extra bucks. Everyone had a system, from the corner newsboy to the sexton in the church, and I liked listening to people tell me how they picked their combinations. The numbers came from everywhere. From birthdays and dreams, from batting averages and the price of potatoes, from cracks in the pavement, license plates, laundry lists, and the attendance at last Sunday's prayer meeting. The chances of winning were almost nil, so no one held it against me when they lost, but on those rare occasions when somebody hit the mark, I got turned into a messenger of good tidings. I was the Count of Lucky Dough, the fat-wadded Duke of Largesse, and I loved watching people's faces light up when I forked over the money. All in all, it wasn't an unpleasant job, and when Bingo finally promoted me again, I was almost sorry to leave.

From numbers I was shifted over to gambling, and by 1936 I was chief operating boss of a betting parlor on Locust Street, a snug, smoke-filled joint hidden away in the back room of a dry-cleaning establishment. The customers would arrive with their rumpled shirts and pants, drop them off at the front counter, and then push their way past the racks of hanging clothes to the secret room in the rear. Almost everyone who stepped into that place made some crack about getting taken to the cleaners. It was a standing joke with the men who worked under me, and after a while we began making bets on how many people would come out with it on a given day. As my bookkeeper Waldo McNair once put it: 'This is the only place in the world where they empty your pockets and press your pants at the same time. Blow your wad on the ponies, and you still can't lose your shirt.'

I ran a good little business in that room behind Benny's Cleaners. Traffic was heavy, but I hired a kid to keep it spic-and-span for me, and I always saw to it that butts were put out in ashtrays and not on the floor. My ticker-tape machines were the last word in modern equipment, with hookups to every major hippodrome around the country, and I kept the law off my back with regular donations to the private pension funds of half a dozen cops. I was twenty-one years old, and any way you looked at it I was sitting pretty. I lived in a classy room at the Featherstone Hotel, I had a closetful of suits that a wop tailor had cut for me at half price, I could trot out to Wrigley and take in a Cubs game any afternoon I pleased. That was already good, but on top of that there were women, lots of women, and I made sure my crotch saw all the action it could handle. After facing that terrible decision in Philadelphia seven years before, my balls had become exceedingly precious to me. I'd given up my shot at fame and fortune for their sake, and now that Walt the Wonder Boy was no more, I figured the best way to justify my choice was to use them as often as I could. I was no longer a virgin when I reached Chicago, but my career as a cocksman didn't get fully off the ground until I joined up with Bingo and had the cash to buy my way into any bloomers I fancied. My cherry had been lost to a farm girl named Velma Childe somewhere in western Pennsylvania, but that had been fairly rudimentary stuff: fumbling around with our clothes on out in a cold barn, our faces raw with saliva as we groped and grappled our way into position, not exactly certain what went where. A few months later, on the strength of the hundred-dollar bill I found in Minneapolis, I'd had two or three experiences with whores, but for all intents and purposes I was still a rank novice when I hit the streets of Hogtown. Once I settled into my new life, I did everything I could to make up for lost time.

So it went. I made a home for myself in the organization, and I never felt the smallest pang about throwing in my lot with the bad guys. I saw myself as one of them, I stood for what they stood for, and I never breathed a word to anyone about my past: not to Bingo, not to the girls I slept with, not to anyone. As long as I didn't dwell on the old days, I could deceive myself into thinking I had a future. It hurt too much to look back, so I kept my eyes fixed in front of me, and every time I took another step forward, I drifted farther away from the person I'd been with Master Yehudi. The best part of me was lying under the ground with him in the California desert. I'd buried him there along with his Spinoza, his scrapbook of Walt the Wonder Boy clippings, and the necklace with my severed finger joint, but even though I went back there every night in my dreams, it drove me crazy to think about it during

228

the day. Killing Slim was supposed to have squared the account, but in the long run it didn't do a bit of good. I wasn't sorry for what I'd done, but Master Yehudi was still dead, and all the Bingos in the world couldn't begin to make up for him. I strutted around Chicago as if I were going places, as if I were a regular Mr Somebody, but underneath it all I was no one. Without the master I was no one, and I wasn't going anywhere.

I had one chance to pull out before it was too late, a single opportunity to cut my losses and run, but I was too blind to go for it when the offer fell in my lap. That was in October of 1936, and I was so puffed up with my own importance by then, I thought the bubble would never burst. I'd ducked out of the cleaner's one afternoon to attend to some personal business: a shave and a haircut at Brower's barbershop, lunch at Lemmele's on Wabash Avenue, and then on to the Royal Park Hotel for some hanky-panky with a dancer named Dixie Sinclair. The rendezvous was set for two thirty in suite 409, and my pants were already bulging at the prospect. Six or seven yards before I reached Lemmele's door, however, just as I rounded the corner and was about to go in for my lunch, I looked up and saw the last person in the world I was expecting to see. It stopped me dead in my tracks. There was Mrs Witherspoon with her arms full of bundles, looking as pretty and smartly turned out as ever, rushing toward a taxi at a hundred and ten miles an hour. I stood there with a lump forming in my throat, and before I could say anything, she glanced up, flicked her eyes in my direction, and froze. I smiled. I smiled from one ear to the other, and then followed one of the most astonishing double-takes I've ever seen. Her jaw literally dropped open, the packages slipped out of her hands and scattered on the sidewalk, and a second later she was flinging her arms around me and planting lipstick all over my newly shaven mug.

'There you are, you rascal,' she said, squeezing me for all

she was worth. 'Now I've got you, you goddamn slippery son-of-a-bitch. Where the hell have you been, kiddo?'

'Here and there,' I said. 'Around and about. Up and down, down and up, the usual story. You look swell, Mrs Witherspoon. Really grand. Or should I be calling you Mrs Cox? That's your name now, isn't it? Mrs Orville Cox.'

She backed off to get a better look at me, holding me at arms' length as a big smile spread across her face. 'I'm still Witherspoon, honey. I got all the way to the altar, but when the time came to say "I do", the words got stuck in my throat. The dos turned into don'ts, and here I am seven years later, still a single girl and proud of it.'

'Good for you. I always knew that Cox guy was a mistake.'

'If it hadn't been for the present, I probably would have gone through with it. When Billy Bigelow brought back that package from Cape Cod, I couldn't resist taking a peek. A bride's not supposed to open her presents before the wedding, but this one was special, and once I unwrapped it, I knew the marriage wasn't meant to be.'

'What was in the box?'

'I thought you knew.'

'I never got around to asking him.'

'He gave me a globe. A globe of the world.'

'A globe? What's so special about that?'

'It wasn't the present, Walt. It was the note he sent along with it.'

'I never saw that either.'

'One sentence, that's all it was. *Wherever you are, I'll be with you*. I read those words, and then I fell apart. There was only one man for me, sweetie-pie. If I couldn't have him, I wasn't going to fool around with substitutes and cheap imitations.'

She stood there remembering the note as the downtown crowds swirled past us. The wind fluttered against the brim of her green felt hat, and after a moment her eyes started filling with tears. Before she could let go in earnest, I bent down and gathered up her packages. 'Come on inside, Mrs W.,' I said. 'I'll buy you some lunch, and then we'll order a tub of Chianti and get good and crocked.'

I slipped a ten-spot to the maître d' at the door and told him we wanted privacy. He shrugged, explaining that all the private tables were booked, so I peeled off another ten from my wad. That was good enough to cause an unexpected cancellation, and less than a minute later one of his minions was leading us through the restaurant to the back, where he installed us in a snug, candlelit alcove furnished with a set of red velvet curtains to shield us from the other customers. I would have done anything to impress Mrs Witherspoon that day, and I don't think she was disappointed. I saw the flash of amusement in her eyes as we settled into our chairs, and when I whipped out my monogrammed gold lighter to get her Chesterfield going, it suddenly seemed to hit her that little Walt wasn't so little anymore.

'We're doing all right for ourselves, aren't we?' she said.

'Not bad,' I said. 'I've been running pretty hard since you last saw me.'

We talked about this and that, circling around each other for the first few minutes, but it didn't take long for us to start feeling comfortable again, and by the time the waiter came in with the menus, we were already talking about the old days. As it turned out, Mrs Witherspoon knew a lot more about my last months with the master than I thought she did. A week before he died, he'd written her a long letter from the road, and everything had been spelled out to her: the headaches, the end of Walt the Wonder Boy, the plan to go to Hollywood and turn me into a movie star.

'I don't get it,' I said. 'If you and the master were quits, what was he doing writing you a letter?'

'We weren't quits. We just weren't going to get married, that's all.'

'I still don't get it.'

'He was dying, Walt. You know that. You must have known it by then. He found out about the cancer not long after you were kidnaped. A fine little mess, no? Talk about hell. Talk about your rough patches. There we were, scrambling around Wichita trying to scrape up the money to free you, and he comes down with a goddamn fatal disease. That's how all the marriage talk got started in the first place. I was gung-ho to marry him, you see. I didn't care how long he had to live, I just wanted to be his wife. But he wouldn't go for it. "You hitch up with me," he said, "and you'll be marrying a corpse. Think of the future, Marion" – he must have said those words to me a thousand times – "think of the future, Marion. This Cox fellow isn't too bad. He'll give us the money to spring Walt, and then you'll be set up in style for the rest of your days. It's a sweet deal, sister, and you'd be a fool not to jump at it." '

'Sweet fucking Christ. He really loved you, didn't he? I mean, he really fucking loved you.'

'He loved us both, Walt. After what happened to Aesop and Mother Sioux, you and I were the whole world to him.'

I had no intention of telling her how he'd died. I wanted to spare her the gory details, and all through drinks I managed to hold her off – but she kept pressing me to talk about the last part of the trip, to explain what happened to us after we got to California. Why hadn't I gone into the movies? How long had he lived? Why was I looking at her like that? I started to tell her how he'd slipped off gently in his sleep one night, but she knew me too well to buy it. She saw through me in about four seconds, and once she understood that I was covering up something, it was no use pretending anymore. So I told her. I told her the whole ugly story, and step by step I crawled down into the horror of it again. I didn't leave anything out. Mrs Witherspoon had a right to know, and once I got started, I couldn't stop. I just talked on through her tears, watching her makeup smudge

232

and the powder run off her cheeks as the words tumbled out of me.

When I got to the end, I opened my jacket and pulled the gun from the holster strapped around my shoulder. I held it in the air for a moment or two and then set it down on the table between us. 'Here it is,' I said. 'The master's gun. Just so you know what it looks like.'

'Poor Walt,' she said.

'Poor nobody. It's the only thing of his I've got left.'

Mrs Witherspoon stared at the small, oak-handled revolver for ten or twelve seconds. Then, very tentatively, she reached out and put her hand on top of it. I thought she was going to pick it up, but she didn't. She just sat there looking at her fingers as they closed around the gun, as if touching what the master had touched allowed her to touch him again.

'You did the only thing you could,' she finally said.

'I let him down is what I did. He begged me to pull the trigger, and I couldn't do it. His last wish – and I turned my back on him and made him do it himself.'

'Remember the good times, that's what he told you.'

'I can't. Before I get to the good times, I remember what it was like when he told me to remember them. I can't get around that last day. I can't go back far enough to remember anything before it.'

'Forget the gun, Walt. Get rid of the damn thing and wipe the slate clean.'

'I can't. If I do that, he'll be gone forever.'

That was when she stood up from her chair and left the table. She didn't say where she was going, and I didn't ask. The conversation had turned so heavy, so awful for both of us, we couldn't say another word and not go crazy. I put the gun back in the holster and looked at my watch. One o'clock. I had plenty of time until my appointment with Dixie. Maybe Mrs Witherspoon would be back, and maybe she wouldn't. One way or the other, I was going to sit there and eat my

233

lunch, and afterward I was going to prance over to the Royal Park Hotel and spend an hour with my new flame, bouncing on the bed with her silky gams wrapped around my waist.

But Mrs W. hadn't flown the coop. She'd merely gone to the ladies' to dry her tears and freshen up, and when she returned about ten minutes later, she was wearing a new coat of lipstick and had redone her lashes. Her eyes were still red around the rims, but she shot me a little smile when she sat down, and I could see that she was determined to push the conversation onto a different subject.

'So, my friend,' she said, taking a bite of her shrimp cocktail, 'how's the flying business these days?'

'Packed away in mothballs,' I said. 'The fleet's been grounded, and one by one I've been selling off the wings for scrap.'

'And you don't feel tempted to give it another whirl?'

'Not for all the crackers in Kalamazoo.'

'The headaches were that bad, huh?'

'You don't know the meaning of bad, toots. We're talking high-voltage trauma here, life-threatening toaster burns.'

'It's funny. I sometimes hear conversations. You know, sitting in a train or walking down the street, little snatches of things. People remember, Walt. The Wonder Boy made quite a stir, and a lot of people still think about you.'

'Yeah, I know. I'm a fucking legend. The problem is, nobody believes it anymore. They stopped believing when the act folded, and by now there's nobody left. I know the kind of talk you mean. I used to hear it, too. It always ended up in an argument. One guy would say it was a fake, the other guy would say maybe it wasn't, and pretty soon they'd be so pissed off at each other they'd stop talking. But that was a while ago. You don't hear so much of it anymore. It's like the whole thing never happened.'

'About two years ago they ran an article about you somewhere, I forget which paper. Walt the Wonder Boy, the little

234

lad who fired the imagination of millions. Whatever happened to him, and where is he now? That kind of article.'

'He fell off the face of the earth, that's what happened to him. The angels carried him back to where he came from, and no one's ever going to see him again.'

'Except me.'

'Except you. But that's our little secret, isn't it?'

'Mum's the word, Walt. What kind of person do you take me for anyway?'

Things loosened up quite a bit after that. The busboy came in to haul off the appetizer plates, and by the time the waiter returned with the main course, we'd drunk enough to be ready for a second bottle.

'I see you haven't lost your taste for the stuff,' I said.

'Booze, money, and sex. Those are the eternal verities.'

'In that order?'

'In any order you like. Without them the world would be a sad and dismal place.'

'Speaking of sad places, what's new in Wichita?'

'Wichita?' She put down her glass and gave me a gorgeous shit-eating grin. 'Where's that?'

'I don't know. You tell me.'

'I can't remember. I packed my bags five years ago and haven't set foot in that town since.'

'Who bought the house?'

'I didn't sell it. Billy Bigelow lives there with his chatterbox wife and two little girls. I thought the rent would give me some nice pin money, but the poor sap lost his job at the bank a month after they moved in, and I've been letting him have it for a dollar a year.'

'You must be doing okay if you can afford that.'

'I pulled out of the market the summer before the crash. Something to do with ransom notes, cash deliveries, drop-off points – it's all a bit blurry now. It turned out to be the best thing that ever happened to me. Your little misadventure saved my life, Walt. Whatever I was worth then, I'm worth ten times that now.'

'Why stay in Wichita with that kind of dough, right? How long since you moved to Chicago?'

'I'm just here on business. I go back to New York tomorrow morning.'

'Fifth Avenue, I'll bet.'

'You bet right, Mr Rawley.'

'I knew it the second I saw you. You look like big money now. It gives off a special smell, and I like sitting here breathing in the vapors.'

'Most of it comes from oil. That stuff stinks in the ground, but once you convert it into cash, it does release a lovely perfume, doesn't it?'

She was the same old Mrs Witherspoon. She still liked to drink, and she still liked to talk about money, and once you uncorked a bottle and steered her onto her favorite subject, she could hold her own with any cigar-chomping capitalist this side of Daddy Warbucks. She spent the rest of the main course telling me about her deals and investments, and when the plates were carted off again and the waiter slid back in with the dessert menus, something went click, and I could see the lightbulb go on in her head. It was a quarter to two by my watch. Come fire or flood, I aimed to be out of there in half an hour.

'If you want in, Walt,' she said, 'I'll be happy to make a place for you.'

'Place? What kind of place?'

'Texas. I've got some new wildcat rigs down there, and I need someone to watch over the drilling for me.'

'I don't know the first thing about oil.'

'You're smart. You'll catch on fast. Look at the progress you've made already. Nice clothes, fancy restaurants, money in your pocket. You've come a long way, sport. And don't

236

think I haven't noticed how you've cleaned up your grammar. Not one "ain't" the whole time we've been together.'

'Yeah, I worked hard on that. I didn't want to sound like an ignoramus anymore, so I read some books and retooled my word-box. I figured it was time to step out of the gutter.'

'That's my point. You can do anything you want to do. As long as you put your mind to it, there's no telling where you might go. You watch, Walt. Come in with me, and two or three years from now we'll be partners.'

It was a hell of an endorsement, but once I'd soaked up her praise I snubbed out my Camel and shook my head. 'I like what I'm doing now. Why go to Texas when I've got everything I want in Chicago?'

'Because you're in the wrong business, that's why. There's no future in this cops-and-robbers stuff. You keep it up, and you'll either be dead or serving time before your twenty-fifth birthday.'

'What cops-and-robbers stuff? I'm clean as a surgeon's fingernails.'

'Sure. And the pope's a Hindu snake charmer in disguise.'

Dessert was wheeled in after that, and we nibbled at our eclairs in silence. It was a bad way to end the meal, but we were both too stubborn to back down. Eventually, we made small talk about the weather, threw out some inconsequential remarks about the upcoming election, but the juice was gone and there was no getting it back. Mrs Witherspoon wasn't just peeved at me for turning down her offer. Chance had thrown us together again, and only a bungler would pass up the call of fate as blithely as I had. She wasn't wrong to feel disgusted with me, but I had my own path to follow, and I was too full of myself to understand that my path was the same as hers. If I hadn't been so hot to run off and plant my pecker in Dixie Sinclair, I might have listened to her more carefully, but I was in a rush, and I couldn't be bothered with any soul-searching that day. So it goes. Once your groin gets the upper hand, you lose the ability to reason.

We skipped coffee, and when the waiter delivered the check to the table at ten past two, I snatched it out of his fingers before Mrs Witherspoon could grab hold of it.

'My treat,' I said.

'Okay, Mr Big Time. Show off if it makes you happy. But if you ever wise up, don't forget where I am. Maybe you'll come to your senses before it's too late.' And with that she reached into her purse, pulled out her business card, and laid it gently in my palm. 'Don't worry about the cost,' she added. 'If you're belly-up by the time you remember me, just tell the operator to reverse the charges.'

But I never called. I stuck the card in my pocket, fully intending to save it, but when I looked for it before going to bed that night, it was nowhere to be found. Given the tusseling and tugging those trousers were subjected to immediately following lunch, it wasn't hard to guess what had happened. The card had fallen out, and if it hadn't already been tossed into the trash by a chambermaid, it was lying on the floor in suite 409 of the Royal Park Hotel.

I was an unstoppable force in those days, a comer to beat all comers, and I was riding the express train with a one-way ticket to Fat City. Less than a year after my lunch with Mrs Witherspoon, I landed my next big break when I went out to Arlington one sultry August afternoon and put a thousand dollars on a long shot to win the third race. If I add that the horse was dubbed Wonder Boy, and if I further add that I was still in the thrall of my old superstitions, it won't take a mind reader to understand why I bit on such a hopeless gamble. I did crazy things as a matter of routine back then, and when the colt came in by half a length at forty to one, I knew there was a God in heaven and that he was smiling down on my craziness.

The winnings provided me with the clout to do the thing I most wanted to do, and I promptly set about to turn my dream into reality. I requested a private counsel with Bingo in his penthouse apartment overlooking Lake Michigan, and once I laid out the plan to him and he got over his initial shock, he grudgingly gave me the green light. It wasn't that he thought the proposition was unworthy, but I think he was disappointed in me for setting my sights so low. He was grooming me for a place in the inner circle, and here I was telling him that I wanted to go my own way and open a nightclub that would occupy my energies to the exclusion of all else. I could see how he might interpret it as an act of betrayal, and I had to tread carefully around that trap with some fancy footwork. Luckily, my mouth was in good form that evening, and by showing how many advantages would accrue to him in terms of both profit and pleasure, I eventually brought him around.

'My forty grand can cover the whole deal,' I said. 'Another

guy in my shoes would tip his hat and say so long, but that's
not how I conduct business. You're my pal, Bingo, and I want
you to have a piece of the action. No money down, no work
to fuss with, no liabilities, but for every dollar I earn, I'll give
you twenty-five cents. Fair is fair, right? You gave me my
chance, and now I'm in a position to return the favor. Loyalty
has to count for something in this world, and I'm not about
to forget where my luck came from. This won't be any two-
bit cheese joint for the hoi polloi. I'm talking Gold Coast with
all the trimmings. A full-scale restaurant with a Frog chef,
top-notch floor shows, beautiful girls slithering out of the
woodwork in skin-tight gowns. It'll give you a hard-on just
to walk in there, Bingo. You'll have the best seat in the house,
and on nights when you don't show up, your table will sit
there empty – no matter how many people are waiting outside
the door.'
   He haggled me up to fifty percent, but I was expecting
some give-and-take and didn't make an issue of it. The
important thing was to win his blessing, and I did that by
jollying him along, steadily wearing down his defenses with
my friendly, accommodating attitude, and in the end, just to
show how classy he was, he offered to kick in an extra ten
thousand to see that I did up the place right. I didn't care.
All I wanted was my nightclub, and with Bingo's fifty percent
subtracted from the take, I was still going to come out ahead.
There were numerous benefits in having him as a partner,
and I would have been kidding myself to think I could get
along without him. His half would guarantee me protection
from O'Malley (who ipso facto became the third partner) and
help keep the cops from breaking down the door. When you
threw in his connections with the Chicago liquor board, the
commercial laundry companies, and the local talent agents,
losing that fifty percent didn't seem like such a shabby
compromise after all.
   I called the place Mr Vertigo's. It was smack in the heart of

240

the city at West Division and North LaSalle, and its flashing neon sign went from pink to blue to pink as a dancing girl took turns with a cocktail shaker against the night sky. The rhumba rhythm of those lights made your heart beat faster and your blood grow warm, and once you caught the little stutter-step syncopation in your pulse, you didn't want to be anywhere except where the music was. Inside, the decor was a blend of high and low, a swank sort of big town comfort mixed with naughty innuendos and an easy, roadhouse charm. I worked hard on creating that atmosphere, and every nuance and effect was planned to the smallest detail: from the lip rouge on the hat-check girl to the color of the dinner plates, from the design of the menus to the socks on the bartender's feet. There was room for fifty tables, a good-size dance floor, an elevated stage, and a long mahogany bar along a side wall. It cost me every cent of the fifty thousand to do it up the way I wanted, but when the place finally opened on December 31, 1937, it was a thing of sumptuous perfection. I launched it with one of the great New Year's Eve parties in Chicago history, and by the following morning Mr Vertigo's was on the map. For the next three and a half years I was there every night, strolling among the customers in my white dinner jacket and patent leather shoes, spreading good cheer with my cocky smiles and quick-tongued patter. It was a terrific spot for me, and I loved every minute I spent in that raucous emporium. If I hadn't messed up and blown my life apart, I'd probably still be there today. As it was, I only got to have those three and a half years. I was one-hundred-percent responsible for my own downfall, but knowing that doesn't make it any less painful to remember. I was all the way at the top when I stumbled, and it ended in a real Humpty Dumpty for me, a spectacular swan-dive into oblivion.

But no regrets. I had a good dance for my money, and I'm not going to say I didn't. The club turned into the number-one hot spot in Chicago, and in my own small way I was just as much a celebrity as any of the bigwigs who came in there. I hobnobbed with judges and city councilmen and ball players, and what with all the showgirls and chorines to audition for the flesh parades I presented at eleven and one every night, there was no lack of opportunity to indulge in bedroom sports. Dixie and I were still an item when Mr Vertigo's opened, but my carryings-on wore her patience thin, and within six months she'd moved to another address. Then came Sally, then came Jewel, then came a dozen others: leggy brunettes, chain-smoking redheads, big-butted blondes. At one point I was shacked up with two girls at the same time, a pair of out-of-work actresses named Cora and Billie. I liked them both the same, they liked each other as much as they liked me, and by pulling together we managed to produce some interesting variations on the old tune. Every now and then, my habits led to medical inconveniences (a dose of the clap, a case of crabs), but nothing that put me out of commission for very long. It might have been a putrid way to live, but I was happy with the hand I'd been dealt, and my only ambition was to keep things exactly as they were. Then, in September 1939, just three days after the German Army invaded Poland, Dizzy Dean walked into Mr Vertigo's and it all started to come undone.

I have to go back to explain it, all the way back to my tykehood in Saint Louis. That's where I fell in love with baseball, and before I was out of diapers I was a dyed-in-the-wool Cardinals fan, a Redbird rooter for life. I've already mentioned how thrilled I was when they took the 'twenty-six series, but that was only one instance of my devotion, and after Aesop taught me how to read and write, I was able to follow my boys in the paper every morning. From April to October I never missed a box score, and I could recite the batting average of every player on the squad, from hot dogs like Frankie Frisch and Pepper Martin to the lowest journeyman scrub gathering splinters on the bench. This went on during the good years with Master Yehudi, and it continued during the bad years that followed. I lived like a shadow, prowling the country in search of Uncle Slim, but no matter how dark things got for me, I still kept up with my team. They won the pennant in 'thirty and 'thirty-one, and those victories did a lot to buck up my spirits, to keep me going through all the trouble and adversity of that time. As long as the Cards were winning, something was right with the world, and it wasn't possible to fall into total despair.

That's where Dizzy Dean enters the story. The team dropped to seventh place in 'thirty-two, but it almost didn't matter. Dean was the hottest, flashiest, loudest-mouthed rookie ever to hit the majors, and he turned a crummy ball club into a loosey-goosey hillbilly circus. Brag and cavort as he did, that cornpone rube backed up his boasts with some of the sweetest pitching this side of heaven. His rubber arm threw smoke; his control was uncanny; his windup was a wondrous machine of arms and legs and power, a beautiful thing to behold. By the time I got to Chicago and settled in as Bingo's protégé, Dizzy was an established star, a big-time force on the American scene. People loved him for his brashness and talent, his crazy manglings of the English language, his brawling, boyish antics and fuck-you pizzazz, and I loved him, too, I loved him as much as anyone in the world. With life growing more comfortable for me all the time, I was in a position to catch the Cards in action whenever they came to town. In 'thirty-three, the year Dean broke the record by striking out seventeen batters in a game, they looked like a first-division outfit again. They'd added some new players to the roster, and with thugs like Joe Medwick, Leo Durocher, and Rip Collins around to quicken the pace, the Gas House Gang was beginning to jell. 'Thirty-four turned out to be their glory year, and I don't think I've ever enjoyed a baseball season as much as that one. Dizzy's kid brother Paul won nineteen games, Dizzy won thirty, and the team fought from ten games back to overtake the Giants and win the pennant. That was the first year the World Series was broadcast on the radio, and I got to listen to all seven games sitting at home in Chicago. Dizzy beat the Tigers in the first game, and when Frisch sent him in as a pinch runner in the fourth, the lummox promptly got beaned with a wild throw and was knocked unconscious. The next day's headlines announced: *X-Rays of Dean's Head Reveal Nothing*. He came back to pitch the following afternoon but lost, and then, just two days later, he shut out Detroit 11–0 in the final game, laughing at the Tiger hitters each time they swung and missed at his fastballs. The press cooked up all kinds of names for that team: the Galloping Gangsters, River Rowdies from the Mississippi, the Clattering Cardinals. Those Gas Housers loved to rub it in, and when the score of the final game got out of hand in the late innings, the Tiger fans responded by pelting Medwick with a ten-minute barrage of fruits and vegetables in left field. The only way they could finish the series was for Judge Landis, the commissioner of baseball, to step in and pull Medwick off the field for the last three outs.

Six months later, I was sitting in a box with Bingo and the boys when Dean opened the new season against the Cubs in Chicago. In the first inning, with two down and a man on base, the Cubs' cleanup hitter Freddie Lindstrom sent a wicked line drive up the middle that caught Dizzy in the leg and knocked him down. My heart skipped a beat or two when I saw the stretcher gang run out and carry him off the field, but no permanent damage was done, and five days later he was back on the mound in Pittsburgh, where he hurled a five-hit shutout for his first win of the season. He went on to have another bang-up year, but the Cubs were the team of destiny in 1935, and by knocking off a string of twenty-one straight wins at the end of the season, they pushed past the Cards and stole the flag. I can't say I minded too much. The town went gaga for the Cubbies, and what was good for Chicago was good for business, and what was good for business was good for me. I cut my teeth on the gambling rackets in that series, and once the dust had settled, I'd maneuvered myself into such a strong position that Bingo rewarded me with a den of my own.

On the other hand, that was the year when Dizzy's ups and downs began to affect me in a far too personal way. I wouldn't call it an obsession at that point, but after watching him go down in the first inning of the opener at Wrigley – so soon after the skull-clunking in the 'thirty-four series – I began to sense that a cloud was gathering around him. It didn't help matters when his brother's arm went dead in 'thirty-six, but even worse was what happened in a game against the Giants that summer when Burgess Whitehead scorched a liner that hit him just above the right ear. The ball was hit so hard that it caromed into left field on a fly. Dean went down again, and though he regained consciousness in the locker room seven or eight minutes later, the initial diagnosis was a fractured skull. It turned out to be a bad concussion, which left him woozy for a couple of weeks, but an inch or so the other way and the big guy would have been pushing up daisies instead of going on to win twenty-four games for the season.

The following spring, my man continued to curse and scuffle and raise hell, but that was only because he didn't know any better. He triggered brawls with his brushback pitches, was called for balks two games in a row and decided to stage a sit-down strike on the mound, and when he stood up at a banquet and called the new league president a crook, the resulting fracas led to some fine cowboy theater, especially after Diz refused to put his signature on a self-incriminating formal retraction. 'I ain't signin' nothin'' was what he said, and without that signature Ford Frick had no choice but to back down and rescind Dean's suspension. I was proud of him for behaving like such a two-fisted asshole, but the truth

245

was that the suspension would have kept him out of the All-Star Game, and if he hadn't pitched in that meaningless exhibition, he might have been able to hold off the hour of doom a little longer.

They played in Washington, D.C., that year, and Dizzy started for the National League. He breezed through the first two innings in workmanlike fashion, and then, after two were gone in the third, he gave up a single to DiMaggio and a long home run to Gehrig. Earl Averill was next, and when the Cleveland outfielder lined Dean's first pitch back to the mound, the curtain suddenly dropped on the greatest right-hander of the century. It didn't look like much to worry about at the time. The ball hit him on the left foot, bounced over to Billy Herman at second, and Herman threw to first for the out. When Dizzy went limping off the field, no one thought twice about it, not even Dizzy himself.

That was the famous broken toe. If he hadn't rushed back into action before he was ready, it probably would have mended in due time. But the Cardinals were slipping out of the pennant race and needed him on the mound, and the dumb-cluck yokel fool assured them he was okay. He was hobbling around on a crutch, the toe was so swollen he couldn't get his shoe on, and yet he donned his uniform and went out and pitched. Like all giants among men, Dizzy Dean thought he was immortal, and even though the toe was too tender for him to pivot on his left foot, he gutted it out for the whole nine innings. The pain caused him to alter his natural delivery, and the result was that he put too much pressure on his arm. He developed a sore wing after that first game, and then, to compound the mischief, he went on throwing for another month. After six or seven times around, it got so bad that he had to be yanked just three pitches into one of his starts. Diz was lobbing canteloupes by then, and there was nothing for it but to hang up his spikes and sit out the rest of the season.

Even so, there wasn't a fan in the country who thought he was finished. The common wisdom was that a winter of idle repose would fix what ailed him and come April he'd be his old unbeatable self again. But he struggled through spring training, and then, in one of the great bombshells in sports history, Saint Louis dealt him to the Cubs for $185,000 in cash and two or three warm bodies. I knew there was no love lost between Dean and Branch Rickey, the Cards' general manager, but I also knew that Rickey wouldn't have unloaded him if he thought there was some spit left in the appleknocker's arm. I couldn't have been happier that Dizzy was coming to Chicago, but at the same time I knew his coming meant that he was at the end of the road. My worst fears had been borne out, and at the ripe old age of twenty-seven or twenty-eight, the world's top pitcher was a has-been.

Still, he provided some good moments that first year with the Cubs. Mr Vertigo's was only four months old when the season started, but I managed to sneak off to the park three or four times to watch the Dizmeister crank out a few more innings from his battered arm. There was an early game against the Cards that I remember well, a classic grudge match pitting old teammates against each other, and he won that showdown on guile and junk, keeping the hitters off-stride with an assortment of dipsy-doodle floaters and change-ups. Then, late in the season, with the Cubs pushing hard for another pennant, Chicago manager Gabby Hartnett stunned everyone by giving Dizzy the nod for a do-or-die start against the Pirates. The game was a genuine knuckle-biter, joy and despair riding on every pitch, and Dean, with less than nothing to offer, eked out a win for his new hometown. He almost repeated the miracle in the second game of the World Series, but the Yanks finally got to him in the eighth, and when the assault continued in the ninth and Hartnett took him out for a reliever, Dizzy left the mound to some of the wildest, most thunderous applause I've ever heard. The whole joint was on its feet, clapping and cheering and whistling for the big lug, and it went on for so long and was so loud, some of us were blinking away tears by the time it was over.

That should have been the end of him. The gallant warrior takes his last bow and shuffles off into the sunset. I would have accepted that and given him his due, but Dean was too thick to get it, and the farewell clamor fell on deaf ears. That's what galled me: the son-of-a-bitch didn't know when to stop. Casting all dignity aside, he came back and played for the Cubs again, and if the 'thirty-eight season had been pathetic – with a few bright spots sprinkled in – 'thirty-nine was pure, unadulterated darkness. His arm hurt so much he could barely throw. Game after game he warmed the bench, and the brief moments he spent on the mound were an embarrassment. He was lousy, lousier than a hobo's mutt, not even the palest facsimile of what he'd once been. I suffered for him, I grieved for him, but at the same time I thought he was the dumbest yahoo clod on the face of the earth.

That was pretty much how things stood when he walked into Mr Vertigo's in September. The season was winding down, and with the Cubs well out of the pennant race, it didn't cause much of a stir when Dean showed up one crowded Friday night with his missus and a gang of two or three other couples. It certainly wasn't the moment for a heart-to-heart talk about his future, but I made a point of going over to his table and welcoming him to the club. 'Pleased you could make it, Diz,' I said, offering him my hand. 'I'm a Saint Louis boy myself, and I've been following you since the day you broke in. I've always been your number-one backer.'

'The pleasure's all mine, pal,' he said, engulfing my little hand in his enormous mitt and giving a cordial shake. He started to flash one of those quick, brush-off smiles when his expression suddenly grew puzzled. He frowned for a second, searching his memory for some lost thing, and when it didn't

248

come to him, he looked deep into my eyes as if he thought he could find it there. 'I know you, don't I?' he said. 'I mean, this ain't the first time we've met. I just can't place where it was. Way back somewhere, ain't I right?'

'I don't think so, Diz. Maybe you caught a glimpse of me one day in the stands, but we've never talked before.'

'Shit. I could swear you ain't no stranger to me. Damnedest feeling in the world it is. Oh well,' he shrugged, beaming me one of his big yap grins, 'it don't matter none, I guess. You sure got a swell joint here, mac.'

'Thanks, champ. The first round's on me. I hope you and your friends have a good time.'

'That's why we're here, kid.'

'Enjoy the show. If you need anything, just holler.'

I'd played it as cool as I could, and I walked away feeling I'd handled the situation fairly well. I hadn't sucked up to him, and at the same time I hadn't insulted him for going to the dogs. I was Mr Vertigo, the downtown sharpie with the smooth tongue and elegant manners, and I wasn't about to let Dean know how much his plight concerned me. Seeing him in the flesh had broken the spell somewhat, and in the natural course of things I probably would have written him off as just another nice guy down on his luck. Why should I care about him? Whizzy Dizzy was on his way out, and pretty soon I wouldn't have to think about him anymore. But that's not the way it happened. It was Dean himself who kept the thing alive, and while I'm not going to pretend we became bosom buddies, he stayed in close enough contact to make it impossible for me to forget him. If he'd just drifted off the way he was supposed to, none of it would have turned out as badly as it did.

I didn't see him again until the start of the next season. It was April 1940 by then, the war in Europe was going full tilt, and Dizzy was back – back for yet another stab at reviving his tumbledown career. When I picked up the paper and read that he'd signed another contract with the Cubs, I nearly choked on my salami sandwich. Who was he kidding? 'The ol' soup bone ain't the buggy whip it used to be,' he said, but Christ, he just loved the game too damned much not to give it another try. All right, dumbbell, I said to myself, see if I care. If you want to humiliate yourself in front of the world, that's your business, but don't count on me to feel sorry for you.

Then, out of the blue, he wandered back into the club one night and greeted me like a long-lost brother. Dean wasn't someone who drank, so it couldn't have been booze that made him act like that, but his face lit up when he saw me, and for the next five minutes he gave me an all-out dose of herkimer-jerkimer bonhomie. Maybe he was still stuck on the idea that we knew each other, or maybe he thought I was somebody important, I don't know, but the upshot was that he couldn't have been more delighted to see me. How to resist a guy like that? I'd done everything I could to harden my heart against him, and yet he came on in such a friendly way that I couldn't help but succumb to the attention. He was still the great Dean, after all, my benighted soulmate and alter ego, and once he opened up to me like that, I fell right back into the snare of my old bedevilment.

I wouldn't say that he became a regular at the club, but he stopped by often enough over the next six weeks for us to strike up more than just a passing acquaintance. He came in alone a few times to eat an early supper (dowsing every dish with gobs of Lea & Perrins steak sauce), and I'd sit with him shooting the breeze while he chomped down his food. We skirted baseball talk and mostly stuck to the horses, and since I gave him a couple of excellent tips on where to put his money, he began listening to my advice. I should have spoken up then and told him what I thought about his comeback, but even after he muddled through his first starts of the season, disgracing himself every time he stepped onto the field, I didn't say a word. I'd grown too fond of him by then, and with the sad sack trying so hard to make good, I couldn't bring myself to tell him the truth.

After a couple of months, his wife Pat persuaded him to go down to the minors to work on a new delivery. The idea was that he'd make better progress out of the spotlight – a frantic ploy if there ever was one, since all it did was support the delusion that there was still some hope for him. That's when I finally got up the nerve to say something, but I didn't have the guts to push hard enough.

'Maybe it's time, Diz,' I said. 'Maybe it's time to pack it in and head home to the farm.'

'Yeah,' he said, looking about as dejected as a man can look. 'You're probably right. Problem is, I ain't fit for nothin' but throwin' baseballs. I flunk out this time, and I'm up shit's creek, Walt. I mean, what else can a bum like me do with hisself?'

Plenty of things, I thought, but I didn't say it, and later that week he left for Tulsa. Never had a great one fallen so far so fast. He spent a long, miserable summer in the Texas League, traveling the same dusty circuit he'd demolished with fastballs ten years before. This time he could barely hold his own, and the rinky-dinks and Mickey Mousers sprayed his pitches all over the lot. Old delivery or new, the verdict was clear, but Dizzy went on busting his chops and didn't let the rough treatment get him down. Once he'd showered and dressed and left the park, he'd go back to his hotel room with a stack of racing forms and start phoning his bookies. I handled a number of bets for him that summer, and every time he called we'd jaw for five or ten minutes and catch up on each other's news. The incredible thing to me was how calmly he accepted his disgrace. The guy had turned himself into a laughingstock, and yet he seemed to be in good spirits, as gabby and full of jokes as ever. What was the use of arguing? I figured it was only a matter of time now, so I played along with him and kept my thoughts to myself. Sooner or later, he was bound to see the light.

The Cubs recalled him in September. They wanted to see if the bush-league experiment had paid off, and while his performance was hardly encouraging, it wasn't as dreadful as it might have been. Mediocre was the word for it – a couple of close wins, a couple of shellackings – and therein hung the final chapter of the story. By some ditsy, screwball logic, the Cubs decided that Dean had shown enough of his old flair to warrant another season, and so they went ahead and asked him back. I didn't find out about the new contract until after he left town for the winter, but when I did, something inside me finally snapped. I stewed about it for months. I fretted and worried and sulked, and by the time spring came around again, I understood what had to be done. It wasn't as if I felt there was a choice. Destiny had chosen me as its instrument, and gruesome as the task might have been, saving Dizzy was the only thing that mattered. If he couldn't do it himself, then I'd have to step in and do it for him.

Even now, I'm hard-pressed to explain how such a twisted, evil notion could have wormed its way into my head. I actually thought it was my duty to persuade Dizzy Dean that he didn't want to live anymore. Stated in such bald terms, the whole thing smacks of insanity, but that was precisely how I planned to rescue him: by talking him into his own murder. If nothing else, it proves how sick my soul had become in the years since Master Yehudi's death. I'd latched onto Dizzy because he reminded me of myself, and as long as his career flourished, I could relive my past glory through him. Maybe it wouldn't have happened if he'd pitched for some town other than Saint Louis. Maybe it wouldn't have happened if our nicknames hadn't been so similar. I don't know. I don't know anything, but the fact was that a moment came when I couldn't tell the difference between us anymore. His triumphs were my triumphs, and when bad luck finally caught up with

252

him and his career fell apart, his disgrace was my disgrace. I couldn't stand to live through it again, and little by little I began to lose my grip. For his own good, Dizzy had to die, and I was just the man to urge him into making the right decision. Not only for his sake, but for my sake as well. I had the weapon, I had the arguments, I had the power of madness on my side. I would destroy Dizzy Dean, and in so doing I would finally destroy myself.

The Cubs hit Chicago for the home opener on April tenth. I got Diz on the horn that same afternoon and asked him to stop by my office, explaining that something important had come up. He tried to get me to come out with it, but I told him it was too big to discuss on the phone. If you're interested in a proposition that will turn your life around, I said, you'll come. He was tied up until after dinner, so we set the appointment for eleven o'clock the next morning. He showed up only fifteen minutes late, sauntering in with that loose-jointed stride of his and rolling a toothpick around on his tongue. He was wearing a worsted blue suit and a tan cowboy hat, and while he'd put on a few pounds since I'd seen him last, his complexion had a healthy tint after six weeks in the Cactus League sun. As usual, he was all smiles when he walked in, and he spent the first couple of minutes talking about how different the club looked in the daytime without any customers in it. 'Reminds me of an empty ballpark,' he said. 'Kinda creepy like. Still as a tomb, and a helluva lot bigger.'

I told him to take a seat and fixed him up with a root beer from the ice box behind my desk. 'This will take a few minutes,' I said, 'and I don't want you getting thirsty while we talk.' I could feel my hands starting to shake, so I poured myself a shot of Jim Beam and took a couple of sips. 'How's the wing, old timer?' I said, settling back into my leather chair and doing my best to look calm.

'Same as it was. Feels like there's a bone stickin' out of my elbow.'

'You got knocked around pretty hard in spring training, I heard.'

'Them's just practice games. They don't mean nothin'.'

'Sure. Wait till it really counts, right?'

He caught the cynicism in my voice and gave a defensive shrug, then reached for the cigarettes in his shirt pocket. 'Well, little guy,' he said, 'what's the scoop?' He shook out a Lucky from his pack and lit up, blowing a big gust of smoke in my direction. 'From the way you talked on the phone, it sounded like life and death.'

'It is. That's exactly what it is.'

'How so? You got a patent on a new bromide or somethin'? Christ, you come up with a medicine to cure sick arms, Walt, and I'll give you half my pay for the next ten years.'

'I've got something better than that, Diz. And it won't cost you a cent.'

'Everything costs, fella. It's the law of the land.'

'I don't want your money. I want to save you, Diz. Let me help you, and the torment you've been living in these past four years will be gone.'

'Yeah?' he said, smiling as if I'd just told a moderately amusing joke. 'And how you aimin' to do that?'

'Any way you like. The method's not important. The only thing that counts is that you go along with it – and that you understand why it has to be done.'

'You've lost me, kid. I don't know what you're talkin' about.'

'A great person once said to me: "When a man comes to the end of the line, the only thing he really wants is death." Does that make it any clearer? I heard those words a long time ago, but I was too dumb to figure out what they meant. Now I know, and I'll tell you something, Diz – they're true. They're the truest words any man ever spoke.'

Dean burst out laughing. 'You're some kidder, Walt. You got that wacko sense of humor, and it don't never let up.

That's why I like you so much. There ain't no one else in this town that comes out with the ballsy things you do.'

I sighed at the man's stupidity. Dealing with a clown like that was hard work, and the last thing I wanted was to lose my patience. I took another sip of my drink, sloshing the spicy liquid around in my mouth for a couple of seconds, and swallowed. 'Listen, Diz,' I said. 'I've been where you are. Twelve, thirteen years ago, I was sitting on top of the world. I was the best at what I did, in a class by myself. And let me tell you, what you've accomplished on the ball field is nothing compared to what I could do. Next to me, you're no taller than a pygmy, an insect, a fucking bug in the rug. Do you hear what I'm saying? Then, just like that, something happened, and I couldn't go on. But I didn't hang around and make people feel sorry for me, I didn't turn myself into a joke. I called it quits, and then I went on and made another life for myself. That's what I've been hoping and praying would happen to you. But you just don't get it, do you? Your fat hick brain's too clogged with cornbread and molasses to get it.'

'Wait a second,' Dizzy said, wagging his finger at me as a sudden, unexpected glow of delight spread across his face. 'Wait just a second. Now I know who you are. Shit, I knowed it all along. You're that kid, ain't you? You're that goddamned kid. Walt . . . Walt the Wonder Boy. Christ almighty. My daddy took me and Paul and Elmer out to the fair one day in Arkansas, and we seen you do your stuff. Fuckin' out of this world it was. I always wondered what happened to you. And here you are, sittin' right across from me. I can't fuckin' believe it.'

'Believe it, friend. When I told you I was great, I meant great like nobody else. Like a comet streaking across the sky.'

'You were great, all right, I'll vouch for that. The greatest thing I ever saw.'

'And so were you, big man. As great as they come. But

you're over the hill now, and it breaks my heart to see what you're doing to yourself. Let me help you, Diz. Death isn't so terrible. Everybody has to die sometime, and once you get used to the idea, you'll see that now is better than later. If you give me the chance, I can spare you the shame. I can give you back your dignity.'

'You're really serious, ain't you?'

'You bet I am. As serious as I've ever been in my life.'

'You're off your trolley, Walt. You're fuckin' looped outa your gourd.'

'Let me kill you, and the last four years will be forgotten. You'll be great again, champ. You'll be great again, forever.'

I was going too fast. He'd thrown me off balance with that Wonder Boy talk, and instead of circling back and modifying my approach, I was charging ahead at breakneck speed. I'd wanted to build up the pressure slowly, to lull him with such elaborate, airtight arguments that he'd eventually come round on his own. That was the point: not to force him into it, but to make him see the wisdom of the plan for himself. I wanted him to want what I wanted, to feel so convinced by my proposal that he would actually beg me to do it, and all I'd done was leave him behind, scaring him off with my threats and half-baked platitudes. No wonder he thought I was crazy. I'd let the whole thing get out of hand, and now, just when we should have been getting started, he was already standing up and making his way for the exit.

I wasn't worried about that. I'd locked the door from the inside, and it couldn't be opened without the key – which happened to be in my pocket. Still, I didn't want him pulling on the knob and rattling the frame. He might have started shouting at me then to let him out, and with half a dozen people working in the kitchen at that hour, the ruckus surely would have brought them running. So, thinking only about that small point and ignoring the larger consequences, I opened the drawer of my desk and removed the master's gun. That was the mistake that finally did me in. By pointing that gun at Dizzy, I crossed the boundary that separates idle talk from punishable crimes, and the nightmare I'd set in motion could no longer be stopped. But the gun was crucial, wasn't it? It was the linchpin of the whole business, and at one moment or another it was bound to come out of that drawer. Pull the trigger on Dizzy – and thus go back to the desert and do the job that was never done. Make him beg for death in the same way Master Yehudi had begged, and then undo the wrong by summoning the courage to act.

None of that matters now. I'd already botched it by the time Dizzy stood up, and pulling out the gun was no more than a desperate attempt to save face. I talked him back into the chair, and for the next fifteen minutes I made him sweat a lot more than I'd ever intended to. For all his swagger and size, Dean was a physical coward, and whenever a brawl broke out he'd duck behind the nearest piece of furniture. I already knew his reputation, but the gun terrorized him even more than I thought it would. It actually made him cry, and as he sat there moaning and blubbering in his seat, I almost pulled the trigger just to shut him up. He was begging me for his life – not to kill him, but to let him live – and it was all so upside-down, so different from how I'd imagined it would be, I didn't know what to do. The standoff could have gone on all day, but then, just around noon, someone knocked on the door. I'd left clear instructions that I wasn't to be disturbed, but someone was knocking just the same.

'Diz?' a woman's voice said. 'Is that you in there, Diz?'

It was his wife, Pat: a bossy, no-nonsense piece of work if there ever was one. She'd come by to pick up her husband for a lunch date at Lemmele's, and of course Dizzy had told her where she could find him, which was yet another potential snag I'd neglected to think of. She'd barged into my club looking for her henpecked better half, and once she collared the sous-chef in the kitchen (who was busy chopping spuds and slicing carrots), she made such a nuisance of herself that the poor sap finally spilled the beans. He led her up the stairs and down the hall, and that was how she happened to be standing in front of my office door, pounding on the white veneer with her angry bitch knuckles.

Short of planting a bullet in Dizzy's head, there was nothing I could do but put away the revolver and open the door. The shit was sure to hit the fan at that point – unless the big guy came through for me and decided to play mum. For ten seconds my life dangled from that gossamer thread: if he was too embarrassed to tell her how scared he'd been, he'd keep the imbroglio to himself. I put on my warmest, most debonnaire smile as Mrs Dean stepped into the room, but her sniveling husband gave the whole thing away the instant he set eyes on her. 'The little fucker was gonna kill me!' he said, blurting out the goods in a high-pitched, incredulous voice. 'He was holdin' a gun to my head, and the little fucker was gonna shoot!'

Those were the words that knocked me out of the nightclub business. Instead of keeping their reservation at Lemmele's, Pat and Dizzy tramped out of my office and headed straight for the local precinct to swear out a complaint against me. Pat told me they were going to do as much when she slammed the door in my face, but I didn't stir a muscle. I just sat behind my desk and marveled at how stupid I was, trying to collect my thoughts before the bulls showed up to cart me away. It took them less than an hour, and I went off without a peep, smiling and cracking jokes when they put the cuffs around my wrists. If not for Bingo, I might have done some serious time for my little stab at playing God, but he had all the right connections, and a deal was struck before the case ever came to court. It was just as well that way. Not only for me, but for Dizzy too. A trial wouldn't have been good for him – not with all the flak and scandal-mongering that would have gone with it – and he was perfectly happy to accept the compromise. The judge gave me a choice. Plead guilty to a lesser charge and do six to nine months at Joliet, or else leave Chicago and enlist in the army. I opted to walk through the second door. It wasn't that I had any great desire to wear a uniform, but I figured I'd outstayed my welcome in Chicago and that it was time to move on.

Bingo had pulled strings and paid bribes to keep me out of the can, but that didn't mean he had any sympathy for what I'd done. He thought I was nuts, ninety-nine-point-nine-percent nuts. Bumping off a guy for money was one thing, but what kind of dimwit would go after a national treasure like Dizzy Dean? You had to be stark raving mad to cook up a thing like that. That's what I probably was, I said, and didn't try to explain myself. Let him think what he wanted to think and leave it at that. There was a price to pay, of course, but I wasn't in any position to argue. In lieu of cash for services rendered, I agreed to compensate Bingo for his legal help by signing over my share of the club to him. Losing Mr Vertigo's was hard on me, but not half as hard as giving up the act had been, not a tenth as hard as losing the master. I was nobody special now. Just my old ordinary self again: Walter Claireborne Rawley, a twenty-six-year-old GI with a short haircut and a pair of empty pockets. Welcome to the real world, pal. I gave my suits to the busboys, I kissed my girlfriends good-bye, and then climbed aboard the milk train and headed for boot camp. Considering what I was about to leave behind me, I suppose I was lucky.

By then, Dizzy was gone, too. His season had consisted of one game, and after Pittsburgh shelled him for three runs in the first inning of his first start, he'd finally called it quits. I don't know if my scare tactics had knocked some sense into him, but I felt glad when I read about his decision. The Cubs gave him a job as their first-base coach, but a month later he got a better offer from the Falstaff Brewing Company in Saint Louis, and he went back to the old town to work as a radio announcer for the Browns and Cardinals games. 'This job ain't gonna change me none,' he said. 'I'm just gonna speak plain ol' pinto-bean English.' You had to hand it to the big clodhopper. The public went for the folksy garbage he spewed out over the airwaves, and he was such a success at it that they kept him on for twenty-five years. But that's another story, and I can't say that I paid much attention to him. Once I left Chicago, it had nothing to do with me anymore.

IV

My eyes were too weak for flight school, so I spent the next four years crawling through the mud. I became an expert in the habits of worms and other creatures who slither along the ground and prey on human skin for nourishment. The judge had said the army would make a man of me, and if eating dirt and watching limbs fly off soldiers' bodies is proof of manhood, then I suppose the Honorable Charles P. McGuffin called it right. As far as I'm concerned, the less said about those four years the better. At first, I thought seriously about swinging a medical discharge for myself, but I could never find the courage to go through with it. My plan was to start levitating again in secret – and bring on such violent, crippling attacks of pain that they'd be forced to send me home. The problem was, I had no home to go to anymore, and once I'd mulled over the situation for a little while, I realized that I preferred the uncertainty of combat to the certain torture of those headaches.

I didn't distinguish myself as a soldier, but I didn't disgrace myself either. I did my job, I avoided trouble, I hung in there and didn't get killed. When they finally shipped me back in November 1945, I was burned out, incapable of thinking ahead or making plans. I drifted around for three or four years, mostly up and down the east coast. The longest stretch was in Boston. I worked as a bartender there, supplementing my income by playing the horses and sitting in on a weekly poker game at Spiro's pool hall in the North End. It was only medium-stakes action, but if you keep on winning those ones and fives, it begins to add up. I was just on the point of putting together a deal to open a place of my own when my luck turned sour. My nest egg dribbled away, I went into debt, and before many moons had passed, I had to sneak out of town to slough off the loan sharks I was in hock to. From there I went to Long Island and found a job in construction. Those were the years when suburbs were sprouting up around the cities, and I went where the money was, doing my bit to change the landscape and turn the world into what it looks like today. All those ranch houses and tidy lawns and spindly little trees wrapped in burlap – I was the guy who put them there. It was dreary work, but I stuck with it for eighteen months. At one point, for reasons I can't explain, I let myself get talked into marriage. It didn't last more than half a year, and the whole experience is so foggy to me now, I have trouble remembering what my wife looked like. If I don't think hard about it, I can't even remember her name.

I had no idea what was wrong with me. I had always been so fast, so quick to pounce on opportunities and turn them to my advantage, but now I felt sluggish, out of sync, unable to keep up with the flow. The world was passing me by, and the oddest thing about it was that I didn't care. I had no ambitions. I wasn't on the make or looking for an edge. I just wanted to be left in peace, to scrape along as best I could and go where the world took me. I'd already dreamed my big dreams. They hadn't gotten me anywhere, and now I was too exhausted to think of any new ones. Let someone else carry the ball for a change. I'd dropped it a long time ago, and it wasn't worth the effort to bend down and pick it up.

In 1950, I moved across the river to a low-rent apartment in Newark, New Jersey, and started my ninth or tenth job since the war. The Meyerhoff Baking Company employed over two hundred people, and in three eight-hour shifts we churned out every baked good imaginable. There were seven different varieties of bread alone: white, rye, whole wheat, pumpernickel, raisin, cinnamon raisin, and Bavarian black. Add in twelve kinds of cookies, ten kinds of cakes, six kinds of doughnuts, along with breadsticks, breadcrumbs, and dinner rolls, and you begin to understand why the factory was in

264

operation twenty-four hours a day. I started out on the assembly line, adjusting and preparing the cellophane wrappers that went around the pre-sliced loaves of bread. I figured I'd stick around for a few months at most, but once I caught the hang of it, it turned out to be a decent place to earn a living. The smells in that factory were so pleasant, and with the aroma of fresh bread and sugar wafting continually through the air, the hours didn't drag as heavily as they had on my other jobs. That was part of it in any case, but even more important was the little redhead who started making eyes at me about a week after I got there. She wasn't much to look at, at least not compared to the showgirls I'd horsed around with in Chicago, but there was a bemused flicker in those green eyes that struck a chord with me, and I didn't waste much time in getting to know her. I've made only two good decisions in my life. The first one was following Master Yehudi onto that train when I was nine years old. The second one was marrying Molly Fitzsimmons. Molly put me together again, and considering the kind of shape I was in when I landed in Newark, that was no small job.

Her maiden name was Quinn, and she was this side of thirty when we met. She'd married her first husband straight out of high school, and five years later he was drafted into the army. By all accounts, Fitzsimmons was a friendly, hardworking mick, but his war had been less lucky than mine. He took a bullet at Messina in 'forty-three, and since then Molly had been on her own, a young widow without any kids looking after herself and waiting for something to happen. God knows what she saw in me, but I fell for her because she made me feel comfortable, because she brought out my old wise-cracking self and knew a good joke when she heard one. There was nothing flashy about her, nothing to make her stand out in a crowd. Pass her on the street, and she was just another working stiff's wife: one of those women with pudgy hips and a broad bottom who didn't bother to put on makeup unless she was going out to a restaurant. But she had spirit, Molly did, and in her own quiet, watchful way, she was as sharp as any person I've ever known. She was kind; she didn't bear grudges; she stood up for me and never tried to turn me into someone I wasn't. If she was a bit of a slob as a housekeeper and something less than a good cook, that didn't matter. She wasn't my servant, after all, she was my wife. She was also the one true friend I'd had since my days in Kansas with Aesop and Mother Sioux, the first woman I'd ever loved.

We lived in a second-floor walkup apartment in the Ironbound section of Newark, and since Molly wasn't able to bear children, it was always just the two of us. I made her quit her job after the wedding, but I stuck with mine, and over the years I rose through the ranks at Meyerhoff's. A couple could get by on one salary back then, and after they promoted me to foreman of the night shift, we had no money worries to speak of. It was a modest life by the standards I'd once set for myself, but I'd changed enough not to care about that anymore. We went to the movies twice a week, we ate out on Saturday night, we read books and watched the tube. In the summer, we drove down to the shore at Asbury Park, and nearly every Sunday we got together with one of Molly's relatives. The Quinns were a large family, and her brothers and sisters had all married and begotten children. That gave me four brothers-in-law, four sisters-in-law, and thirteen nieces and nephews. For a man with no kids of his own, I was up to my elbows in youngsters, but I can't say I objected to my role as Uncle Walt. Molly was the good fairy godmother, and I was the court jester: the chunky little guy with all those quips and slapstick gags, Rootie Kazootie rolling down the steps of the back porch.

I spent twenty-three years with Molly – a good long run, I suppose, but not long enough. My plan was to grow old with her and die in her arms, but cancer came along and took her from me before I was ready to let go. First one breast went, then the other breast, and by the time she was fifty-five, she wasn't there anymore. The family did what it could to help, but it was an awful period for me, and I spent the next six or seven months in an alcoholic stupor. It got so bad that I eventually lost my job at the factory, and if two of my brothers-in-law hadn't hauled me off to a drying-out clinic, there's no telling what might have happened to me. I stayed for a full sixty-day cure at Saint Barnabas Hospital in Livingston, and that's where I finally started dreaming again. I don't mean daydreams and thoughts about the future, I mean actual sleep dreams: vivid, movie-show extravaganzas almost every night for a month. Maybe it had something to do with the drugs and tranquilizers I was taking, I don't know, but forty-four years after my last performance as Walt the Wonder Boy, it all came rushing back to me. I was back on the circuit with Master Yehudi, traveling from town to town in the Pierce Arrow, doing my act again every night. It made me incredibly happy, and it brought back pleasures I'd long since forgotten I could feel. I was walking on water again, strutting my stuff before gigantic, overflowing crowds, and I could move through the air without pain, floating and spinning and prancing with all of my old virtuosity and assurance. I'd worked so hard to bury those memories, had struggled for so many years to hug to the ground and be like everyone else, and now it was all surging up again, blasting forth in a nightly display of Technicolor fireworks. Those dreams turned everything around for me. They gave me back my pride, and after that I was no longer ashamed to look at the past. I don't know how else to put it. The master had forgiven me. He'd canceled out my debt to him because of Molly, because of how I'd loved her and mourned her, and now he was calling out to me and asking me to remember him. There's no way to prove any of this, but the effect was undeniable. Something had been lifted inside me, and I walked out of that drunk tank as sober as I am now. I was fifty-eight years old, my life was in ruins, and yet I didn't feel too bad about it. When all was said and done, I actually felt pretty good.

Molly's medical bills had wiped out whatever cash we'd managed to save. I was four months behind on the rent, the landlord was threatening to evict me, and the only thing I owned was my car – a seven-year-old Ford Fairlane with a dented grille and a faulty carburetor. About three days after I left the hospital, my favorite nephew called me from Denver about a job. Dan was the bright one in the family – the first college professor they'd ever had – and he'd been living out there with his wife and son for the past few years. Since his father had already told him how hard-up I was, I didn't waste my breath telling fibs about my big bank account. The job wasn't much, he said, but maybe a change of scenery would do me good. What sort of job? I asked. Maintenance engineer, he replied, trying not to make it sound too funny. You mean a janitor? I said. That's it, he said, a mop jockey. A position had opened up in the building where he taught his classes, and if I felt like moving to Denver, he'd put in a word for me and swing the deal. Sure, I said, why the hell not, and two days later I packed some things into the Ford and set off for the Rocky Mountains.

I never did make it to Denver. It wasn't because the car broke down, and it wasn't because I had second thoughts about becoming a janitor, but things happened along the way, and instead of winding up in one place, I wound up in another. It's really not hard to explain. Coming so soon after all those dreams in the hospital, the trip brought back a flood of memories, and by the time I crossed the Kansas border, I couldn't resist making a short, sentimental detour to the south. It wasn't so far out of the way, I told myself, and Dan wouldn't mind if I was a little slow in getting there. I just wanted to spend a few hours in Wichita – and go back to Mrs Witherspoon's house to see what the old place looked like. Once, not long after the war, I'd tried to look her up in

New York, but there was no listing for her in the phone book, and I'd forgotten the name of her company. For all I knew she was dead now, just like everyone else I'd ever cared about.

The city had grown a lot since the 1920s, but it still wasn't my idea of a good time. There were more people, more buildings, and more streets, but once I adjusted to the changes, it turned out to be the same backwater pancake I remembered. They called it the 'Air Capital of the World' now, and it gave me a good laugh when I saw that slogan plastered on billboards around town. The chamber of commerce was referring to all the aircraft companies that had set up factories there, but I couldn't help thinking about myself, the original birdboy who'd once called Wichita his home. I had some trouble finding the house, which made my tour a bit more thorough than I'd planned. Way back when, it had been located on the outskirts of town, sitting by itself on a dirt road that led to open country, but now it was part of the residential hub, and other houses had been built around it. The street was called Coronado Avenue, and it came with all the modern accoutrements: sidewalks, street lamps, and a blacktop surface with a white stripe running down the middle. But the house looked good, there was no question about that: the shingles gleamed white under the gray November sky, and the little trees that Master Yehudi had planted in the front yard towered over the roof like giants. Whoever owned the place had been treating it well, and now that it was so old, it had taken on the air of something historic, a venerable mansion from a bygone age.

I parked the car and walked up the steps of the front porch. It was late afternoon, but a light was on in a first-floor window, and now that I was there, I figured I had to go through with it and ring the bell. If the people weren't ogres, they might even let me in and show me around for old time's sake. That was all I was hoping for: just a glimpse. It was cold

269

out on the porch, and as I stood there waiting for someone to appear, I couldn't help thinking back to the first time I'd come to this house, half-dead from losing my way in that infernal blizzard. I had to ring twice before I heard footsteps stirring within, and when the door finally opened, I was so wrapped up in remembering my first encounter with Mrs Witherspoon, it took a couple of seconds before I realized that the woman standing in front of me was none other than Mrs Witherspoon herself: an older, frailer, more wrinkled version to be sure, but the same Mrs Witherspoon for all that. I would have known her anywhere. She hadn't gained a pound since 1936; her hair was dyed the same snazzy shade of red; and her bright blue eyes were as blue and bright as ever. She was seventy-four or seventy-five by then, but she didn't look a day over sixty – sixty-three tops. Still dressed in fashionable clothes, still holding herself erect, she came to the door with a burning cigarette wedged between her lips and a glass of Scotch in her left hand. You had to love a woman like that. The world had gone through untold changes and catastrophes since I'd last set eyes on her, but Mrs Witherspoon was the same tough broad she'd always been.

I recognized her before she recognized me. That was understandable, since time had taken a more drastic toll on my looks than on hers. My freckles had all but vanished now, and I'd turned into a squat, dumpy sort of guy with thinning gray hair and a set of Coke-bottle lenses perched on my nose. Hardly the dashing smoothy she'd dined with at Lemmele's thirty-eight years before. I was dressed in dull workaday clothes – lumber jacket, khaki pants, cordovan shoes, white socks – and my collar was turned up to ward off the chill. She probably couldn't see much of my face, and what she could see was so haggard, so worn out from my struggle with the booze, there wasn't anything to be done but to tell her who I was.

The rest goes without saying, doesn't it? Tears were shed,

stories were told, we gabbed and carried on until the wee small hours. It was auld lang syne on Coronado Avenue, and I doubt there could have been a better reunion than the one we had that night. I've already given the gist of what happened to me, but her story was no less strange, no less unexpected than mine. Instead of parlaying her millions into more millions during the Texas wildcat boom, she'd sunk her drills into dry ground and gone bust. The oil game was largely guesswork back then, and she made one too many bad guesses. By 1938, she'd lost nine-tenths of her fortune. That still didn't qualify her as a pauper, but she was no longer in the Fifth Avenue league, and after floating a few more ventures that didn't pan out, she finally packed it in and returned to Wichita. She thought it would be only temporary: a few months in the old house to take stock and then on to the next bright idea. But one thing led to another, and by the time the war came she was still there. In what can only be called a startling about-face, she got caught up in the patriotic fervor of the time and spent the next four years working as a volunteer nurse at the Wichita VA Hospital. I was hard-pressed to imagine her doing that Florence Nightingale bit, but Mrs W. was a woman of many surprises, and if money was her strong point, it was by no means the only thing she thought about. After the war she went into business again, but this time she stayed in Wichita, and little by little she built it into a nice profitable concern. With Laundromats of all things. It sounds funny after all that high-stakes speculation in stocks and oil – but why not? She was one of the first to see the commercial possibilities of the washing machine, and she got a jump on her competitors by entering the field early. By the time I showed up in 1974, she had twenty Laundromats scattered around the city and another twelve in neighboring towns. The House of Clean, she called them, and all those dimes and quarters had turned her into a wealthy woman again.

And what about men? I asked. Oh, lots of men, she

271

answered, more men than you could shake a stick at. And Orville Cox – what about him? Dead and gone, she said. And Billy Bigelow? Still among the living. As a matter of fact, his house was just around the corner. She'd brought him into the Laundromat business after the war, and he'd worked as her manager and right-hand man until his retirement six months ago. Young Billy was pushing seventy now, and with two heart attacks already behind him, the doctor had told him to go easy on the pump. His wife had died seven or eight years back, and with his kids all grown and gone, Billy and Mrs Witherspoon were still in close touch. She described him as the best friend she'd ever had, and from the way her voice softened when she said it, I gathered that relations between them went beyond simple shop talk about washers and dryers. Ah ha, I said, so patience finally won out, and sweet little Billy got what he wanted. She threw me one of her devilish winks. Sometimes, she said, but not always. It depends on my mood.

It didn't take much arm-twisting to get me to stay. The janitor thing was only a stopgap measure, and now that something better had turned up, I didn't have to think twice about changing my plans. The salary was only a small part of it, of course. I was back where I belonged, and when Mrs Witherspoon invited me to step in and take over Billy's old job, I told her I'd start first thing in the morning. It didn't matter what the work was. If she'd invited me to stay on to scrub the pots in her kitchen, I would have said yes to that, too.

I slept in the same top-floor room I'd occupied as a boy, and once I learned the business, I did all right for her. I kept the washing machines humming, I jacked profits up, I persuaded her to expand in different directions: a bowling alley, a pizza joint, a pinball arcade. With all the college kids pouring into town every fall, there was a demand for quick food and cheap entertainment, and I was just the man to provide those things. I put in long hours and worked my buns off, but I liked being in charge of something again, and most of my schemes turned out pretty well. Mrs Witherspoon called me a cowboy, which from her mouth was a compliment, and for the first three or four years we galloped along at a sprightly clip. Then, very suddenly, Billy died. It was another heart attack, but this one took place on the twelfth fairway of the Cherokee Acres Country Club, and by the time the medics got to him, he had already breathed his last. Mrs W. went into a tailspin after that. She stopped going to the office with me in the morning, and little by little she seemed to lose interest in the company, leaving most of the decisions in my hands. I'd been through something like that with Molly, but it wasn't much good telling her that time would take care of it. The one thing she didn't have was time. The man had worshiped her for fifty years, and now that he was gone, no one was ever going to replace him.

One night in the midst of all this, I heard her sobbing through the walls as I lay upstairs reading in bed. I went down to her room, we talked for a while, and then I took her in my arms and held her until she drifted off to sleep. Somehow or other, I wound up falling asleep, too, and when I woke in the morning I found myself lying under the covers with her in the large double bed. It was the same bed she'd shared with Master Yehudi in the old days, and now it was my turn to sleep beside her, to be the man she couldn't live without. It was mostly a matter of comfort, of companionship, of preferring to sleep in one bed rather than two, but that isn't to say the sheets didn't catch fire every now and then. Just because you get old, that doesn't mean you stop getting the urge, and whatever qualms I had about it in the beginning soon went away. For the next eleven years we lived together like husband and wife. I don't feel I have to make any apologies for that. Once upon a time I'd been young enough to be her son, but now I was older than most grandfathers, and when you get to be that age, you don't have to play by the rules anymore. You go where you have to go, and whatever it takes to keep on breathing, that's what you do.

She stayed in good health for most of the time we were together. In her mid-eighties she was still drinking a couple of Scotches before dinner and smoking the occasional cigarette, and most days saw her with enough spunk to doll herself up and go out for a spin in her giant blue Cadillac. She lived to be ninety or ninety-one (it was never clear which century she'd been born in), and things didn't get too rough for her until the last eighteen months or so. Towards the end she was mostly blind, mostly deaf, mostly unable to get out of bed, but she remained herself for all that, and rather than put her into a home or hire a nurse to take care of her, I sold off the business and did the dirty work myself. I owed her that much, didn't I? I bathed her and combed her hair; I carried her around the house in my arms; I wiped the shit from her ass after every accident, just as she had once wiped mine.

The funeral was a bang-up affair. I made sure of that and didn't stint on the extras. Everything belonged to me now – the house, the cars, the money she'd made for herself, the money I'd made for her – and since there was enough in the cookie jar to keep me going for another seventy-five or hundred years, I decided to throw her a big send-off, the biggest bash Wichita had ever seen. A hundred and fifty cars joined in the motorcade to the cemetery. Traffic was tangled up for miles around, and once the burial was over, mobs tramped through the house until three o'clock in the morning, swilling liquor and stuffing their maws with turkey legs and cakes. I'm not going to say I was a respectable member of the community, but I'd earned some respect for myself over the years, and people around town knew who I was. When I asked them to come for Marion, they turned out in droves.

That was a year and a half ago. For the first couple of months I moped around the house, not quite sure what to do with myself. I'd never been fond of gardening, golf had bored me the two or three times I'd played it, and at seventy-six I didn't have any hankering to go into business again. Business had been fun because of Marion, but without her around to liven things up, there wouldn't have been any point. I thought about getting away from Kansas for a few months and seeing the world, but before I could make any definite plans, I was rescued by the idea of writing this book. I can't really say how it happened. It just hit me one morning as I climbed out of bed, and less than an hour later I was sitting at a desk in the upstairs parlor with a pen in my hand, scratching away at the first sentence. I had no doubt that I was doing something that had to be done, and the conviction I felt was so strong, I realize now that the book must have come to me in a dream – but one of those dreams you can't remember, that vanish the instant you wake up and open your eyes on the world.

I've worked on it every day since last August, pushing along from word to word in my clumsy old man's script. I started out with a school composition book from the five-and-ten, one of those hardbound things with a black-and-white marble cover and wide blue lines, and by now I've filled nearly thirteen of them, about one a month for every month I've been working. I haven't shown a single word to anyone, and now that I'm at the end, I'm beginning to think it should stay that way – at least while I'm still kicking. Every word in these thirteen books is true, but I'd bet both my elbows there aren't a hell of a lot of people who'd swallow that. It's not that I'm afraid of being called a liar, but I'm too old now to waste my time defending myself against idiots. I ran into enough doubting Thomases when Master Yehudi and I were on the road, and I have other fish to fry now, other things to keep me busy after this book is done. First thing tomorrow morning, I'll go downtown to the bank and put all thirteen volumes in my safe-deposit box. Then I'll go around the corner and see my lawyer, John Fusco, and have him add a clause to my will stating that the contents of that box should be left to my nephew, Daniel Quinn. Dan will know what to do with the book I've written. He'll correct the spelling mistakes and get someone to type up a clean copy, and once *Mr Vertigo* is published, I won't have to be around to watch the mugwumps and morons try to kill me. I'll already be dead, and you can be sure I'll be laughing at them – from above or below, whichever the case may be.

For the past four years a cleaning woman has been coming to the house several times a week. Her name is Yolanda Abraham, and she's from one of the warm-weather islands – Jamaica or Trinidad, I forget which. I wouldn't call her a talkative person, but we've known each other long enough to be on fairly cozy terms, and she was a great help to me during Marion's last months. She's somewhere between thirty and thirty-five, a round black woman with a slow, graceful walk and a beautiful voice. As far as I know, Yolanda doesn't have a husband, but she does have a child, an eight-year-old named Yusef. Every Saturday for the past four years, she's parked her offspring in the house with me while she does her work, and having watched this kid in action for more than half his life, I can say in all fairness that he's one monumental pain in the ass, a junior hooligan and wise-talking brat whose sole mission on earth is to spread mayhem and bad will. To top it off, Yusef is one of the ugliest children I've ever set eyes on. He has one of those jagged, scrawny, asymmetrical little faces, and the body that comes with it is a pathetic, sticklike bundle of bones – even if pound for pound it happens to be stronger and more supple than the bodies of most fullbacks in the NFL. I hate the kid for what he's done to my shins, my thumbs, and my toes, but I also see myself in him when I was that age, and since his face resembles Aesop's to an almost appalling degree – so much so that Marion and I both gasped the first time he walked

276

into the house – I continue to forgive him everything. I can't help myself. The boy has the devil in him. He's brash and rude and incorrigible, but he's lit up with the fire of life, and it does me good to watch him as he flings himself headlong into a maelstrom of trouble. Watching Yusef, I now know what the master saw in me, and I know what he meant when he told me I had the gift. This boy has the gift, too. If I could ever pluck up my courage to speak to his mother, I'd take him under my wing in a second. In three years, I'd turn him into the next Wonder Boy. He'd start where I left off, and before long he'd go farther than anyone else has ever gone. Christ, that would be something to live for, wouldn't it? It would make the whole fucking world sing again.

The problem is the thirty-three steps. It's one thing to tell Yolanda I can teach her son to fly, but once we got past that hurdle, what about the rest? Even I'm sickened by the thought of it. Having gone through all that cruelty and torture myself, how could I bear to inflict it on someone else? They don't make men like Master Yehudi anymore, and they don't make boys like me either: stupid, susceptible, stubborn. We lived in a different world back then, and the things the master and I did together wouldn't be possible today. People wouldn't stand for it. They'd call in the cops, they'd write their congressman, they'd consult their family physician. We're not as tough as we used to be, and maybe the world's a better place because of it, I don't know. But I do know that you can't get something for nothing, and the bigger the thing you want, the more you're going to have to pay for it.

Still, when I think back to my dreadful initiation in Cibola, I can't help wondering if Master Yehudi's methods weren't too harsh. When I finally got off the ground for the first time, it wasn't because of anything he'd taught me. I did it by myself on the cold kitchen floor, and it came after a long siege of sobbing and despair, when my soul began to rush out of my body and I was no longer conscious of who I was. Maybe

277

the despair was the only thing that really mattered. In that case, the physical ordeals he put me through were no more than a sham, a diversion to trick me into thinking I was getting somewhere – when in fact I was never anywhere until I found myself lying face-down on that kitchen floor. What if there were no steps in the process? What if it all came down to one moment – one leap – one lightning instant of transformation? Master Yehudi had been trained in the old school, and he was a wizard at getting me to believe in his hocus-pocus and high-flown talk. But what if his way wasn't the only way? What if there was a simpler, more direct method, an approach that began from the inside and bypassed the body altogether? What then?

Deep down, I don't believe it takes any special talent for a person to lift himself off the ground and hover in the air. We all have it in us – every man, woman, and child – and with enough hard work and concentration, every human being is capable of duplicating the feats I accomplished as Walt the Wonder Boy. You must learn to stop being yourself. That's where it begins, and everything else follows from that. You must let yourself evaporate. Let your muscles go limp, breathe until you feel your soul pouring out of you, and then shut your eyes. That's how it's done. The emptiness inside your body grows lighter than the air around you. Little by little, you begin to weigh less than nothing. You shut your eyes; you spread your arms; you let yourself evaporate. And then, little by little, you lift yourself off the ground.

Like so.

278